Sleepy Hollow

DAX VARLEY

Sleepy Hollow
Copyright 2013 by Dax Varley
All rights reserved

The Horseman…he is real. He came for me.

I sat, gazing out my chamber window. A ground mist had collected, hovering over the glen. Then I heard him, distant at first, approaching within the fog. His race with the night thundered a rhythm. My heart drummed to each beat.

Within moments, I saw him—a headless outline of black within a gray cloud. As though sensing my eyes upon him, he slowed his phantom steed, circling once. The horse reared, pawing the haze. The Horseman quickly drew his sword and sliced the air.

I dropped down below the windowsill, my breath coming in shallow gasps. Had I doomed myself by daring to peek? I quivered, hugging my knees.

He is not real. He is not real.

Moments passed. Then slowly, I inched to the edge of the sill. Hiding in the shadows, I moved the curtain just a whisper.

The Horseman was still there, but now he'd turned…toward my window. My heart hammered and my blood ran as cold as the Hudson River.

He knows I'm watching.

His hand reached out—beckoning…inviting…bewitching me. A gray breath of evil played upon my neck, and my name wafted through the mist.

Katrina.

I struggled against the force that summoned me, tightening every muscle, every nerve, refusing to move an inch. My body quaked, but I kept my mind as sharp as the Horseman's blade. *I will not come. I will not.*

Still he remained. No wind. No stars. Just the ivory fog. And that hand…

Katrina.

When I thought I couldn't hold back a second more, he spurred his massive steed. And like a midnight blast, he flew, charging across the countryside.

I collapsed, trembling, heaving. Finding strength, I crawled upon my bed. I dared not move. I dared not sleep. I lay within my quilt, knotted in fear.

The Horseman...he is real. He came for me. And I knew not when he'd return.

It's a simple game, really. A game that I call "Someday." I close my eyes, spin a globe, and then draw it to a stop with my finger. When I open my eyes, there it is—the place I'll visit "someday." My diaries were filled with someday destinations. Vienna. Cairo. Burma. Someday I would visit every one.

"Katrina," Father snapped, pointing to the inkblot I'd dripped on a billing slip. "Pay attention. I can't have sevens resembling twos."

Oh rot. We'd been working the ledgers for over an hour, and the numbers were bleeding together before my bleary eyes. Our 1300 acres had produced a particularly abundant harvest, and Father insisted on registering every grain. I picked up the blotter and rolled it over the fat droplet, then glanced at the remaining notes and vouchers. *Sigh.* I'd rather jab this quill in my eye than continue tabulating. But as always, I pressed on. Being the only child of the wealthiest man in Sleepy Hollow meant that "someday" I was to inherit this farm—keep his empire intact. But that was the "someday" Father had planned.

Some ten minutes later, the door to Father's study opened. Hans Van Ripper, an old farmer, came in, nervously tapping his hat to his leg. His face was dark and shadowed, and he heaved like he'd limped all the way here.

Father rose from his chair. "What it is, Hans?"

Van Ripper cut his eyes to me, then back. "Better tell you in private."

"Go on, Katrina," Father said, making shooing motions with his hands.

"Father, I'm eighteen. Certainly old enough to hear –"

"Go!" he ordered.

"Fine." At least I was getting a break from the ledgers. But there was something behind Van Ripper's tense expression that told me this was news I needed to hear. I rose, passed between the two of them, and then quietly closed the door. I made a few thumping noises to sound like I'd retreated, then, as lightly as possible, placed my ear to the door.

There was a strained silence in the room. Perhaps they were making sure I'd gone. Then Van Ripper uttered, "The Horseman has killed again."

A thousand pinpricks needled my skin. I pressed my palms to the door for support. *The Horseman's back.*

"Good God," Father boomed. "Who has he claimed?"

"The schoolmaster," Hans answered, "Nikolass Devenpeck. Found the body myself."

The air thinned. I struggled for breath. *Nikolass?* True, he was always clumsy, dry, and poorly dressed, but he was a fine teacher who'd only settled here last winter. Before then the children had been educated at home, as I had. *Why him?*

There was some foot shuffling, then Father asked, "And you're sure it was the Horseman?"

Van Ripper's gravelly voice lowered. "His headless body was layin' in a circle of scorched grass. Same as the others."

The others. Old Brower and Cornelius Putnam—two villagers beheaded. But that was three years ago. *Then.*

"I'm waging the schoolteacher tried to outrun the Horseman on foot," Van Ripper wheezed. "His old dapple, Gunpowder, was found grazing near the school."

"And his head?" Father asked.

"Several of us scoured the nearby field, but it weren't nowhere to be found."

Their words wavered in and out as I leaned heavier on the door. For three years there had been no word. No sightings. No deaths. And now…?

More foot shuffling. Father pacing. "I thought this nightmare was behind us."

"Will it ever be?" Van Ripper asked. "You know as well as I that Sleepy Hollow is a haunted place."

Bile clogged my throat. I couldn't shake the chilling image of Nikolass—a heap of blood and limbs, sprawled upon a circle of blackened ground.

Father briefly stopped his pacing. "Do you know if anyone's disturbed the Horseman's grave?"

"Who would dare?" Van Ripper snapped.

Not a soul.

In life, the Horseman had been a Hessian mercenary whose head was severed by a cannonball. His body lies in the far reaches of the church cemetery, the only marker a crude headstone that reads:

Hessian Swine
Dismantled 1778

The grave is hidden among a mass of creeping vines and cockleburs. No villager would risk going near it.

There was a thick silence on the other side of the door, then Van Ripper spoke again. "Baltus, you know the Horseman does not rise of his own accord."

I had always heard this—rumors that someone controlled the Hessian, conjuring him to enact their own revenge. But the schoolmaster? *Nikolass, what had you done?*

Father's footfall was heavy as he crossed the room. "There will be panic among the villagers. Go and assemble the Council. I shall be there shortly."

I spun, meaning to hurry off. But I only made it a few feet when I realized—*Blast!*—the hem of my dress was stuck between the door and the jamb. I tugged hard, but it was wedged tight.

The knob turned. I pressed myself to the wall, hoping the door would hide me when Van Ripper opened it. Once he'd passed, I could slip down the hall undetected. But it was Father who emerged, slinging it open. It swung back, slamming into me. *Oomph!*

He peeked around, his face ruddy with anger. "Katrina, get back in here and finish the numbers. I'll be back later this afternoon."

I tugged my creased skirt from the door hinge as Van Ripper pushed past me.

"Father—" I started.

"And don't you dare leave this house." He lifted his coat from the peg. "Do you understand me?"

"Yes." Though I doubted my hands would stop trembling long enough for me to write. All my sevens would definitely resemble twos. "But, Father…has the Horseman returned?"

He shrugged his coat on, not bothering to meet my eye. "You were listening. What do you think?"

I handed him his scarf. "What will we do?"

He pitched it around his neck and sighed. "Pray."

Pray? Absolutely. I prayed that my "someday" would soon be at hand.

* * *

A bright September sun shone down upon the funeral, sweeping shadows across the crypts, stone crosses, and weeping angels. The air smelled of maple and spices. And the birds sang as the village mourned.

We gathered near the newly dug grave while the reverend stirred us with passages of rebirth and heavenly treasure. And while my mind should have been on the proceedings, I couldn't help glaring across the far field of gravestones to the spot where the Horseman lay. These past three nights I waited…wondered…listened—falling asleep to the sound of my heart beating in my ears. *Will this be the night he comes back for me?*

My close friend, Elise, nudged me out of my daze. "Stop

staring," she murmured. "You'll only provoke him."

"Don't worry," I told her. "He doesn't rise during the day."

"But he may sense your eyes upon him. God only knows which one of us is next."

God only knows.

Once the last prayer was uttered, we trudged back to the church for the feast waiting inside. Elise and I dallied behind Father as we moved toward the church.

"Has your father given any indication as to why the Horseman chose Nikolass?" she whispered as we trod the dirt path.

"Father keeps Council business to himself. What about yours? Anything?"

"The same. He stomps about, grumbling under his breath."

The Council is a committee of grumblers. "I still can't imagine what offense Nikolass committed."

She suppressed a smile. "Besides wearing shoe buckles?"

I slapped my hand to my mouth to cover a snorting laugh. Then I gave her a sidelong glance "So rude."

"Really, Kat, no one wears shoe buckles anymore."

"That's hardly grounds for execution."

As we rounded to the front of the church, I spotted Brom, our overseer, standing near the doors. He was handsomely dressed in black, except for the ridiculous fox-skin cap on his head.

Father stopped abruptly and gripped Brom's arm. "What on earth are you doing here?"

Brom shrugged like the answer was obvious. "I've come to pay my respects. Isn't that what funerals are for?"

Father's forehead crimpled. "I left you in charge."

"Don't worry, Baltus. Fearful slaves work quick and hard. Now that the Horseman has risen, they won't chance being out after dark. And anyway, I intend to make my stay short."

Father placed his hand on Brom's shoulder. "See that you do."

"Came to pay your respects?" I asked after Father had gone inside. "You might've tried wearing a decent hat."

His cocked brow disappeared under his cap. "I'm proud of this one. I trapped and skinned this fox myself."

"I know. You've told me a thousand times."

He leaned close. "But you love it."

I pushed his face away.

He turned his attention to Elise. "Surely you'd like to hear my heroic tale."

"Which version?" she snipped. Whisking her handkerchief, she shooed him back.

He tipped the ugly cap as we walked around him.

We stepped through the double doors of our small church and weaved through the people and pews to the very front. Several tables were arranged next to the pulpit, each set with ample amounts of roast duckling, ham, puddings, and pies.

"It all looks so delicious," Elise said.

"Especially these." I pointed to a large batch of strawberry fritters, then scooped a generous portion onto my plate.

Elise swatted my hand. "Pig."

I pinched off the edge of one and popped it in my mouth. "These are dark times. I'm allowed."

She raised a brow. "When were you never?"

I'd barely finished filling my plate when Brom swept over and took it from me. The man had the prowess of a cat and the intelligence of a baboon.

"Wait," I said. "That's not yours."

He flashed his devil-may-care grin. "Of course it is. See? The other wives are serving their husbands."

What an idiot. "Oh dear. You must've forgotten. I'm not your wife."

He plucked up a fritter and bit in. "Then consider it practice."

He will not *steal my fritters.* I snatched the plate back, nearly spilling my precious hoard.

"Why do you taunt me like this?"

"Me? It's you who's doing the taunting." He nodded toward Father, who was across the room, talking with the Council. "Baltus says we merely have to set a date."

"Hmmm... He hasn't told me. But let me know which day you decide so I can be occupied elsewhere."

Elise stepped between us. "Come, Kat, before he starts naming your children."

We searched the packed church for a place to sit, but the assembly had overtaken the best seats. Unless we climbed to the belfry or impaled ourselves on the pipe organ, Elise and I were forced to settle next to the village busybody, Henny Van Wart. If there was no news to spread, Henny invented her own. I once heard that the minister sneezed during prayer, and because of Henny, the entire Hollow knew about it before he uttered "Amen."

"So tragic," Henny said, holding her platter in one hand and a drumstick in the other. "And no family to speak of."

I nodded as I nibbled, not wanting to spur her into one of her outrageous tales. But a nod is conversation enough for Henny. She continued.

"I hear his wife and daughter were taken by Indians some ten or so years ago. No telling what unspeakable acts befell them."

More nodding on my part.

"Poor Mr. Devenpeck found himself so distraught, he turned to drink to cure his grief, and, well, you know how that goes."

Not firsthand, but I didn't let on.

"He suffered a tumultuous tumble from society, and after some five years or so, picked himself up and started over."

As Henny's tongue wagged out her story, she waved the drumstick around like a choirmaster's baton. Twice I dodged it to avoid getting poked in the eye.

"So," she sighed, "the man finally got his life back in order, only to have the Horseman make short work of it."

Elise looked down at her meat pie like it was Nikolass's severed head. "I just don't understand, of all the villagers, why him?"

Though it was a question that had endlessly plagued me, I nudged Elise with my knee. *Don't encourage her.*

"Oh, I suspect it was some form of sacrilege on the part of Mr. Devenpeck," Henny clucked.

"Sacrilege?" Elise and I spouted together.

Oh, Henny, what have you cooked up now?

She drew so close I could smell the meaty seasonings on her breath. "It seems he used pages of old copybooks to patch the schoolhouse windows, and when there were none to spare, he used pages from a hymnal."

"I hardly find that sacrilegious," I said. "Why would a hymnal be of more value than repairs to the school?"

Henny craned back like I'd committed a sacrilege of my own. "Because they contain praises to God!"

I tilted my head, considering it. "So you're saying God summoned the Horseman to rise up against the teacher because He was offended by Nikolass's actions to protect the children from all manner of weather and bugs?" Absurd.

"Of course God didn't summon the Horseman, but he obviously ignored Nikolass's prayers while the Hessian…" Here she paused, and using the drumstick, made an imaginary slash across her bulky neck.

I lifted my chin. "Well, I think he was an honorable man

and an innocent victim." If indeed Nikolass Devenpeck had been plagued by years of grief and drink, he certainly didn't need to be remembered as godless too. "And," I added, "he didn't need a hymnal. As I recall, he had all the psalms memorized."

Henny eyed me suspiciously. "I didn't know you knew the schoolmaster so well."

"I didn't. I only saw him at Sunday service...*which* he attended regularly."

Henny narrowed her eyes, giving me a slantwise look. "Hmmm... He was more than twice your age, but a comely man to be sure. I can see why you had eyes for him."

I choked on a fritter making its way down. "No. *No.* I didn't have eyes for him."

She lowered her voice. "Now, now, dear. Your secret is safe with me."

"I have nothing to hide." I turned to Elise, who was struggling for composure. No help there.

Henny's gray-speckled eyes danced. "Don't you worry, Katrina, I will not tell a single soul."

Only the entire village. "There was *nothing* between Mr. Devenpeck and me."

Henny nodded once, condescendingly, as though promising to keep a secret.

"Urrrgh!" *Why didn't I keep my mouth shut?* I rose, clutched my plate tightly, and stomped off.

Elise sprang up and came after me. She was trying unsuccessfully not to giggle.

"It's not funny," I said, wanting badly to flick some of my fritter crumbs in her face.

She placed her hand on my shoulder in an attempt to settle my rattled nerves. "Stop worrying, Kat. Henny Van Wart is just a large sail of foul wind. No one listens to her."

"Everyone listens to her."

"But no one believes her."

She was right, of course, but it didn't ease my frustration. Though I still had several fritters that could. We found a quiet corner behind the altar.

I was about to take an ample bite when my friend Marten Piers shoved his way through a group of standing mourners. They glared, curling their lips in distaste. And no wonder. He was still wearing his fishing garments—gray breeches and shirt (smeared with who knows what), and a red knit cap that he tugged off, revealing hair as tangled as his casting net.

"Katrina," he blurted, panting like he'd just raced up from the docks. It had to be dire for him to come dressed as he was.

Elise put her handkerchief to her nose. "Dear Lord, Marten, you smell like mackerel."

He took a step back, but kept his eyes to mine. "Katrina, come, I must speak with you."

I hopped up from the chair. "What's wrong?"

"Just come," he said, nodding toward the door. "I haven't much time."

As I was setting aside my plate, Brom stepped forward, blocking the way. "Much time for what?"

More of that catlike agility. If he'd been born twenty years earlier he could've served as a military spy.

Marten's face momentarily dipped, then he stood taller, chin raised. "I didn't expect to see you here."

Brom crossed his arms, challenging. "At least I dressed for the occasion."

Except for the hat.

"Marten," I said, "let's go." I hitched my skirt, ready to rush out.

But Marten stood firm, still facing Brom.

"Marten," I repeated.

I shoved him hard, spitting away the taste of his kiss. "Were you kicked in the head?" I stomped back toward my horse. I swear, in all the years I'd known Brom, he'd never once tried to take advantage of me. Why would he break that trust now?

He rushed forward, blocking my path, his chestnut eyes glimmering. "What's wrong? Too soon after your lover's demise?"

And now he was speaking in riddles. "What on earth are you talking about?"

He cocked a brow. "Still mourning the loss of old Nikolass? Missing your midnight trysts?"

He could only have heard that from one person. "Henny?"

His laughter shook some birds from a tree. "Who else? According to her, you're the reason he came to Sleepy Hollow in the first place."

I clenched my fists. "That woman." Again I tried to leave. Again he blocked the way.

"Calm down," he said, still chuckling. "No one believes the prattles of that old witch."

Nevertheless. "Brom, step out of the way now or I'll tell Father how you lied to lure me here."

"I didn't lie. This *is* farm business."

"How?" If I had a shred of patience left, it was thinning fast.

He stood taller as a gleam lit his eyes. "I spoke with Baltus. He's giving me this acreage to build a house."

Maybe it was me who'd been kicked in the head. My mouth lopped open and I was momentarily speechless. What he'd said made no sense. The only man-made structure here was an old granary. Father would never allow this place to be ruined. "You're a bigger liar than Henny. Why on earth would he offer it to you?"

He held up his hands like it was crystal clear. "So we'll have a place to live once we're married." He reached for another kiss, but I shoved him off. Then I searched his eyes for the truth. "Brom, did you go behind my back and ask Father for my hand?"

"It was going to happen eventually, and you're already eighteen."

"It was never going to happen, and it never will. Would you get that through your thick head?"

He huffed a huge sigh as he gazed across the landscape, then he brought his eyes back to mine. "Be logical, Katrina."

"Logical?"

"It's a good business match."

Yes, Father's guarantee that he'll stay on as overseer. What Brom lacked in civility, he made up for in productivity. Our farm had earned far more under his supervision.

"Oh, so now I'm just an asset for bargaining?"

His mouth twitched until he finally admitted, "There's also the fact that I love you. You know that."

And something I'd always tried to ignore. "Brom, I don't have those feelings for you." Even if I did, I could never put up with his endless brawling and half-witted stunts. He, along with Marten and Garritt, were always up to some foolishness—especially after an evening at the River Song tavern. Where there was mischief, Brom was involved—be it cockfights, racing, or ridiculous pranks like upending an outhouse or stringing wire to knock a rider from his horse. I would be marrying a child.

"I won't marry you, Brom. *Or* allow you to spoil this beautiful property by building a house on it." I stormed by him, but he caught me by the waist.

"Now, now," he whispered. "Settle down."

I pried his hands off. "That's my point. I won't settle

down. I'll never settle down. Especially with someone who spends most evenings reveling and gambling and—"

He drew a quick breath. "Katrina, I assure you, I am done with carousing and foolish games."

"And that is supposed to sway me?"

He rose a little taller, piercing me with his eyes. "This marriage makes good sense."

"To you," I said, stomping around him. "You can bully everyone else, Brom, but you won't bully me. And given a choice"—I threw myself upon my horse—"I'd rather marry the Horseman."

* * *

That night I dreamt of Nikolass in his coffin. His body sinking into the wooden flooring, his folded hands hardening like stone. The gaping wound where his head once sat served as a doorway for all manner of parasites. They crept like sap oozing from pine bark—millipedes, woodlice, ticks, scorpions, maggots, and mites. Wiggling and squirming and eating their way through him.

My bed curtain rustled against me, and though I didn't fully awake, I jumped as if one of the insects had made its way out of his coffin—out of my dream—and scuttled up my arm. Wrestling with sleep, I was powerless to fling it off. It writhed its way under my skin, and I could do nothing but lie motionless and suppressed. A silent shriek engulfed me, yet I could not expel it. I burned from my struggle to scream. The bed curtains closed in, and I became trapped in a coffin of my own. I fought for breath, inhaling leeches and snails and other manner of grave dwellers. *Wake up! Wake up!* But the paralysis kept its hold.

Beyond this, I heard him…the Horseman, whipping toward our farm.

Dear God! I will not come. I will not.

The Horseman only rose at night. At dawn, he returned to his grave, his cell, with only the maggots and mites for company. Would he take me there with him? Would this nightmare become my reality?

As he drew nearer my senses heightened, and I woke up gasping for air. But just as quickly, I froze. My dream had vanished, but the Horseman had not. He rode close by, hooves beating against the heavy clay of the road leading to our farm. Perspiration covered me. My nightdress clung to my skin. Yet a chill washed over me like a rippling tide.

I will not go.

He journeyed closer. Had my dream mystically drawn him, or had he purposely waited till now for my capture?

Curiosity ate at me like the insects in my dream. I gathered the courage to slip from my bed and take the tiniest peek through my window. I strained to see, but he rode in shadow. Still, he approached. I waited and watched, my mouth parched, my heart banging against my chest. Moments later, the black clouds parted and the moonlight shone upon him. I exhaled for the first time in what seemed like an eternity. It was only Brom, riding past our farm to his cabin. I didn't know the hour, but could sense it was late…or early, rather. Far past midnight.

And he'd said he was done with carousing and foolish games.

I eased back onto my bed, my nerves a shattered mess. The Horseman had not come, yet I could feel his cold breath upon me.

* * *

Over the next week, Sleepy Hollow became ghostly and withdrawn. While there were no credible sightings of the Horseman, rumors of witchcraft spread like the Tappan Zee. The slaves took precautions, wearing all manner of crude charms and enchantments. Simon, our house servant, carved a protective talisman for me from a black willow root—an oblong pendant with a spiraling eye. I discreetly wore it tucked into my bodice. Of course, with Father insisting I remain inside, I had nothing to dread. Other than being imprisoned in my own home.

Twice I sent messages to the dock, hoping to reach Marten, but he sometimes spent a week or more on the water. What had he wanted to tell me? Just when I thought I might literally burst, he finally showed up.

"Marten, I've been so worried," I whispered, stepping onto the piazza.

He placed a finger to his lips and led me away from the door. "Katrina, I've done it."

I searched his eyes. "Done…what?" This was Marten, the boy who always reached for the impossible, yet never came close.

"I have arranged for the purchase of a ship."

I stood, thunderstruck. No wonder he'd burst in at the funeral.

He bent his knees to be eye level with me. "Did you hear me?"

"Yes," I said, blinking away my shock. He'd always talked of owning his own vessel, but on his wages? I never dreamed it'd be a reality. "But…how?"

He scratched his head, looking away.

Gripping his chin, I turned his gaze back to mine. "Where did you get the money?"

He waved it off. "Don't worry. It's taken care of."

"I worry, Marten. I always worry. And even more so since we're whispering."

He placed his hands on my arms and lowered us onto one of the wooden benches.

"Marten," I urged, "why so secretive?"

"Because," he said, "when it arrives, I'm leaving the Hollow for good. And I want you to come with me."

Though Marten and I were only friends, we'd always sworn that one day we'd leave Sleepy Hollow and sail off to exotic ports unknown. I never thought it'd actually come to pass. Was this my escape? Had my "someday" finally arrived?

My heartbeat quickened and a thousand thoughts flickered through my mind. "When?"

"Not for a few weeks."

"Weeks?" *He offers a chance at escape, then tells me this?*

He rubbed his hands together, fidgeting. "No one's more frustrated than I. But it's currently sailing up from the West Indies. And it'll need some repairs and preparations."

I didn't hide my disappointment. "A lot can happen in a few weeks."

"Or in the blink of an eye." His ominous tone was reflected on his face. "Keep in mind, there are *other* arrangements to be made."

"What other arrangements?"

His expression flattened as he leaned close. "Katrina, think. Your father would spare no expense to hunt us down and bring you back. And with his wealth and power…"

Father would definitely find a way. Not to mention the unspeakable things Brom would do to Marten if we were caught.

"But don't worry," he said. "I'll work it out." He nudged me and winked. "I'm clever that way."

I couldn't keep the smile from my face. "Yes, you certainly are."

"In the meantime," he said, "don't breathe a word to anyone. Only you and the necessary parties know I've purchased this ship. If you're to go with me, it must remain secret."

I nodded. The only person I'd even consider telling was Elise, but I'd never risk it.

"I must go," he said, rising, "but I'll return soon with more news."

I walked him to the steps. "Marten." He turned his soft blue eyes to mine. "Thank you."

He gave me a warm smile, then left.

* * *

I had only seen Garritt, the notary's son, once in all that time, and that was at Sunday service. I gasped at the sight of him. A walking death. His eyes were red veins and his pallor like sour milk. I tried to speak with him, but he kept evading me...and everyone else, for that matter.

Rumor was, when he wasn't working for his father, he was hiding behind a glass of rum. So it was quite unexpected to see him at the town meeting that evening, sitting next to his father and squirming like a schoolboy. His russet hair hung stringy and unkempt, though he'd occasionally rake his trembling fingers through it. He had always been so witty and full of laughter. I had to find out what had set him on edge.

Due to the late hour, the meeting was not well attended. The church, serving as our town hall, was only half filled. Magistrate Harding, along with the other councilmen—Father, Notary de Graff, Hans Van Ripper, Reverend Bushnell and Caspar Jansen (Elise's father)—were present. The topic of news was the arrival of the new schoolmaster, expected within the next few days. Since Father was the one who hired him, he presided, standing over the seated members.

"His name is Ichabod Crane," he announced. "And he'll be coming to us from Connecticut. His references are reputable and his credentials impressive."

Ichabod? What a ridiculous name. No doubt he'd be old and dumpy with a bald pate, shiny as a polished kettle.

Father placed a hand on Van Ripper's shoulder. "Of course he'll be lodging at the Van Ripper farm, just as Nikolass had. But being the hospitable community that we are, I expect Mr. Crane will be a dinner guest for many of us over time. Keep in mind, we are extremely lucky to have him take over the position of schoolmaster."

But is it lucky for Mr. Crane?

"So as not to jinx our good fortune," he went on, "I propose that we keep the circumstances of his predecessor's death to ourselves."

That sparked some mumbling among the gathering. The notary's head snapped to Father. "You'd have us lie to him?"

Garritt slumped, his face wincing in pain.

The magistrate rose, his mouth puckered in a scowl. I'd never seen the man when he didn't look like someone had cheated him at cards. "We're not asking anyone to condemn their soul. But in the interest of the Hollow, maybe we can avoid a direct answer to that question should Mr. Crane ask."

"Besides," Father said, "I addressed it in my letter to him. I admit I wasn't truthful, stating that Mr. Devenpeck had died of natural causes. But do you think he would've agreed to come otherwise?"

How would you explain that in a letter?

Dear Mr. Crane, we are gratified with your decision to accept our offer of employment as schoolmaster of Sleepy Hollow. We're confident that you'll find our community both amiable and enriching, with the exception of our headless ghost who unfortunately, took a disliking to our former teacher and sliced off his head. Sincerely, etc.

But there was one thing I didn't understand, and I risked voicing it. "Won't having him to dinner be putting him in danger? That would be after nightfall."

Half of the Council bristled, while Father bored a hole through me with his glare.

Hans Van Ripper's face twisted into a grimace—a look he never wore well. "I'm providin' his shelter, but I can't be responsible for all his meals."

Father held up a hand to calm him. When he spoke, he addressed the assembly, not me. "It's been discussed. The Council sees no reason that the Horseman would be a threat to Mr. Crane."

This brought a stilled hush over the room.

The notary lowered his quill. "Though I doubt the secret of Devenpeck's death will stay secret for long."

No doubt at all. Henny Van Wart would probably break out in hives trying to hold it in.

Father tapped his knuckles on the table. "It is the education of our children at stake here." He threw another glare at me. "We'll carry on in our *usual* manner."

Usual, in this case, meaning I stay quiet. Seeing as how I was lucky to be out of the house, I pledged to keep my mouth shut.

As Father continued with more tidbits about welcoming Mr. Crane, I noticed Garritt glance back toward the church doors. Curious, I looked too. Brom stood there like a sentry guarding a palace. He must have just slipped in. I turned back toward the altar, aware of how safe I felt inside the church. I held on to that security, knowing that once the meeting was over I'd be in my father's carriage, exposed to the mysticism of the night and all the perils of darkness. There would be no window separating me from the beckoning Horseman.

After further town business, Reverend Bushnell led us in prayer. We adjourned to a draw of coffee and pie. Garritt still sat, staring at the floor. I picked up a cup of coffee, intending to take it to him. As I crossed the room, Brom slinked over and plucked the cup from its saucer.

"Will you stop doing that?" I said. "I'm not serving you."

He cocked a brow. "You will."

I was two breaths away from knocking that scalding coffee all over him.

"The harvest party is nearing," he said with a confident smile. "The perfect time and place to announce our engagement."

The man was hopeless.

I patted his chest. "That sounds wonderful, Brom. I hope you and your delusions live happily ever after."

He simply snickered.

Paying no further attention to him, I crossed over to where Garritt sat. He looked to be holding back tears. I settled beside him. "Garritt, what's wrong?"

"Katrina…" he whispered. I waited for him to continue, but he only held my gaze.

"Please, tell me. Is there anything I can do? Is there anything you need?"

"Katrina," he repeated. This time I thought he might pour out his soul. But his demeanor went from anxious to cautious as he looked over my head at someone standing behind me.

"Yes," Brom boomed. "*Need* anything? A coffee perhaps?" He held up the cup he'd just snatched from me.

Garritt turned back, arms folded. "I need nothing from you."

"Ah, come on," Brom said. "Have some pie."

I turned to Brom, firing my anger. "Would you stop?"

My words rolled off him like water on a stone wall. "I'm only trying to help."

"You can help by leaving."

Garritt closed his eyes and placed his hands over his ears. What in the world was causing this torment?

"Garritt," I tried again. "Please. I do want to help you."

He tossed a look at Brom, then me. Then he rocked

forward and glared like a madman. Chills scuttled down my spine. "I saw him."

Brom set aside his coffee and knelt eyelevel to him. "Saw who?"

Garritt didn't hesitate. "The Horseman."

Dear God. "You saw him?"

Brom merely shook his head. How could he have so little compassion?

"Yes," Garritt answered. "Last night. I'd been penning some contracts for Father. I stepped outside for a moment…" His face pinched. "The Horseman was there, waiting. He charged me." Garritt's hands quaked as perspiration beaded his brow. "God, it was like nothing I'd ever seen. His horse snorted smoke and its hooves fired white sparks like flint on steel." He paused for composure, yet his body still shook. "But unlike the legend, he didn't carry a sword." Here, he gave Brom a stern, beleaguered look. "It was a scythe. And he meant to have my head."

Brom still showed no shock or sympathy. "Obviously you escaped unharmed."

"Unharmed?" I blurted. "Can't you see he's tormented?

Garritt rubbed his face so hard I thought he might peel away skin.

"What did you do?" I asked, reminding myself to breathe.

He shifted his eyes toward me. "I barely made it inside. The Horseman lingered, circling our house twice. Then approached the window next to my bed." Tears now fell. "He ran his scythe against the glass, scoring a blackened slash within the pane." He clamped his fists to his ears. "I can't stop hearing that noise."

I imagined the teeth-gnashing shriek echoing through his head. I leaned closer. "Why did you not report this?"

He brushed the wetness from his cheeks. "For fear that no

one would believe me."

"After Nikolass's death? Don't be absurd. You must say something."

He winced, then rubbed his brow. "Please, Katrina, I'd rather not speak of it."

"But you should," I said, clutching his sleeve. "Do it now while everyone is gathered."

Brom plucked my hand from Garritt's coat. "Relax. It was probably just a bad dream. "

Garritt whipped him a fiery look. "It was no dream!" I dodged the spittle from his rage.

Brom rose, nodding. "Fine. If you're convinced, so am I." He picked up his coffee and took a sip. "I say we devise a clever plan to destroy this headless brute once and for all."

I stood and met his eye. "Are you insane?" A redundant question. "He should report it to the Council."

He puffed his chest, choosing to ignore me. "Come, Garritt. We'll conspire at the tavern. Surely there is some tangible manner of defeating a ghost. We'll simply put our *heads* together on this." A curl of a smile played on his lips.

Garritt pushed up from the pew and straightened his waistcoat. He sniffled back his remaining tears. "No. I promised Father I'd accompany him tonight, but hereafter I'm staying in."

"Garritt—" I started.

"And I'll not report it." He brushed past me and hurried to where his father stood.

Brom scoffed, shaking his head. "The boy's gone stark raving mad."

I shoved him hard, spilling the coffee down the front of his vest. "You're the only madman here."

I turned quickly, planning to plead with Garritt again, but Brom clutched my arm, holding me back. "He needs a drink more than he needs you."

I jerked free. "He needs someone he can trust."

When I turned back, Garritt and his father had gathered their things. I stood trembling as they pushed through the church doors and into the night.

Yes, Father, we'll all carry on in our usual manner.

* * *

I didn't see Garritt in the days that followed. He kept good to his word of staying in. No one else had seen him either. His father made excuses, and rumors of his drinking grew worse.

Poor Garritt. The boy who used to chase me across the fields and leap out our hayloft window was now a dark shell. The Horseman had seen to that. His mark upon Garritt's window must serve as a constant reminder. I felt I should say something, but didn't want to betray his trust.

Then word came that Ichabod Crane had arrived. Two days afterward, Father suggested that Elise and I go to the schoolhouse to welcome him. We were to put on our brightest smiles, be cordial, and act as though nothing were amiss. I happily obliged. It's hard not to smile when you're finally given a reprieve.

Placing a basket of apples, plums, and blackberry muffins into the buggy, we rode lazily to the school.

"Hmmm..." Elise said, stretching her chin up toward the delft-blue sky. "I bet he's a warty, toothless old toad with bulging eyes and a croaking voice."

I gave her a sidelong glance. "With a name like Ichabod, would you expect anything less?"

Her face soured. After some thought, she added, "Though I do expect he'll be better dressed than Mr. Devenpeck."

How could he not? "Well, he is from Connecticut. And Father says he's a scholar."

"That would mean no drooping wig, faded gabardine, or shoe buckles."

I shook my head. "Oh, believe me, if he's as ancient as he sounds, there *will* be shoe buckles."

Elise sputtered a giggle.

My thoughts went to poor Nikolass, who'd always seemed so innocent and quiet. "But it's sad when you think about it. Mr. Devenpeck was pleasant and kind. And aside from his dreadful clothing, he was a fairly nice-looking man."

"Ah!" She pointed a finger at my face. "You did have eyes for him."

"No." I twisted her finger, shoving it away. "Ugh. The man was well into his thirties."

"And so were his breeches," she added.

"Elise! You're shameless." Our eyes met, and we both broke into a fit of laughter.

Thankfully, God didn't smite us for speaking ill of the dead, and we soon arrived at our destination.

"Remember," Elise said, her voice low, "we're going to give him this fruit basket, make some nice remarks about the weather, politely warn him about Henny, and then excuse ourselves and go."

It sounded like a fair plan. But before stepping down, I said, "Wait." I removed a napkin and set aside two of the blackberry muffins. "Afterward we'll ride down to the river. We can sit for a while and watch the boats." I planned to hold on to my freedom as long as I could.

She tilted her head toward me. "The boats or those brawny young dock workers unloading cargo?"

I quirked a brow. "Can you think of a better pastime?"

She snatched up the basket. "Come on, let's hurry."

We breezed into the open schoolhouse and...empty. There were indications that someone had been rearranging desks, patching holes, and stacking firewood. A cozy contrast to the original state of the quarters.

The school had once been the home of Bartholomeus Smedt, a troll of a man with no kith or kin. He shied away from society, preferring the life of a hermit. I heard many a wild story about old Bartholomeus while growing up. When he died two years ago, the Council took over his property. Inside the weathered one-room house they found only a straw pallet, some crockery, and an iron stove. But it was what they found in his earthen root cellar that proved most interesting. It served as a repository for all manner of weapons. He'd stockpiled a vast number of muskets and pistols, and a considerable amount of gunpowder. It was determined that he had not been a soldier, but a scavenger of war—stealing weapons from the dead. The munitions were cleared away, and when Mr. Devenpeck arrived, he quickly learned to keep the cellar locked as it proved a favorite hideout for truant children.

Pushing aside a stack of books on the desk, I set the basket down. I pointed to a coat, draped over the back of a chair. "Where do you suppose he is?"

Elise shrugged. "Maybe he just stepped out."

"Stepped out where?"

We walked around the schoolyard to the old birch near the brook. Then I saw him, ambling toward us. My heart danced like never before. This young man was eons from the warty old toad we'd imagined. He couldn't have been more than three years older than us. And with his waistcoat unfastened and white cambric shirt rolled at the cuffs, he hardly seemed the teacher sort. Though he did carry what looked like a small journal and a lead pencil in his hand.

As we grew closer, his mouth curved into an endearing smile. "Good afternoon," he called to us.

"Good afternoon," we returned.

Up close proved even better. His dark hair fell in wisps, framing his angelic face. His smiling lips accentuated the dimple on his cheek. And his eyes—*Those eyes!*—as green as our meadow, shimmering with morning dew.

Elise practically stumbled, pushing in front of me. "You must be Ichabod Crane. I'm Elise Jansen. We, uh, looked for you inside, but you weren't there, so we came here, so here you are, and here we are and..." She rushed and bungled every word. I might've come to her rescue if I hadn't been so absorbed in him myself.

"I'm sorry I wasn't there. It's just that"—he pointed back toward the brook—"there's a comfortable patch of clover near the water. It's an excellent spot to relax and think." He tucked the small book and pencil into his pocket, and turned those fabulous eyes to me. "And you must be..."

I blinked away my awe. "Katrina...Van Tassel."

His face suddenly came alive. "A relation to Baltus Van Tassel?"

"Yes. He's my father."

"I have to say, I'm extremely grateful to him."

"We're grateful as well," Elise blurted. Her cheeks blushed when she realized she'd said that out loud. But then, I'd be grateful too if I weren't planning an escape on Marten's ship.

She quickly regained her composure and slowed her words. "It's a pleasure to meet you."

His eyes sparkled like the glimmer on the brook. "Likewise. Come, let's go inside."

The trees were alive with birdsong as he accompanied us back to the school. Or maybe that was my heart singing. It took tremendous willpower to keep from staring, while questions raced through my mind. *What's it like in Connecticut? Why'd you trade it for the dullness of Sleepy Hollow? What were you writing in that notebook? And how did such an adorable creature as yourself end up with a name like Ichabod?* Ugh. There's not even a suitable nickname for that.

I was hoping Elise would blurt out some of these for me, but she kept her remarks to the weather. That was safe territory for her.

Once inside the school, Ichabod spotted the basket we'd left on his desk. He picked up one of the ruby apples and cocked a brow. "An apple for the teacher?"

"Fresh from our orchard," Elise said. Her flaxen lashes batted like moth wings. I nudged her foot with mine. She kept a tight smile as she nudged back.

Ichabod polished the apple on his rolled sleeve then brought it to his mouth. "Goodness, if everyone here is this generous, I'll have no regrets leaving home." Juicy bits sputtered as he crunched down.

Elise giggled like a five-year-old. But his remark brought back that niggling question. "Why did you leave?" I asked. I hadn't meant to be so forward, but honestly, why would anyone as young as he want to live here?

Elise, still keeping that tight smile, lightly nudged me with her elbow. "Kat, maybe we should let him get settled before we start hurling personal questions."

He waved it off. "I don't mind. The truth is Hartford was closing in on me. I was needing a little peace and quiet. I've found there's plenty of that. I think I'll thrive well here."

Unless the Horseman takes a fancy to you.

He sat down on the corner of his desk and held the basket out. "Would you like to share?"

Elise politely declined. I, on the other hand, took one of the blackberry muffins. I nicked off a tiny bite as I glanced about the schoolroom. He certainly appeared earnest. The rows of desks were uniformly lined, a copybook atop each one. On his desk were the stacks of books I'd earlier pushed aside. I stepped by him and drew two of them toward me. *Gulliver's Travels* and *Robinson Crusoe*.

He twisted around to see. "Those will be part of the studies."

"I love these books," I said, pinching off another taste of my muffin.

"You've read them?" He leaned close enough that I could smell the tang of apple on his breath. My stomach fluttered faster than Elise's eyelashes.

"My father has an extensive library," I answered, trying to stay focused. "And since I've traveled so little, books have always been my escape."

"No better holiday," he said.

I beg to differ.

Elise nudged between us and picked up a small book the color of red clay. The title, imprinted in gold, read: *The Thousand and One Nights—Persian Tales.* Her face brightened. "I've heard of this one." She ran her hand across the cover. "The stories are quite exotic."

"And adventurous," he added.

"Adventure," she purred.

"Yet hardly teaching material," I pointed out.

His face blushed an adorable pink. "No, that one is part of my own collection."

I couldn't think of one man in Sleepy Hollow who'd own a collection of exotic, adventurous tales. None that they could display on an open shelf anyway.

Other books on his desk included *The Iliad, Candide,* and *Don Quixote.* Impressive. Our new schoolmaster was indeed well read.

But then another book caught my eye. This one tattered from use. Clippings of paper bookmarked many of the pages, and the binding was broken and loose. When I reached for it, he fumbled, racing to pick it up first. Too late. It was already in my hand.

He dropped back like I'd done something hurtful.

I held the book carefully for fear it might fall apart. The cover contained a vile sketch of horned beings dancing among flickering tongues of fire as slithering snakes coiled around their naked bodies. The title, stamped in small print, read: *New England Witchcraft*. I instinctively touched Simon's talisman, still hidden inside my bodice.

Ichabod squirmed, and I knew this was not a book I was meant to see. "That one too is personal."

Ah, have I uncovered an evil secret behind those beautiful eyes?

"You've spent a good deal of time with this book," I said, handing it to him. "Do you believe in the black arts?"

He opened a drawer and quickly slipped the book inside. "Yes. Very much."

My eyes were drawn to the pocket of his waistcoat, and the notebook he'd concealed. I was now more eager than ever to know what things he'd written inside.

Again Elise stepped between us. "Then you'll love Sleepy Hollow. It's always been a place of specters and spirits and the supernatural."

"Really?" he said, his confidence returning.

Before she could open her mouth again, I quickly nudged her foot. "Ichabod, I'm sure you'll hear all kinds of wild tales. The people here are quite superstitious."

He set the apple down and dusted his hands. "All based on intriguing lore, I'm sure."

Don't be too sure.

I sensed more damaging words bubbling from Elise, so I quickly hooked my arm though hers. "I fear we've taken up too much of your time. We should let you get back to work."

His eyes settled on mine and held. "Not at all. It's been a pleasant distraction."

I swear, his enticing gaze could melt bronze.

"Enjoy the treats." I still held Elise close, urging her toward the door.

"Wait," she said, slipping her arm free. Once again, she batted those lashes as she addressed him. "My family would like you to dine with us this evening. You can meet my two brothers. They'll be students of yours when the school reopens."

"I'd love to," he answered, his voice soft. "And you can tell me more about the legends of Sleepy Hollow."

She trembled with glee. "Come at six. We're the farm closest to Van Ripper's."

"I'm looking forward to it. And thank you again. It was a pleasure meeting you both."

Though he'd addressed the pair of us, his eyes locked with mine. *My God, you're amazing.* It took every ounce of strength I had to walk out that door.

* * *

"And we thought he'd be an old toad," Elise said as we rode away from the school. She leaned back and took one of the muffins I'd set aside.

"Wait…"—I reached for it—"Aren't those for our trip to the river?"

She giggled like a giddy child. "Kat, really. After seeing Ichabod? Do you really want to spoil that image by staring at those boys on the dock?"

I answered by grabbing the other muffin.

"I can't believe it," she said, gazing dreamily at the azure sky. "His every feature was perfection. Hair, eyes, mouth, and…" she placed her hand to her heart. "…that charming smile."

Captivating was the word I'd use.

She sighed so heavily that loose crumbs fell onto her skirt.

"I really must thank your father for bringing us such a delicious schoolmaster."

I laughed. "I'm sure delicious was not a requirement." Though it was a benefit.

Her head was so far in the clouds, I didn't think she'd even heard me. "I have to get home and pick out a dress for dinner."

A spike of jealously stung me. It was my father who'd hired Ichabod. Why weren't we the first to invite him?

"But I'm sick of all my plain old frocks." She swept the crumbs from her dress as she pouted. Then she whipped toward me. "Kat, you have a beautiful wardrobe. May I please borrow one of yours?" She leaned close, her hands in prayer position. "Pleeeeease?"

That spike of jealousy became a spear. But then I wondered, *Why should I even care?* My sights were on the open Atlantic and wherever Marten steered us.

"You don't have to beg," I told her.

Her face lit once again. "Thank you, thank you, thank you, thank you."

While I didn't want to dump ash on her glowing passion, I couldn't help but be curious. "How'd you feel about that book?"

She turned back to me, eyebrows knitted. "Which book?"

"That book of witchcraft. He'd read it cover to cover...*many* times. Like he has an obsession."

She waved it away. "*Interest*, not obsession."

"He grew strangely uncomfortable when the subject came up."

Elise's smile returned. "Then tonight, I'll make sure it doesn't come up. There will only be laughter and enjoyment."

In a village threatened by a murdering ghost, I hoped that would be so.

* * *

It was in church on Sunday when I saw Ichabod again. The pews were filled and he sat just on the edge of the second row, hymnal and Bible both resting on his lap.

Well, Ichabod, you haven't burst into flames. Maybe I'd misjudged your interest in witchcraft.

I searched about for Garritt, but he was not there. I thought surely he'd find refuge in the church. His father sat among the elders, and though his brown suit was pressed and proper, his face had more wrinkles than an old hound. I vowed no matter what, I'd visit the de Graff home this afternoon and speak with Garritt myself. I ached to know how he was doing.

Reverend Bushnell preached a lengthy sermon, but I barely noticed. My eyes were on Ichabod. When he rose to sing, his fingers traced along the words in the hymnal. And with each hymn his voice grew louder. Either he was trying to fit in or out-sing Mrs. Twiggs, who, in spite of the hymnal, always got the words wrong.

When the last prayer was finally delivered, I searched for Elise. I had to know more about his visit at dinner. The only word I'd gotten from her was a note she'd sent by way of her younger brother, Dirk. It simply said: *Delicious*.

I had just reached her when Henny Van Wart interceded.

"Come, come, come, come, come," Henny said, herding us to a corner near the front. Elise and I pushed in next to Sally Groot and Gertie Marris, who cradled her infant son.

Henny fidgeted like a fly caught in goose grease. "I have such news of our newest resident I thought I might burst. Had I perished halfway through the sermon, I would have found a way to resurrect myself so you good ladies would not be kept from this vital information."

"Henny—" I started.

"Shh, shh, shh, shh, shh," she blustered. "It turns out our schoolmaster left his native Connecticut just in the nick of time.

Had we not offered him a position here, heaven knows where he'd be. Probably tarred and feathered, still dashing away from an angry mob."

Gertie's jaw dropped. "Why?"

Henny barely took a breath before continuing. "He hails from Hartford, you see—a city that circulates several newspapers and periodicals. Using an assumed name, he published a lewd serial in one of the publications." She lowered her voice. "Tales of debauchery."

Sally and Gertie gasped. I, on the other hand, was more intrigued than alarmed.

Their amazement only enlivened Henny. "Each week it featured horrific topics that glorified all manner of vulgar behavior. When the upstanding citizens of Hartford learned that it was he, they literally chased him out of town with cudgels and pitchforks. I dare-say he ran all the way here."

I tried to visualize a gathering of city folk with pitchforks. Absurd.

Elise bubbled with anxiety. "What types of things did he publish?"

"Dreadful things," Henny answered, placing a hand to her heart. "Tales of smugglers, gamblers, prostitution—"

"And don't forget my favorite," came a soft voice behind us. I turned to see Ichabod leaning against the pulpit, his eyes bright with amusement. "A particularly engrossing piece that involved men dressed in women's apparel. Quite shocking."

Henny gasped, her face turning one shade darker than a turnip. "I dare-say!"

"It provided me extra money while studying at the university. You should consider publishing, Mrs. Van Wart. I'm sure you could produce a riveting weekly scandal sheet."

I gulped back my laughter and could see Elise suppressing a grin as well.

"I would do nothing of the sort," Henny said. "I am not one to indulge in such tasteless behavior." She hitched her head high, nose in the air. "Come, ladies." She turned and stormed away. Sally and Gertie lingered a moment then awkwardly followed.

Elise and I erupted into fits of giggles.

"Sorry," I sputtered, covering my mouth with my hand. "It's just that no one ever stands up to Henny."

"Was any of that true?" Elise asked, her eyes anxious and starry.

"Yes," he answered, a little more timid. "I published a lot of stories back home."

I raised a brow in question. "Tales of debauchery?"

His playful smile melted my heart. "That would depend on how you define the word. But no, nothing like Mrs. Van Wart suggested." He leaned close. "And none of my heroes would be caught dead in a corset."

That conjured an intriguing image. "So...no pitchforks?"

He looked down at the seat of his breeches. "Hmmm... No holes. No pitchforks."

I held up a finger. "For all we know, you could just be a fast runner."

He lifted his foot and looked at the sole of his shoe. "Nope."

"But what kinds of stories did you publish?" Elise asked, fawning.

This he answered with a fair amount of pride. "Tales of courage, love, adventure—rogues and risk-takers, rubes and royalty. My mind is overrun with fantasy."

Elise swooned over his every word. "Much like those Persian tales?"

"My stories are quite different. Perhaps I could share one with you the next time I visit your farm."

She clutched her hands together, beaming. "I'd love that. We could have you back before week's end."

"Perfect." He then turned to me, his eyes dancing beneath his dark lashes. "There's one particular story of mine that might interest you, Katrina. I could bring it this evening."

"This evening?"

"Yes." He pointed toward Father, grumbling with the councilmen in their usual corner. "Baltus has invited me to dinner."

I worked to keep my composure. "That's wonderful. I look forward to it." Here was my chance to learn if *he* was a rogue or risk-taker.

Elise's jaw tightened. "How lucky you are"—she gritted her teeth—"to be the first to enjoy his work."

If her teeth ground any tighter, they'd shatter from her mouth. And if that wasn't enough, she daggered me with her glare as well.

Before I could reply, Marten approached, head lowered. This time he wore appropriate attire. "Katrina, I must speak with you." He spoke quietly, but I detected a sense of urgency in his tone.

Please don't tell me our plans are off.

"Privately," he added.

Elise suddenly relaxed—delighted, I'm sure, that I was leaving her to a full helping of Ichabod.

"Excuse us," I said.

Marten led me behind the pulpit.

Once out of sight, I gripped his arm. "What's happened? Has the purchase fallen through?"

"Shhh." He shook his head. "No. Not that."

I exhaled relief.

"It's Garritt," he said. "I've been to his house twice this week. He won't see me."

Marten and Garritt were the closest of friends. I could see Garritt turning anyone away but him.

"Has he indicated why?" I didn't mention the Horseman, though I was sure Brom had informed him of Garritt's encounter.

"No, but I think he's panicked."

What I saw at the meeting that night was more than panic. It was pure madness. "Have you spoken with his father?"

"He says Garritt's extremely ill. Doctor Goodwine is calling it hysteria. Daily bloodlettings haven't helped, and they've tried all manner of vinegars and draughts." He looked at me as though I'd have a solution.

There was one unspoken question between us. "Has he told them of the Horseman?"

Marten shook his head. "I don't think so."

"Why not? After what happened to Mr. Devenpeck, surely they'd be looking for a way to help him, not cure him."

Marten moved in close, his voice low. "Katrina, do you believe him? That he truly saw the Horseman?"

"Why wouldn't I? Why would there even be a doubt?"

"It's possible that he ate something disagreeable and Devenpeck's death triggered a hallucination."

"He ate something disagreeable? Oh, Marten, listen to yourself. "

"But there are cases of people who've become hysterical just from ingesting bad grain."

"And there are cases of people who were bewitched and murdered just like our former schoolmaster. Garritt has somehow attracted the wrath of the Horseman, and we must do what we can to help him."

Marten stepped back, giving in, but the worry never left his face.

I placed a hand on his. "Listen, I'll ride out to his place this afternoon and persuade Notary de Graff to let me in."

Marten leaned close, eyes narrowed. "Katrina, that could take some bewitching from you."

* * *

It was well after three before I could sneak out undetected. Being a Sunday, I knew Brom would not be near the stables. He only abided by the Sabbath when it came to work. I took every precaution not to encounter him. I quietly saddled Dewdrop and rode away.

A scattering of cotton clouds dotted the sky. The scent of pine and spruce filled the air, and the chattering of woodland creatures accompanied me. Had this not been such a grave endeavor, I would've relished the afternoon sun on my face.

The fall air was cool, normal for this time of year, but as I approached the de Graff home, I gaped. At present, the trees of Sleepy Hollow wore an array of autumn colors—a blending of lime, jade, ash, gold, and coral. But the trees on their property were barren and dry, as though they'd been embraced by some pestilence or blight. Their rotting limbs resembled skeletal fingers, all pointing toward the house.

The Horseman's handiwork.

The grass had also succumbed to some unnatural plague. Withered and scorched. It looked as through fire had rained down upon it.

What must the notary think?

Dewdrop slowed to a canter as we neared the property line.

"Come on, girl," I said.

She stopped, refusing to take another step.

I snapped the reins. "Make haste."

She remained firm, nodding and braying distress.

"Fine, then." I dismounted, intending to lead her the rest of the way, but she fought, pulling back and nearly dragging me to the ground. Her ears pricked, and her black eyes grew wild with fear, arousing a sense of dread that rippled my flesh. But I couldn't turn back. Garritt was enclosed in this hellish terrain. I had to see him.

I towed Dewdrop back to one of the living trees—"You're just making this more difficult!"—and secured her to a limb. She wrestled with the branch. It felt more like a warning than an attempt at escape. *Animals sense danger.* I quickly turned away, refusing to heed.

It was only fifty paces back to the de Graff property, but one step into it and—*Holy God!*—the air grew bitterly cold. I pulled my shawl tighter around my arms, wishing I'd worn wool instead. There'd been no forewarning that the Horseman had left his mark upon the climate here too.

I walked in haste, drawing closer and closer. The house itself looked the same. The small saltbox structure stood firm as always, the paint and trim unmarred. The dark smoke of the chimney disappeared into the graying sky.

As I reached the porch, I noticed a medicinal wreath on the door. No doubt placed there to ward off disease. But rather than green and aromatic, the sprigs appeared to have been touched by flame. Whatever it meant to keep out had burned its way through.

With a trembling hand, I tapped lightly on the door. Within moments Notary de Graff appeared, his waistcoat unbuttoned and his shirt hanging loose. He looked woefully weary, as though all strength had abandoned him.

"Katrina. We were not expecting you."

"Many pardons, notary. I'm here to see Garritt." How foolish of me not to bring a gift—mutton soup or sweet cakes. Something to show my goodwill.

"You know that Garritt isn't well. He cannot receive guests."

"I am aware, but this is urgent."

He narrowed his gaze. "In what manner?"

"I…uh…" Since the only urgency was my desire to talk to Garritt, I had to pull a reason out of thin air. Then I remembered the talisman that Simon had made for me. I uncovered it from my bodice. "I have brought him this."

The notary reached out and touched the carved trinket, running a finger across the spiral. "Very intricate. Is this some rare charm?"

"Yes, sir. It is for health and protection."

Other men in Sleepy Hollow might scoff at such a thing, but the kindled wreath on the door told me that the notary was a man of superstition.

"That's very generous of you, Katrina." He held out his hand. "I shall deliver it to him with your good wishes."

"I wish to deliver it myself." I spoke as calmly as possible, trying to hide my panic.

He briskly shook his head. "That's not possible."

"Please, I'll take no more than a minute."

He began to slowly close the door. "I should be attending my son. I'll give him your regards."

"Wait!" I removed the talisman from my neck. "Here."

The notary gave me a disheartened smile. "This is very kind of you."

And with those words, he shut me out.

I stepped off the small porch, my spirits low. It made sense that Garritt would close himself away from the Horseman, but close out his friends as well?

The whistling wind whipped across the property. It was like cold fingers raking my flesh. I heard my name whispered within the gust—*Katrina*—and felt *his* pale breath upon my neck. Or had it just been my imagination, stirred by the bleak surroundings? *I hope.*

Anyone else would've ridden straight home, but it was my

stubborn nature that guided me. I quietly slipped around to the side of the house, tiptoeing toward the back.

I lingered in the chill with the presumption that the notary would deliver the talisman to Garritt straight away. How long he'd remain, I could only guess. I had no sense of time—it being void here—and let instinct guide me.

I pressed myself to the wall and ticked off seconds in my head. *One…two…three…*With my eyes closed, the stale air reeked stronger. It clung to my skin and I could taste it on my tongue. But I wouldn't lose count…*thirty-five…thirty-six…thirty-seven…* Something brushed past my ankle! I jerked aside, shaking my skirts. *What in the name of…?* The ground moved! It spiraled and churned like the inner workings of a clock. How was that possible?

My heart pounded as I knelt for a closer look. *Oh God!* I leapt back, clapping my hands to my mouth. *Snakes!* Masses of them—brown and speckled like the barren soil. They moved chaotically, weaving about with no sense of direction. Their tongues flickered. Their bodies coiled. Two fought over a field mouse, still squirming for its life. Another had swallowed its own tail.

With my hands still pressed to my mouth—*I will not cry out*—I treaded gingerly through them. Then, finding my footing, I crept around to Garritt's window.

He had not exaggerated the Horseman's mark. It ran diagonally through the center of the pane, raven black with eyelash thin cracks branching from it.

My need to see Garritt pushed me forward. I rapped once, quickly jerking my hand away. It was like tapping the surface of a frozen pond, burning my knuckles. I wrapped my hand in my shawl and knocked again. "Garritt," I called through the glass. "Come to the window."

I waited, my heart ticking the seconds. "Garritt."

I saw movement behind the curtains. Slight, but there nonetheless. I tapped again. This drew him over. He lifted the curtain just enough to peer out. His eyes drew to the Horseman's mark and he pulled back. "Meet me at the other window," he said.

I rounded the corner to the one facing the back of the property. Garritt was already there, his pallor practically transparent and his eyes baggy and red. The talisman hung from his neck. He lifted the window just enough that we might speak without strain. His gaze shifted beyond me, looking left and right.

"Go, Katrina. It's not safe here."

"Why have you not told your father of the Horseman?"

He winced, drawing back. "This is not your concern. Please, leave. I couldn't bear it if you came to harm."

Why must he be so stubborn?

"Garritt, simply confess your encounter. Measures will be taken to keep you safe."

"I can't. And besides, I've already made my own plans."

"What plans?"

He hesitated, eyes shifting again. "I'm refusing the bloodlettings to gain strength, then I'll sneak out and ride away. The Horseman only keeps to this vicinity. He won't pursue me outside the Hollow."

"Garritt, I've an even better idea. Speak with Marten. He's purchased a ship. He and I are going to sail away. You can come with us."

His weary eyes grew wide. "Marten bought a ship?"

"Yes," I said, now smiling. "It will be here in a few weeks and —"

"*Weeks?*" His shoulders sank and he raked his fingers through his matted hair. "Katrina, I won't last that long."

I feared he was right. "Please, Garritt, there has to be

something I can do to help you."

"You can help me by staying quiet."

"But –"

"No one must know. Now leave."

After all I'd risked, it'd been a fruitless attempt. There was no reason to continue pressing him. "Very well. But I do hope you'll change your mind."

"I won't." He reached for the talisman. "You should have this back. You'll need it more than me."

"No," I said, shaking my head. "You keep it. To protect you until you're safely away."

He clutched it in his hand. "Thank you."

Our eyes held for a moment, then he said, "Go, before you're discovered."

I stepped away, tightening my shawl.

"Katrina."

I turned.

"Be careful." With those words, he closed the window.

* * *

Garritt's deathly face haunted me all the way home. I told myself there was nothing more I could do. And I kept repeating it as I counted down the minutes to Ichabod's arrival. I was weak-kneed with anticipation, yet determined to remain levelheaded. Still, I changed out of my church dress and into a shimmering violet gown with silver trim.

What's wrong with a little dazzle to brighten the evening?

Stepping out onto our piazza, I breathed in the evening air. The western sky blazed with streaks of spun gold and deep burgundy. What a contrast to the environment of Garritt's surroundings. How would this sunset look through his eyes? A boy in hell. A boy marked by the Horseman.

A hand touched my shoulder and I blanched.

"Jumpy, are we?"

"Brom!" I clutched my fists to my heart. "Don't sneak up on me like that." How did he always appear out of nowhere?

He arched an eyebrow. "I wasn't sneaking. You were in a daze."

I brushed his hand away. "Still."

Brom had dinner with us every Sunday evening. Although I'd wished tonight he'd gone carousing instead.

He puffed his chest and rocked back on his heels. "So tonight we dine with the honorable Mr. Crane."

"Honorable being the pertinent word," I said. "Try to behave yourself…if you're capable."

"I promise not to lick the mutton drippings off my fingers."

"I was referring to your sharp tongue."

He grinned and pulled me close, nuzzling his lips to my neck. "I shall be a proper gentleman."

I unwound his arms from my waist. "Then start now."

He stepped back, laughing like a fool. I would've kicked him had I not been worried about losing the bow on my slipper.

The clip-clop of hooves echoed softly from the road. Momentarily, Ichabod approached…on what appeared to be the most cussed of all horses. It shambled forth, flicking its tail and flaring its nostrils. As they neared the hitching rail, the dapple stopped, backed up, and circled clockwise…twice.

"Steady," Ichabod said, patting the animal's smoky mane.

"Quite the cavalier," Brom whispered. I poked him with my elbow.

Ichabod dismounted, and with a little goading, led the horse to hitch. "Meet Gunpowder," he said, patting the horse's hindquarters.

Brom lifted a brow. "Looks as though he's lost his spark."

In several long strides, Ichabod joined us on the piazza. "I can only assume by his name that he'd had spirit in his day.

Now it's purely spunk. Van Ripper loaned him to me with the assurance that 'An ornery horse is better than a mile on foot.'" His raspy imitation made me giggle.

"Well, you certainly showed that beast who's boss," Brom scoffed.

Ichabod, being the only gentleman present, ignored the comment and turned his attention to me. "Katrina, you look radiant this evening."

Judging by his fitted suit and teal waistcoat, I could say the same for him. But then, he could wear sackcloth and be just as delicious.

"Why, thank you, Ichabod."

The front door pushed open and Father stood, filling the entry. "Were you planning to leave our guest out there with the frogs and insects?"

"We wouldn't hear of it," Brom said with a sweeping *after you* gesture.

I boldly hooked my arm through Ichabod's and escorted him inside.

Though Brom looked on gently, I knew deep down his soul rumbled. I didn't care. It was time to show him that our engagement was simply a product of his imagination, no matter what blessing Father may or may not have bestowed.

Simon had laid a lovely table with our delft pottery and pewter candlesticks. Brom quickly took the seat next to mine. I was fine with that. Sitting across from Ichabod allowed me the opportunity to look into his eyes and study his face. Expressions speak as clearly as words, and I wanted to know *everything* about him.

"So tell us," Father said, passing the soup tureen, "are you adjusting to our simple ways here at Sleepy Hollow?"

Ichabod lifted the dish from him. "I am, sir. It's like a breath of fresh air. Just the change I needed."

"Too many pitchforks?" I teased.

Father's eyebrows bristled. "What a ridiculous question."

Ichabod waved it off with a smile. "I simply needed a quiet place to clear my head."

Brom chuckled, his eyes on his plate. "If you want your head cleared, you've come to the right place."

Father shot him a threatening look. It was imperative that we stay mum on the subject of the Horseman. Even at the risk of Ichabod's neck. He turned back to Ichabod. "I can't imagine how a schoolroom full of boisterous children could be relaxing, but we're grateful that you came."

"They're not boisterous at all," Ichabod said. "We've only had two days of instruction, but I've found the students quite eager."

"And what form of discipline do you impart?" Father asked. Discipline being Father's specialty.

Brom stabbed a slice of mutton and dropped it onto his plate. "Yes, tell us. Do you rap their knuckles with your ruler or paddle their little bottoms with a board?"

At the moment I wanted to rap his.

"Neither," Ichabod answered without a hint of annoyance. "I've never been a believer in 'spare the rod'. I find communication and bargaining works best."

Father's eyes grew so wide I thought they might roll out of his head. "Bargaining with children? That's absurd."

"Yet it gets results." Ichabod carved into his meat, not the least bit offended by Father's remark. "The children and I have struck an agreement. If they finish their lessons to my satisfaction, they earn a short session of storytelling at the end of the day."

Now I was definitely intrigued. "And what sort of stories do you tell them?"

His mouth curled into a gentle smile. "Ah, I contribute

very little. It's the students who do most of the telling."

Brom harrumphed as he chomped his meat. "I think a lashing would be quicker and less painful than sitting through a lot of bumbling nursery tales."

Ichabod didn't even flinch. He had far more patience than me.

"You would be surprised at the stories they've shared," he said.

Father's brow dipped. "A lot of poppycock, I'd wager."

"I've heard some intriguing accounts. Ancient sailors. Savage Indians. Lost gold." His eyebrows arched as though he'd suddenly remembered "And of course there's a wild yarn about a headless ghost."

A thick silence sat heavy in the room. Did Father really think Ichabod could live here for more than a day without hearing of our notorious Horseman?

Ichabod took of sip of wine and continued. "They are fierce believers in the supernatural. The girls are quite superstitious and won't go near the school's root cellar. They claim the ghost of a Mr. Smedt dwells there, and if they draw close, he'll *burst* through the doors and *grab* their ankles."

I couldn't help but giggle. "Maybe that's just their excuse to avoid that smelly place."

Brom, clearly not amused, actually nodded agreement. "It's a wonder one of the children hasn't fallen in and broken a leg. It should be filled in."

"No," Ichabod said quickly. "I have other plans for it." His expression favored a child who might have a toy taken from him.

Father paused, his fork halfway between him and his plate. "What sort of plans?" He was no doubt worried that Ichabod might ask for a generous donation to carry them out.

Ichabod kept his eyes on his meal. "I intend to lay a sturdy floor. I'll store water and candles and turn it into a suitable shelter against the spring storms."

Father gave a relieved nod. "Sounds sensible."

"I agree," Brom said, wiping his mouth with his napkin (and thankfully not on his sleeve). "If you're determined to restore the thing, I suggest using a good cedar for the planking. It'll resist rot, and the sharp odor will offset that dampened clay smell." His knee brushed mine as he said it. I didn't think it was a conscious gesture, but it relayed to me that he was only being cordial to win my approval.

Ichabod raised his glass. "I will."

Brom's knee pushed closer when he added, "But that's a lot of work for one person. I could lend you one of the slaves."

"Splendid idea," Father said. Of course he'd think it splendid. He'd rather lend a slave than part with some of his money.

Ichabod froze. His breath quickened. "No, thank you, Baltus. That's very generous, but I enjoy a bit of hard labor."

Curious. Was he uncomfortable with the offer, or did he feel he was imposing?

"But you can't cut the timber alone," Brom persisted. His knee pressed closer, and though he seemed oblivious, I tapped it away.

"Simon!" he called toward the kitchen.

Simon approached, awaiting instruction.

Brom promptly provided them. "This Saturday have Isaiah carry some timber to the schoolhouse to help Mr. Crane split and shave wood for planking."

Ichabod blushed as he turned from one to the other, not sure how to handle this awkward encounter. "No, really, that won't be necessary."

Brom's knee found mine again. "I insist."

Oh, Brom, if you really want to impress me, you'd pick up

an ax and volunteer yourself.

"Yes, sir," Simon said, bringing the wine decanter to refill our glasses.

Ichabod's eyes flickered, something formulating behind them. He then directed those lovely green eyes at Simon. "I have a wonderful idea. Why don't we work out an exchange?"

The room went completely mute. We all stopped dead still.

Father gripped the table. "Now you're bargaining with slaves!"

Ichabod's eyes never strayed from Simon's. "You send someone to help me with the woodcutting, and I'll come by on Wednesday afternoons to teach the children."

Father slammed down his fork. "What children?"

Ichabod faced him like it was only a trivial matter. "The slave children, of course."

Father's face pinched so tight I thought it might pop. "Teach the slaves? Whatever for?"

"To educate them, of course."

"To what purpose? They can already read scripture."

Ichabod calmly laid down his fork. "But can they read well? Can they write? And what about arithmetic?"

Father leaned back, nostrils flaring.

I sat on edge, waiting. How long would this exchange go on before Father finally ordered him out of the house? Or worse, ran him straight back to Connecticut?

It was Brom who spoke up. "It's harvest. There's no time for this idiocy."

But was it idiocy? I could see the merit in what Ichabod proposed.

"I'd only be keeping them for a short time," Ichabod said. "Two hours at the most."

"It's a splendid idea," I blurted. Then all eyes were on me. I kept mine trained on Ichabod. "And I'd be happy to assist."

Brom withdrew his leg from mine.

Father seethed with anger. "There will be nothing to assist. This is lunacy."

Ichabod stood his ground. "Baltus, we are coming upon new times. Emancipation laws have already been passed in Connecticut."

"This is not Connecticut!"

I winced. Father would toss him out at any moment.

Ichabod met Father eye to eye. I'd never seen anyone with so much conviction. "Believe me, Baltus, this is to your advantage." Our shy schoolmaster had transformed into a revolutionary.

They glared in a heated match.

Brom wore a slight smirk, but he nearly dropped his utensils when Father said, "All right, Crane. Since it is far easier to agree than to find a new teacher, we'll test it."

I silently sighed relief.

"But," he continued, pointing his knife, "should I smell even a hint of trouble brewing, the Council will deal with you."

Ichabod didn't seem to give a hoot about the Council. He quickly turned to Simon. "How many children are there?"

Simon glanced nervously at Father, then answered. "Seven that are of schoolin' age."

"Then it's settled," Ichabod said. "We'll meet this Wednesday. Sharpen seven short sticks for writing instruments and gather them in a spot with loose soil."

Simon tried to keep a blank face, but I could see a tinge of pleasure peeking through. "Yes, sir."

"And Baltus," Ichabod said, facing Father again, "are you in possession of a globe? I'm afraid mine is too large and bulky."

Father nearly choked on his meat. "I dare-say you've run out of favors with me."

I quickly interceded. "I have a globe. Though it is covered with markings."

Ichabod lifted an eyebrow. "Markings?"

"Yes. I've routed passages to the places I intend to visit someday." *Very soon.*

"A lot of poppycock," Father rumbled. "Katrina's always been a dreamer."

Brom pressed his knee hard against mine. "It's a waste of a perfectly good globe, if you ask me." *No one asked you.* "Katrina will one day inherit this farm. Her duties here won't allow for much travel."

I knocked his knee away hard. "Which is all the more reason to travel now."

"Enough of this," Father said. He pointed his fork at Ichabod. "Just remember, Crane, spend your time on logic. No filling the slaves' heads with ridiculous stories or ideas of emancipation."

Ichabod reverted to the shy teacher he was before. "I shall use the time efficiently."

Clever, Ichabod. You're both a rogue and a risk-taker.

Father waved Simon away, leaving us with a moment of strained silence.

"Speaking of stories," I said to soften the edge in the room, "you promised tonight you'd share one of your published pieces." I wanted so badly to know what sort of tales were spun in that marvelous head.

He patted his breast pocket. "And I never go back on my promises."

Brom's knee found mine again. Enough. I stepped on his foot. He blanched and cut his eyes to me.

Father wavered his hand as though conducting us. "Then eat up so that we may adjourn to the parlor for brandy."

* * *

Father settled into his easy chair and took up his pipe. I chose to sit near the corner, far from Brom and his possessive knee.

Ichabod walked to the fireplace, took out that curious little journal and removed a piece of folded newsprint. From my view I could make out some advertisements—a dentist, paper hangings, and several lotteries—but I was far more interested in the printing on the other side.

Amid the crackling of the fire and the ticking of our mantel clock, he read:

Of Fate and Fortune.

Some ten miles from the city of Easton lay a scant few acres and a modest farm. The farm stood in isolation, with only the oxen and hens for company. On occasion the rumble of a nearby battle could be heard, for the revolution was at its peak and the upheaval vast. But the small farm was so detached, it seemed one of earth's hidden secrets that nothing could penetrate.

The farmer himself, one Philip C. Hartley, was a stout and stubborn gentleman who refused to stay separated from the comings and goings of the city. He not only rode in to sell his plump squash and leafy cabbage, but to also partake in the pleasures of gambling. Hartley's run of luck never ceased, and though he spent a good deal of his winnings on tobacco and rum, he was known throughout Easton as Fortunate Phil.

But his good fortune was not due to any measure on his part. For at home he kept a wife by the name of Rebecca. She was ten years younger and ten times more tolerant than her selfish, demanding husband. Rebecca was lovely and fair, but it was her gift of strong intuition that pleased old Philip most. With his prodding, she would advise him on the best days to plant, hunt, and gamble. And she was never wrong.

While he rewarded her with an occasional new dress or hair combs, Rebecca was not allowed away from the farm. And with no children to keep her company, she spent her days forlorn and lonely—a prisoner in her own home.

After some five years, Rebecca became ill. Her ivory pallor turned gray, and her face soon resembled that of a death mask. Hartley broke his own rule and brought a doctor out to attend her. No tonics eased her. No pill revived her. And so she was left to linger.

Hartley grew agitated and weary. Though his sorrow seemed genuine, it was not the loss of his wife that grieved him, but the loss of the excessive lifestyle that she had afforded him. He was helpless to provide for himself.

Then the fateful day came. Rebecca gazed out the window with dark-rimmed eyes. She requested the grave be dug under her favorite elm, and then, laying out her pink dress, told him that was what she wished to wear.

He fell into tears. His wife, a mere ghost of what she once was, had given him her last requests. What more could he do for this woman who had been faithful to him all this time?

So Hartley took up a shovel and dug. It took the better part of the morning, but soon he had a deep clean hole, worthy of a six-foot coffin. He thrust his shovel into the waiting mound of dirt, wiped his brow, and turned. At that very moment, a stray bullet from the war connected with his head, killing him instantly and knocking him into the gaping hole that he had so vigorously dug for himself.

Rebecca, suddenly taken with a bout of vitality, removed the shovel from the mound and carefully filled in the grave. An hour later, bathed, perfumed, and wearing her pink dress, she rode away from the farm forever.

A thoughtful silence followed. I'd never felt so connected to a tale. I was about to compliment the author when Father grumbled, "That ending certainly had an unexpected twist."

Ichabod's lips crooked into a smile. "It's what we call *irony.*"

Brom sat stiff, gripping the arm of his chair. "And what made you choose that particular story to read?"

Ichabod took a seat near the hearth. He glanced first at Brom, then me, then back to Brom. "Irony."

The shallow look on Brom's face spoke for his mentality. But then, his perception of things were about as narrow as the fireplace poker.

The next two hours were spent on less personal topics such as the weather, farm reports, and the rise of the Federalist Party. I spent that time observing Ichabod, his speech, his mannerisms, and how knowledgeable he was on all subjects. He seemed oddly out of place in Sleepy Hollow. What could possibly have happened in Connecticut that sent him here?

When he rose to leave, Father walked him to the door. "By the way, Crane, you may have heard, each year I open my home for a harvest celebration. It will be on the twenty-eighth. You'll join us, of course." It echoed more as a command than an invitation.

A broad smile lit his face. "I wouldn't miss it."

Brom and I saw him onto the piazza. Gunpowder had managed to loosen his reins and wander some yards away. Ichabod threw up his hands and chuckled. "I swear, if that horse were a woman I'd marry her."

Brom leaned against the railing, arms crossed. "Then spend most of your time trying to tame her."

"Or keep up with her," Ichabod countered.

Their words flickered in and out as I felt a sudden stirring in the air. An odd chill. Though the night was calm, a slight draft brushed my neck, prickling my skin. I held my breath and gazed into the gloaming. *He's out there...waiting.*

"Katrina," Ichabod said, snapping me back around.

"I'm sorry. What did you say?"

His eyes narrowed suspiciously, and then he glanced into the darkness too. "I said"—he turned back— "you have a warm and lovely home."

"Oh. Uh, yes. Thank you."

He could easily detect my agitation. "Thank *you*. It was a wonderful evening." He then nodded at Brom. "Thank you both."

As he started down the steps, I called, "Ichabod!"

Something was there, lurking, just out of sight. Something or someone lying in wait.

He paused, anticipating.

"I –I…" *How do I start? How do I warn him?*

Brom tilted his head, annoyed. The only thing missing was an exasperated sigh.

I was about to pour out the whole story of the Horseman—everything from the night at my window to Garritt's near death. But then I remembered. *Garritt. It's Garritt who's marked. Garritt's the one in danger.* I forced a weak smile. "I was wondering what time we should expect you on Wednesday?"

He relaxed, his smile natural and sweet. "I hope to be here shortly after three."

Our eyes held…a little too long. If he saw some pleading within mine, it never showed. I looked away.

He strode out to Gunpowder and mounted. After some goading, the horse turned. Ichabod gave us a parting wave, and they plodded off.

Once he'd ridden out of sight, Brom caught me by the waist and pulled me aside, away from the windows. "He's gone now. You can stop gawking."

I tugged at his fingers to break his grip. "Let go." The more I pulled, the tighter he held.

He grinned down at me. "You know, Katrina, I'm a dreamer too."

I struggled to squirm free. "I've no doubt. Probably dreaming of tavern girls."

He craned back and cocked a brow. "Have you ever seen a tavern girl?"

How could his fingers lock so tightly? "Not that I'm aware."

"There are only two at the River Song, and they're as lovely as Ichabod's horse."

"Brom, release me now."

"But I haven't told you what I dream of."

I surrendered, going limp. "Tell me."

I didn't think it was possible for him to pull me closer, but somehow he managed. "I dream of our house near the river." He nuzzled my neck. "A side porch. Maple staircase. And a large brass knocker with the head of a lion."

I gripped his ear and twisted it...hard. His eyes widened in surprise.

"Get this through your thick head. There will be no house by the river. And if, by some miracle, there were, I'd most certainly have a say in its structure."

He pulled my hand away and grinned. "Sweetheart, of course you'll have a say. You can choose the location of our bedchamber."

"You *are* a dreamer." I kicked his shin and he released me.

"Katrina, you'll never find anyone who cares for you as much as I do."

I smoothed the wrinkles from my violet dress. "Molesting me is not my idea of affection."

"I admit," he said, "I don't have the manners and education of our Connecticut schoolmaster." He nodded toward Ichabod's trail. "But I can certainly provide more than someone on a schoolmaster's wage."

"With Father's money," I said.

The words hung for a moment, then Brom stepped away, his face dark. "I think you're forgetting that it's my duties as overseer that produces that money. And it's nearly doubled since Baltus put the farm in my hands."

"How can I make you understand? I don't care about the money or being provided for. And I have no desire to be married. Not to you"—I nodded toward Ichabod's trail—"or anyone."

He stared, jaw jutted, then put his finger in my face. "You'll change your mind." With that, he strutted to his horse, mounted, and rode off to his cabin.

Weeks, Marten had told me. Why must it take weeks?

* * *

I barely slept that night, still chilled by the unseen specter near our house. When I did sleep, I dreamt of the Horseman, below my window—his sword…his beckoning hand. I woke twice in a fevered sweat.

But Monday morning finally crept in, and like every Monday it was candle day—a tradition Elise and I started as children. We'd spend the morning dipping candles, laughing, and catching up on gossip. Yes, even the nonsense spun by Henny.

Elise arrived, gleeful and pert, bringing with her a satchel and the gown she'd borrowed. "Thank you *so* much, Kat." She laid the dress on the bed and, floating in a daze, brushed her fingers across the emerald brocade. "It's the color of Ichabod's eyes."

She was right. It was a close match to those eyes I'd looked into so many times last evening.

"How was your dinner with Ichabod?" she asked. "Isn't he magnificent?"

"He's…different."

"To put it mildly." She fluttered her lashes and sighed. "He's so handsome and gallant and…and…"

"Delicious?"

"Sinfully. And look what he brought me." She opened the satchel and brought out his copy of *The Thousand and One Nights—Persian Tales*.

I took it from her and flipped through the vellum pages, awed by the sketches inside. Women peering through veils. Men in plumed turbans. Majestic palaces with spiral domes. "What a generous gift." *Exceedingly generous.*

Her mouth twitched. "Not a gift exactly. He loaned it to me. But he said the tales should play to my romantic nature."

"Oh. He's speaking of romance already?" A pang of envy pricked my heart.

"Not directly. But perhaps he feels it's too soon to profess his love."

I suppressed a smile. "Perhaps." I handed the book back and she gazed on it with love in her eyes.

"Have you read any of the stories?" I asked.

"Just the prologue." She opened to it. "It tells of a king, whose name I can't pronounce." She pointed and I read: *Shahrayar.* What a name. My tongue would stumble over it too.

"This king," she continued, "brought young virgins to his bed each night, and then the next morning he'd have them executed."

"What? That's horrific! And not exactly what I'd deem exotic."

"Wait." She pointed to another word. "This woman" I read the name *Shahazad*—"came to him. She'd devised a plan to stop the killings. Each night she'd tell him a story, but never finish it—always leaving him curious as to what happened next." Elise's eyes bloomed with delight. "After a year had passed, the king grew to love her *and* her stories. He spared her life and kept her as his queen." She sighed.

"And you find that romantic?"

"Don't you?"

"Of course not. The man slaughtered all those young virgins and was never punished for it? That's outrageous."

Elise slumped, tilting her head. "Kat, it's not a *true* account."

"But even the most fantastical fiction should reflect real life in some way. Why was there not an uprising? Surely the fathers of those girls would have conspired revenge."

Elise pushed my brocade dress aside and plopped down on the bed. "I'm sure this is why Ichabod gave the book to me and not you. He knew I wouldn't try to rewrite it."

She had a fair point. It was a valuable piece of literature. Who was I to pick it apart? "You're right." I held up my hands in surrender. "Maybe we can read some of the stories together."

"Only if you promise not to crusade against each one."

"Cross my heart."

She gazed upon the treasured item. "Where is Persia?"

"A very long way from here." I hopped up, took her hand, and tugged her to a standing position. "The fires are ready." Then we hurried outside to the kettles and racks.

Elise snipped the string while I attached it to the hooks. "I want to hear about *your* dinner with Ichabod," she said.

"I assure you, it was not as perfect as yours," I teased.

"I never said mine was perfect. You're forgetting, my stupid little brothers were there. They dominated every conversation, badgering him with questions about school. 'Will the assignments be difficult?' 'Will you allow us some play time?' And Dirk had the audacity to ask, 'Will you be adding a whipping post?'"

I blurted a laugh. "Ichabod prefers bargaining over beating."

Her eyebrows rose. "You must've learned a great deal about him."

"Just that he's unconventional in his thinking." *And a breath of fresh air.*

She helped me lower the first group of strings into the wax. "And that's what I love about him," she uttered.

"It's an admirable trait." But there was so much more of Ichabod to discover…*if I weren't sailing away.*

We placed the strings onto the rack.

"Did he bring one of his stories to share?" she asked.

"Yes. He's a marvelous writer."

Her mouth curved into a sly grin. "A tale of debauchery?"

I laughed, remembering that look on old Henny's face. "Hardly. Father would've booted him right back to Connecticut." *And very nearly did.*

We set about, dipping another set of strings—the heat from the kettle warm on our faces. I gazed out across the field, imagining Ichabod by the brook, journal and pencil in hand. "I wonder how many stories he's published?"

"I don't know," she answered, "but I want to read them all. Or even better, lie next to him, my head on his shoulder, while he reads them to me."

I admit, it did sound like a cozy pastime.

We dipped more and more, watching the wax grow fatter.

Tilting her head, she mused, "I wonder why he doesn't have a wife?"

That came as such a surprise, I nearly dropped the candlewicks. "Elise, he's barely older than us."

She continued as though she hadn't heard me. "Maybe she died?"

"What makes you think he should be married?"

"Because he's perfect."

"I'm sure if we looked hard enough we'd find plenty of flaws." My thoughts turned to that book of witchcraft that he read like a Bible.

"Still," she said, "I bet he had his pick of girls back in Hartford." I could see the cogs in her mind turning. "Surely one would've snared him by now."

I picked up a snippet of string and wrapped it around her ring finger. "Maybe he was waiting for you."

She admired it like it was a gold band. "If only that were

true."

Once the dipping was done, we snipped the wicks and bundled the hardened candles into boxes. I had not told her about Ichabod coming to teach the slave children. Or that I'd be assisting him. *It would only hurt her*, I told myself...several times.

As we gathered our things, Elise suddenly stopped. With squinted eyes, she peered across the field. "Katrina, is that Marten's horse?" She was gazing in the far distance, where Brom's cabin sat.

I stepped onto a stool to see. Indeed it was Marten's horse. And Brom's was hitched next to it.

"I wonder why Marten isn't fishing today?"

I wondered the same. And even more so, why Brom was not out overseeing the farm. What business did they have in his cabin on a late Monday morning?

The wind picked up, and a sudden gust prickled my skin. "Maybe the waters are not right for fishing," I offered. Though deep down I knew that wasn't true.

* * *

Father and I had one thing in common. We always woke up grumpy and cross. Father would huff and growl, communicating with gestures. I, on the other hand, would plod through the house, seeing through blurry eyes. The only person with a smile was Simon, ready with our tea and breakfast. But on this particular Wednesday, I broke my droopy routine.

Simon tilted his head, eyes narrowed. "Something's got you mighty cheerful this morning, Miss Katrina."

"I'm just well rested," I lied. Truthfully, I'd tossed about, a thousand things whisking through my mind. Mostly, the joy that this would not be a typical day, stuck within these walls. I stirred some honey into my cup. "Ichabod comes this afternoon."

Simon shuffled some pots off the stove. "He's a very

generous soul."

I gazed out the kitchen window. "Yes, he is. And thankfully, we're having lovely weather."

"Thankfully," he said, suppressing a grin.

Is he thinking...? "It's just that I'm interested in Ichabod's teaching methods."

Simon still held back that grin. "I'm sure they'll be most interesting."

I stirred in some cream. "The children will benefit greatly."

"It is a blessing," he said, now smiling broadly.

I finally had to ask, "Simon, what is so amusing?"

He lifted the teapot. "I was just thinking that you might want some tea in that cream and honey." He poured.

"Oh...uh..."

"Miss Katrina," he said with a laugh, "it's going to be a wonderful day."

* * *

I prepared by baking two dozen apple dumplings and filling a jug with cider. These were not meant as rewards for good work, but to fill the children's small bellies beforehand. After all, hunger is a gnawing distraction. So is clock-watching. Something I tried not to do.

Ichabod arrived about half past three, juggling four hornbooks, a sum book, and two other texts in his arms. Even though he'd spent the day teaching the village children, his smile was as pleasant and refreshing as if he'd just awakened to a day of sunshine. "I would've been here sooner, but Gunpowder had other plans for me. It took some persuading to get him out of the schoolyard."

I peeked out at the pigheaded beast, which at the moment was using the hitching rail as a scratching post for his gray-speckled breast. "Surely Van Ripper has another horse he could loan you."

"Not unless I want to ride the plow mule. Besides"—he nodded back toward Gunpowder—"he's shown me parts of the valley I never knew existed. Nor could ever find again."

"You don't have to worry about getting lost around here," I said. "As long as you can hear the river, you'll find your way back."

His eyes softened as they met mine. "That's assuring."

Those eyes.

I quickly turned my attention to his supplies. "Let me help you with some of these." I lifted the two texts from his grip, then saw that one was a volume of *Aesop's Fables. No!* Panicked, I quickly opened his coat and shoved it under his arm out of sight.

He blanched, folding to the side as he wrangled the remaining items so they wouldn't fall. He managed to grip the fables with his armpit.

"Sorry," I said, reaching to steady him.

He flinched at my touch.

My face burned ruby hot. "You must think I'm a lunatic." *Or worse!* "Honestly, I didn't mean to be so brash." I slowly reached out and took a couple of the hornbooks from his grasp.

He slipped Aesop out from under his arm. "No, please, don't apologize. It's just that…"—his cheeks reddened slightly as he gave me a shy smile—"I'm…quite ticklish."

"Oh." *Why do I find that so endearing?* I covered my mouth, holding back a giggle.

He rolled his eyes. "I know. Go ahead and laugh."

"I wouldn't." But I wanted to.

He held up the book, turning it front to back. "So tell me, why are we so eager to censor Aesop?"

"Because if Father sees it he'll skin your hide and bury you in Smedt's root cellar."

His face opened in a jest of shock. "Then to save my hide,

I should explain its purpose."

"They are stories," I said.

"But they'll be used for critical thinking. I'll read a short tale, and then have the students try to determine the moral. It stimulates the mind."

I shrugged a little, conceding. "That sounds reasonable."

"And," he added, "I think the children will be inspired to know that Aesop himself had been a slave."

I exaggerated a sigh. "Ichabod, you are one brave man."

Our eyes held for a moment, then a smile lit his face. "Why don't we test that with the children?" He gently took the texts and hornbooks back from me and shifted them to his arm. "So, where is our schoolhouse?"

"This way."

I led him into the kitchen, where I'd placed the plate of dumplings and jug of cider into a hamper. I'd brought out some quilts too. Since the children had no benches or desks, I felt these would ease the discomfort of sitting on the gritty dirt. We carried everything to the spreading maple where Ichabod would teach.

The soil underneath it had been loosened and patted, ensuring each child had a proper writing surface. No doubt a deed Simon had seen to. I'd barely spread the quilts when the children came marching up from the slave quarters.

There were eleven instead of seven—all led by Leta, a strong-willed child of about twelve. After getting them seated she turned to Ichabod. "I invited some others. I didn't think you'd mind. And I sharpened some extra sticks." She held them bundled in her fists.

"Excellent," Ichabod said. "How many did you sharpen?"

I was sure this was a question to test her mathematical abilities, but Leta looked up at him like he was the village idiot. "One for each of them."

"Clever girl," he said.

He then brought out a ledger, quill, and a small pot of ink. "I'll start by taking down your names." He looked first at Leta.

"My name's Leta and I already know how to spell it."

He turned the ledger toward her and offered her the quill. "Would you like to write it in for me? I could help you."

A moment of panic crossed her pretty face. Then, just as quickly she regained her composure. "I don't want to get ink on my fingers."

"Very well," he said. "Would you spell it for me?"

In this she took great pleasure. "L—E—T—A."

"Thank you," he said, suppressing a smile.

Each child in turn stated their name, except for Elijah, a boy of about six. He had the energy of a wild hare. He sprang up from his spot and raced in a circle, giggling and taunting us with "You can't catch me."

As he went for his third turn, Leta reached up and snatched him by the suspenders. He sprang back onto his bottom with a whop. "Sit down, Elijah!" She kept his suspender straps clutched in her hand so he couldn't make for another escape.

"I think it would be safer for all of us," Ichabod said, plucking the boy's stick from his hand, "if young Elijah here used his finger as his writing tool."

I gave each child a dumpling and a cup of cider while Ichabod informed them as to what they could expect from these sessions. They seemed eager for both the food and the knowledge.

They shared the hornbooks, running their fingers along the carved alphabets. Ichabod explained the difference between upper and lowercase letters. Then, starting with the letter A, they practiced writing in the dirt. Some of the children were more skilled, so I took the slower ones aside, helping them to catch up. I found that I enjoyed teaching. I never thought I'd have the patience for it.

Their sharpened sticks served for more than writing. Ichabod used them as counting tools to teach addition and subtraction.

He also formed shapes with them—a square, rectangle, triangle—and had the students look around and name objects and structures that held those geometric shapes. I was mesmerized by his calm voice and patient gestures.

The lessons ended with him sharing the fable of "The Fox and the Grapes." To bring more life to the story, he stood, holding up a dumpling, while small Elijah jumped and jounced, trying unsuccessfully to seize it. Though Ichabod asked them to determine a moral, they tried concocting ways in which the fox could obtain the grapes instead. They had that weary fox pulling carts, riding horses, and waiting for lightning to strike.

As the discussion continued, Elijah still exerted great energy trying to grasp that dumpling. Then, with a frustrated grunt, he drew back his foot and kicked Ichabod hard in the shin. As a manner of reflex, Ichabod bent over and clutched his knee. Elijah plucked the dumpling from his hand, stuffed the entire thing in his mouth, then plopped down on the ground, arms crossed. The children and I bellowed with laughter.

Ichabod sat down, rubbing his shin. He leaned toward me and whispered, "That one will grow up to emancipate them all."

After bringing about order, he told them, "I'll leave two of the hornbooks with you. When there is time, practice your letters and numbers, and I'll check your progress next week."

"If you still have yore head," Leta mumbled under her breath.

"Leta!" I scolded. "Do not speak out of turn."

But Ichabod held up his hand, indicating he'd allow it. He kept his attention on her. "I've heard the tale of your famous horseman. Tell me, why do you think he might take *my* head."

She rolled her eyes as if the answer were simple. "Because he whacked off the first schoolmaster's. It's like arithmetic. He's doing his own subtraction."

"So you believe there is a horseman?" he asked.

"Of course there is," she said. "I've seen him."

I felt a hitch in my chest. "Leta, if this is some game…"

"It's no game, Miss Katrina. I saw him the other night."

I worked to keep my breathing normal. "When?"

"When I went out to the outhouse to do my business. Coming out, I saw him up there." She pointed to a hill near our house.

I turned to look. The trees upon it instantly rustled, as though they knew that I watched.

"He was holding that sickle of his, and his horse pawed the ground like it was fired up, ready to chase somebody down."

Ichabod arched a skeptical brow. "Why didn't you run?"

Again she gave him that "are you thick?" expression. "I did! You think I just stood there like a fool?"

"He didn't come after you?" I asked.

"No, ma'am. He was more interested in what was going on in there." She pointed to the house.

Ichabod rubbed his chin. "What night was this?"

I knew the answer before she said it.

"Sunday."

It was the Horseman I'd sensed.

"You're very calm about this," Ichabod said. "Weren't you frightened?"

"Scared to death! But I have this." She reached under her collar and produced a talisman hanging from a string. It was the same type of charm that Simon had made for me. The one that was now protecting Garritt.

Ichabod lifted the talisman into his hand and stroked it

lightly with his thumb. His expression clouded as he studied it.

Leta tugged it back, like his touch might wear away its power.

He sat back and sighed. "Forgive me, Leta, but I've never been one to believe in ghosts."

Yet you believe in the black arts.

She shrugged. "You'll believe it when yore head is rolling away from yore body."

This earned some giggles from the other children, who'd been listening with wide eyes.

My mind churned. If it was Garritt he sought, then why had the Horseman come here? I held back my anxiety as best I could. The children had enough burdens without me adding further distress.

"Well..." Ichabod rose. "If I'm still in possession of my head next Wednesday, I'll see you all then. Class is dismissed."

Rather than hurrying off, Leta took charge, seeing to it that the children shook out the quilts and folded them neatly. The cups were emptied and placed in the hamper. She ordered each child to say thank you, then led the way, marching them back to their quarters.

I crossed my arms against the chill as we walked back to the house. I could not let go of my fear.

Ichabod watched me from the corner of his eye. "You believe in this horseman too."

I turned quickly, gazing up at him. "I'm so sorry. Someone should've told you before you made the decision to come here."

He lifted a shoulder. "I'm not sure that would've swayed my decision."

"Don't you get it? There is a Horseman. He murdered Nikolass Devenpeck."

"But where's the proof?"

"The Council has proof. And Nikolass was not the first.

Apparently the Horseman follows a pattern."

He still looked doubtful. "That doesn't prove these murders were carried out by a ghost."

"Ichabod, he *is* real. I know. I've seen him myself." I realized I was practically shouting. I lowered my voice when adding, "And not just me. He's marked a dear friend, leaving him tortured and driven to madness."

Our eyes held and a thousand questions crossed his face.

"I know it sounds insane," I said.

"No, it doesn't." He gently clasped my arm. "You're trembling. Let's get you inside."

When we reached the back door, the smell of baked fish greeted us. Simon was busy in the kitchen, tension framing his eyes. "I hope all went well with the children."

"Extremely well," Ichabod assured him. "They are all bright and receptive."

I set the hamper on the sideboard and removed my shawl. "I can attest to that."

Simon's shoulders relaxed as he continued paring potatoes.

I began removing the cups and placing them into the tub for washing. I kept my eyes down, trying to steady my grip. *If Garritt is marked, why was the Horseman here?* Another chill rippled through me.

Ichabod gazed at me, his face a mask of concern. "Katrina, I must be getting back. I promised Van Ripper I'd help—"

"Yes," I blurted before he could say more. "I'd feel better if you're inside before dark."

Simon paused and said, "Thank you kindly, Mr. Crane. I'll be sure Isaiah's there on Saturday with timber and tools."

"Perfect." Ichabod shifted his books from one arm to another.

I managed a weak smile. "I'll see you out."

We stepped onto the piazza, the veil of evening unfolding

before us. Gunpowder, still hitched and waiting, greeted us with a rolling snort.

I followed Ichabod to the hitching rail. He took a moment to place his books in the saddlebag, and then turned. "Katrina..."

"Please, *please* be careful." My eyes cut to the hill and back.

Ichabod glanced over his shoulder. "Don't worry."

"How can I not?"

He took my hand in both of his. "There is no mistaking your fear. Trust me, I do believe you." He stroked my fingers as though they were treasured porcelain. I placed my other hand on his and we stood there, speaking through touch. The night air grew colder, yet the feel of him warmed me.

"I will be careful," he promised, bringing my hand upward and kissing my fingertips. "And if Gunpowder remembers he's a horse, I shall be back at Van Ripper's in a flash."

I reached over and stroked the beast's neck. "He's in your hands," I murmured into his flickering ear.

Ichabod loosened the reins from the hitching rail. The frisky horse seemed eager to go, making Ichabod's mounting a clumsy task. Once in the saddle, he looked down at me with those haunting green eyes. "Take care, Katrina. I shall see you soon."

Then he was off. I watched until he was no longer in sight.

I stood there for a bit, gazing down at my fingertips, still tingling from the brush of his lips. But I finally snapped out of my daze by realizing I was dawdling out in the biting cold without a cloak or shawl. I turned to go inside and... *Dear God!* My breath caught and my knees buckled. The Horseman was there, on the hill, sitting tall upon his steed.

His silhouette loomed larger and more malevolent than when I last saw him—like he bore all the hatred of hell. His scythe rested on his shoulder, the blade touching the sky like a silver crescent moon.

My blood drained as I stood frozen to the spot. Then, like a slap...*Ichabod!*

It could be no coincidence that the Horseman had appeared twice during his visits. It was suddenly clear. Ichabod had become the target.

I must warn him.

Hitching my skirts, I flew around the house, racing toward our stables. My heart thundered against my chest as my unsteady legs carried me.

Ichabod.

Fortune was on my side. One of the stable doors stood open and a lamp flickered within. I ran all the faster, hurrying for my horse.

As I hastened through the door, an arm reached out and grabbed me. I immediately flailed and screamed.

"Whoa, Katrina." It was Brom, struggling to steady me.

"Let go," I cried, fighting to break his grasp.

"Calm down there, little filly."

I had no time for his childishness. "The Horseman is out there."

He gripped me even tighter. "What are you talking about?"

"The Horseman! He's here." I frantically squirmed within his hold.

He loosened his grip but still held on. "Nonsense."

"I just saw him on the hill. He's after Ichabod. I must warn him."

"Settle down. You only imagined it."

"Brom, we're wasting time. Release me." Why was he always so impossible?

He still held on. "Katrina, take a breath."

"Let me go!" I sank my teeth into his hand. He whipped back, startled.

"I have to warn Ichabod." Trembling, I slipped the bit into Dewdrop's mouth and tightened the bridle. *No time for a saddle.* I stepped onto the stall's railings and flung myself onto her back.

Brom gripped the bridle strap, stopping me once again. "And if the Horseman *is* out there, what's to keep him from taking your head?"

"He's not after me."

He glared, eyes tight. "Be reasonable."

I snapped his hand with the reins. "Let go."

He flinched again, surprised, but kept a firm hold. He studied my face, then let out an exasperated sigh. "I'll go instead."

Now I was the one stunned. "W-what?"

"I'll go for you." He put his hands on my waist and hoisted me down.

"But…"

Brom strode out to his waiting horse. I followed, skeptical.

"Why would you offer to do this?" I asked.

He snorted a laugh. "Because Baltus would not forgive me if I let you ride away."

Naturally, it's all a joke to him. "And what will you say to Ichabod?"

He mounted Daredevil and took the reins. "Nothing. I'm not that stupid."

"He has to be warned."

"I'll follow at a distance, making sure he gets to Van Ripper's in one piece."

"Brom, please be careful."

He gazed down at the bite mark on his hand. "It seems I'm much safer out there."

With that, he spurred Daredevil and sped away.

* * *

My thoughts whirled as I sat at dinner, my teacup trembling in my hand. With every blink, the profile of the Horseman appeared—haunting me. *Ichabod. Brom.* How could I have been so selfish to let Brom go in my place?

Father paused from his meal, genuine concern on his face. "What's wrong? You look pale." He touched my cheek, feeling the icy numbness.

I wanted so badly to tell him what had happened, but he was already keeping me prisoner. If he knew about this, I wouldn't even be allowed onto the piazza. "It's nothing."

"Well, you did spend the afternoon with those children, and they carry all manner of disease. I hope it isn't the grippe."

I wish it were that simple "It's just that…I was thinking about Mr. Devenpeck. Have any measures been taken to rid us of the Horseman? Any talk of him rising again?"

"That's not your concern. The Council is taking care of matters."

"It's everyone's concern. What actions have they taken?"

The crow's feet on his eyes creased deeper. "Leave it."

I can't. "What about Old Brower and Cornelius Putnam? What business did the Horseman have with them?"

He gnashed his food like it might escape his mouth. "Leave matters to the men."

"Father, I'm set to inherit this house. Should I leave matters to the men when that day comes?"

"By then you'll have a husband."

My patience was wearing as thin as his. "Are you so sure? What's protecting *you* from the Horseman?"

His chewing slowed. He gulped down his meat, then said, "You're familiar with the André tree?"

That was not what I'd expected to hear. "Yes." The André tree stood just outside Sleepy Hollow. Its gnarled and twisted limbs gave it a vile unearthly look. Many said it'd sprouted from hell, and that its roots served as ropes, binding sinners who did not obey the devil.

But the tree was also a landmark—connected to the tragic story of Major John André, a British sympathizer who assisted Benedict Arnold during the Revolution. It was under that tree that the major was arrested as a spy.

"What of it?" I asked.

He picked through his peas, stabbing three with his fork. "It was concluded that Brower and Putnam were somehow involved in André's capture. The Hessian rose to punish them."

I considered it for a moment. "That makes no sense. André was taken some three years after the Hessian's head was blown off."

"Yes, but it's believed that a Tory lived in our midst and conjured the Horseman to enact the revenge."

Were that true, there were other matters to consider. "Then what of Nikolass? Why would the Hessian come for him?"

Father gave a shrug as he sliced into his beef. "Perhaps he'd been a British sympathizer during the war. We knew so little of him."

Something as dire as that would not have escaped Henny Van Wart. "Who could possibly be the conjurer?"

He cut his eyes to me, then went back to sawing his meat. "If we knew that, he would already be swinging from a noose, now wouldn't he?"

"So there is no solution? No defense?" I asked.

Father sighed. "At present, our only defense is prayer."

"But there has to be something."

"Enough, Katrina. I'm weary of talking about it."

"But what of –"

"Enough!"

I sat back, collecting my thoughts. None of it made sense. Nikolass was a God-fearing man. As was Garritt. Why would God turn a blind eye to them? And what of Ichabod? He'd only just arrived. What could he have done to attract the wrath of the Horseman?

A chill swept over me. If someone is controlling the Horseman, had the conjurer also send him to my window that night?

I placed my napkin on the table. "I've no appetite. May I be excused?"

He tapped his fork against my plate. "You haven't eaten."

"I'm not hungry."

He paused, huffed, then nodded.

Springing up from my chair, I hurried to my room, locked myself inside, then sat, staring out the window. For how long, I could not say. I waited and watched until my eyes would no longer stay open.

It was well after midnight when I was awakened by the sound of Brom's horse, thundering back to his cabin. I could only assume that after Ichabod's safe return, he had spent the rest of the evening at the River Song.

I relaxed upon my pillow, knowing that for tonight both of them were safe.

* * *

I wrote a note to Ichabod, then tore it up. An hour later I wrote another. I destroyed it too. After the third, I was questioning my own sanity, as well as the Horseman's purpose.

I sought out Brom, but he was doing everything in his nature to avoid me. It was a little game he played when he knew I was anxious for something from him. With him, it was always about control.

On Friday, I tried to tempt him by having Leta deliver a basket of apple muffins. I did sincerely want to thank him for his selfless act.

Leta soon returned to the house. "Mr. Brom said he wanted to know why you didn't deliver 'em yoreself—or was you afraid he might bite you back?"

I wish I'd bitten him harder. "When next you see Mr. Van Brunt," I said, "tell him that I would've delivered them myself had I known where he was. He has not kept me apprised of his work schedule."

Obviously Leta had easier access to Brom, because she reported back immediately.

"Mr. Brom said if you'd look out the back window sometime instead of the front, you'd know that his schedule changes with the seasons. And being that you're gonna inherit this farm someday, it might do you some good to stop being a dreamer and pick up a hoe."

Humph! If I picked up a hoe, it would collide with his skull.

"When next you see Mr. Van Brunt, tell him that when I inherit this farm, I intend to sell it and travel far from the vicinity. And where will he be then?"

It wasn't long till Leta was back on our doorstep. "Mr. Brom said he'd most likely be booking passage with you, and for you not to lose your pretty little head over it. Then he told me not to bring him no more messages."

"Ahhhh!" I stamped my foot, my blood rising.

Leta looked at me with wide eyes. "Please don't make me bring any more, 'cause last time he was holding a pitchfork."

"I hope he falls on it!"

I took a deep breath to tamp down my ire. After all, once Marten's ship was ready to sail, it was I who'd have the last say. "Thank you, Leta. There will be no more messages."

I poured her a cup of cider then went about my day.

* * *

Father was gone the next morning. Some business in town. I had business of my own—telling Ichabod about spotting the Horseman.

Around noon, I chanced harnessing Dewdrop to my

cabriolet and riding to the schoolhouse. Ichabod would be there with Isaiah, building the cellar floor. I also brought along a hamper of food, knowing that working men sometimes forget to eat.

I had to hitch Dewdrop to a tree limb because Gunpowder had laid claim to the rail. He stood, nodding, and pacing side to side—most likely a trick to loosen the reins. But it seemed Ichabod had grown wise to it, taking great care to wind and secure them. I doubted his students were as contrary as his horse.

I strolled around to where he and Isaiah were working, pausing briefly to watch Ichabod as he sawed a wooden plank. It rested on two trestles, and he steadied it with his knee. Perspiration beaded his forehead, curling the tips of his ebony hair. The top buttons of his white cambric shirt were unfastened, affording me a view of his glistening chest. I could barely pry my eyes from him as I admired his slender frame. Elise's devilish word immediately sprang to mind. *Delicious.*

His face opened in surprise when he spotted me. "Katrina."

I put on a smile as I carried the hamper forward. *I must tell him.*

He laid down his saw and wiped his face with his sleeve. "What have we here?"

"You'll both need to keep up your strength"—I set the hamper on a block of wood—"So"—I snapped back the cloth covering it—"I brought sausages and beer."

Isaiah paused. They both beamed.

"Watch out, Isaiah," Ichabod said. "She just might spoil us."

Isaiah wiped his hands on a rag. "Miss Katrina is too kind."

We moved away from the splinters and wood shavings and found comfortable spots on the grass. I took out the sausages, along with three tankards and a jug. I poured out the frothy brew. "Enjoy."

They both drank politely, taking moderate sips. I, preoccupied with how to tell Ichabod of the Horseman, tilted my mug to my lips and took two generous gulps –to loosen my nerves a bit.

Ichabod cocked a brow. "Isaiah, remind me to never challenge her to a drinking contest."

Isaiah's face split into a grin. They both drank heartily.

I cut into a sausage, without taking a bite. I had no appetite...and no idea how Ichabod would react when I relayed to him what I'd seen. He'd said he believed me when I pleaded the Horseman's existence. But had he really?

He watched me curiously, sensing something was wrong. "No appetite?"

Not since Wednesday. I forced a smile. "After guzzling my beer, I thought I should show some restraint."

"Ha! Around me? Prim and proper makes me terribly uncomfortable."

I gripped my mug firmly. "I'll try not to extend my pinky."

The sky had turned an iron gray and the air smelled damp and heavy. I glanced over at the timber then cast my eyes upward. "How do you plan to protect all this wood from the rain?"

He feigned panic, pressing a finger to his lips. "Shhhhhhhhh! Don't say that word."

I couldn't help but smile. "Honestly, Ichabod, I'd have never figured you as the superstitious type."

He wavered a finger. "I never take chances when it comes to rousing the devil."

Isaiah discreetly spat three times on the ground.

Ichabod spread his arms. "You see? I'm not the only superstitious one."

"Especially around here," I said. "The Hollow thrives on superstition. There isn't a person in the village who doesn't put his coat on right sleeve first."

"The right sleeve is the right sleeve, and the left sleeve is the wrong sleeve," he joked.

That drew a chuckle from Isaiah. I wished I could feel as lighthearted.

I pointed to the sky. "Yes, but about the…"

He wilted like a wet rag. "You might as well say it now."

"Rain," I whispered.

"Should the"—he pointed upward—"*inevitable* happen, we'll load the timber into the wagon and cover it with oilcloth. But I predict there will only be a thin afternoon drizzle."

"Are your predictions always correct?"

He held up his mug. "Don't place any wagers."

"Can't you simply store the wood in the cellar?"

He took a sip, foam lingering on his lips. "There is more preparation to be done inside. Carrying the planks in and out would just be added work."

"Then have Isaiah bring it back this afternoon," I said. "We'll store it in our barn."

"Oh, no. I've imposed enough already."

"Believe me, Ichabod, a corner of our barn is not an imposition. And besides, we're all anxious to see you succeed."

He slanted his head, looking genuinely touched. "With this type of generosity, how can I fail?"

Isaiah shook the last drops of beer from his tankard. "Miss Katrina, would you like me to rinse these dishes for you?"

"No, leave it. I'll take care of it."

"Then I better get back to the chore," he said, rising. "Beat the..." He grinned widely and pointed up to the sky. "Thank you kindly for the meal."

"You're welcome, Isaiah."

Once he was out of earshot, Ichabod blurted, "Tell me what's wrong. Why have you really come?"

"I saw the Horseman again."

He pushed aside the plates and moved next to me. "Where?"

"At the farm, just after you left. I was terrified he'd go after y—"

We both started when a crow swooped down and perched upon the hamper, inches away. Its black beady eyes observed us, and it cocked its head like someone listening with intent. My heart rose to my throat.

Ichabod waved his hand toward it. "Shoo!"

It remained there, challenging. Then the first sprinkles of rain fell.

"Come," Ichabod said, wrapping his arm around me and helping me into the dank cellar.

"Watch your step. Some of the stones are loose."

He lit a candle and set it on an old three-legged table. "Tell me what happened."

I relayed everything—spotting the Horseman, sending Brom, Father's speculations, and added, "The Council believes the Horseman does not rise on his own."

"Do you believe that?" he asked, his face masked with worry.

I peered into his gentle eyes. "I don't know what to believe. But I'm frightened for all of us."

"That much I can see." He swept back some strands of my dampened hair, his fingers lightly brushing my neck. It sent a new tremor through me.

"Ichabod, what should we do?"

He held my gaze, his eyes expressing trust. "I'll speak with Van Ripper. Perhaps he can tell me something."

"The Council is very secretive. Even with matters of civil

concern." I pulled my shawl tighter around me. "And you're not even supposed to know about the Horseman."

He shook his head. "How could I not? The town empties at dusk. The villagers shut themselves away. And most every door has a cross or hex sign painted on it."

"Perhaps you should put one on the school."

"No," he said. "I'm here to teach the children, not frighten them."

"So you do intend to stay?" I thought surely this would drive him back home.

"Katrina, there is danger everywhere. You can only run from it for so long." We'd moved so near, his breath brushed my cheeks.

I considered his words, realizing it was not just the bustle of Hartford that he'd wished to escape.

We stood close and quiet as the rain tapped the earth above us. His whole presence enveloped me. He smelled of woods and nature and sweat and spice, and I could practically taste it.

"I promise you," he whispered, "I will not leave."

He leaned ever closer.

I did not move.

I did not breathe.

I closed my eyes.

And just as his lips touched mine…

"Katrina," a voice called down.

We parted quickly, composing ourselves.

"Katrina."

It was Brom. *Oh God, I've been caught. What will he tell Father?* I stepped out of the shadows so he could see me.

He was wearing his tricorn instead of his fox cap, and his coat was beaded with mist. His face was sallow and lax as he descended at a leaden pace.

Had he seen?

"Brom," Ichabod greeted.

Brom held up a hand to silence him. "I've come for Katrina." His eyes, clouded and copper, gazed at me like never before. If he were capable, I thought he might cry.

"Brom…what's wrong?"

"It's Garritt," he said. "He's dead."

* * *

The room blurred and my knees gave way. Brom placed his arms around me. "Come. Let's get you home." He carefully led me up the steps.

If Ichabod said anything, I don't remember. I don't even recall looking back at him. All I could see was Garritt's face before me—his expression of torment.

Brom tethered Daredevil to the back of my cabriolet, and together we rode back to the farm.

We sat in silence, hearing only the metrical clapping of the horses' hooves. Chills traveled through my cold and clammy skin. I could barely swallow or catch my breath. It wasn't until we crossed the church bridge that I found my voice. And though I already knew the answer, I still had to ask, "How did it happen?"

Brom seemed reluctant at first, then explained. "The notary woke this morning to find Garritt gone. He'd left him a note saying he was leaving. When de Graff went looking for him, he saw smolder in the distance. Instinct led him. He found Garritt's body lying in a circle of charred grass."

My stomach knotted. "When you say 'he found his body'…"

Brom eyes cut to mine. "His body. Not his head."

I leaned forward and buried my face in my hands.

Why Garritt? Why him?

Once we'd reached home, I went straight to my room and silently shed my tears. Garritt, my sweet friend…dead. God only knew who the next victim would be.

* * *

I spent the next few days stewing, wondering. The Horseman's mark upon Garritt's window was evidence that he did not kill at random. But how *did* he choose his victims? What had each one done to invoke his wrath? These questions continually haunted me. Though I imagined the Council was as flustered as I.

On the day of the funeral, the rain had ceased, but the gray veil lingered. While Garritt and Nikolass had both been murdered by the Horseman, their funerals couldn't have been more different. Garritt was a child of the Hollow. Our grief for him ripped the heart, leaving an emptiness in its place.

Brom and Marten served as pallbearers, pacing grimly to the grave. The procession was slow, as there were many in attendance. And the rain had made the grounds sodden and sluggish, adding to the drudgery. Elise and I hooked arms, helping each other along. With a handkerchief clutched in her gloved hand, she wept in shallow sobs.

Once there, the four of us stood, staring down at the oak coffin. It was as though we were still children, innocent and awed, yet disconnected without Garritt standing alongside us.

The reverend spoke of the glory of heaven, yet I felt no relief or joy. The only solace I took was that Garritt could now be with his mother who had died when we were six. His grave was dug alongside hers, joining them both in heaven and on earth.

Once the service ended, we faced the long walk back, along with the realization that Garritt was taken from us forever. Brom and Marten each offered an arm and escorted us to the church. But as we turned to go, I cast my eyes across the cemetery, toward that grave hidden beneath the weeds. My heart was black with hate. If I could, I would dig up his headless bones and feed them to the wolves.

There was food to be had, but no desire to eat. Most everyone stood, murmuring their sorrows to each other. A line had formed to offer condolences to Notary de Graff. I swept over and took my place. There were many statements of "I am so sorry" and, "He will be missed." Once I approached, I took his hand. "I truly don't know what to say. I loved Garritt so much."

His faded eyes found mine, and he leaned toward me and whispered, "I must speak with you privately. After the service."

I nodded, somewhat aghast. Had Garritt told him of my visit behind the house?

When I turned back, Brom was there. "Come." He guided me back to where Marten stood. Elise had joined her family, still waiting to speak to the notary.

"You should sit," Brom said.

"I'd rather stand." Somehow it felt wrong to relax.

Brom placed a hand on Marten's shoulder. "Watch after her while I get her some tea."

I started to tell him I didn't need watching after, but he'd already hurried away. And he was being kind and civil for once.

Marten fidgeted with his tricorn, turning it corner to corner. In a whisper he asked, "Did you manage to see Garritt last Sunday?"

"Yes." I recalled his tortured face. *Go to safety. And tell no one of my plan to leave.* Why had I agreed?

"Did you speak to him at length?" he asked.

"He only lingered long enough to urge me away."

He stepped closer. "Did he confess anything?"

"Confess?"

"I mean did he give any explanation as to why the Horseman chose him?"

"None." Making sure we were not overheard, I anxiously asked, "Marten, how much longer?"

He brushed back a tumble of hair from his face. "Soon, I hope. And rest assured, those *further* arrangements have already been made."

I won't rest assured until I'm away from this godforsaken place. "What have you arranged?"

"Not here. I'll come by tomorrow and explain."

He'd barely finished his sentence when Brom returned with the tea. I took a sip, finding it as bitter and acrid as this awful day. "I have no taste for this."

"You should drink it," he said.

"Really, I'm fine." *Though far from it.* As I handed it back, someone stepped behind him.

"Pardon me." It was Ichabod, dressed impeccably in black. My heart hitched at the sight of him. He seemed awkwardly out of place, having never met Garritt. "I wanted to express my condolences. I understand he was a dear friend."

Brom stood taller, chin out. "None closer."

"If there's anything I can do," he said, "please do not hesitate to ask." Though these last words were meant for all of us, it was me at whom he looked.

I blushed, thinking of our near-kiss. "That's very generous."

Our eyes lingered for a moment, then he said, "I'll leave you to your mourning."

Though I couldn't voice it, I wanted so much for him to stay.

* * *

I truly wanted to go home and rest, but I had agreed to speak with Garritt's father, and it could only be here. Never again would I set foot on his harrowing property and the sorrow locked within.

Eventually the crowd thinned and I crossed over to where he stood. "You wish to speak with me?"

He took my arm and guided me to the door. He appeared so small and frail—a man left to grieve alone.

Once outside, he led me away from the remaining mourners. He stared down at the ground, his breath shallow. I worried for a moment that he might collapse.

"I know that you defied me." He did not looked up. "You went to Garritt's window and spoke with him."

I was a cornered mouse. "But I had to see him. To understand."

"You knew of his encounter with the Horseman?"

"Yes."

A silver tear fell from his eye. "You knew and you didn't tell me?"

"I was told in the strictest of confidence. I begged him to report it, but he refused."

The notary wept and coughed and wiped his eyes with the back of his hand. "I will live in wonder the rest of my life."

"As will I."

He feebly dug into his pocket and drew out Simon's talisman. "Here. This was found with his body. It was kind of you to offer it."

"You keep it," I said, closing it into his palm. "Perhaps it will do you some good."

A sob escaped him as he nodded. "God be with you, Katrina." With his head hung, he trudged back to the church.

* * *

Fear and grief leaves one achy, so I chose anger instead. Anger directed at whoever controlled the Horseman. If I could discover him, I'd have his head.

And then there was the waiting. Marten had promised to come by. I was itching to know what arrangements he'd made. But it was also Wednesday. Ichabod's day to teach the slave children. My eyes were on the clock. I worried they'd show up at the same time.

To my relief, Marten arrived a little before three. Again we stayed on the piazza so as not to be overheard.

"We must hurry," he said, grappling in his pocket. There was an unusual urgency in his words and his hands trembled. He withdrew a silk cloth, then, holding it in his palm, unfolded each corner, revealing a thin pinchbeck bracelet with six miniature clay roses. "Take this."

"Why? What's it for?"

He clumsily fastened it to my wrist.

It was lovely, but explained nothing. I thought he'd come with news. "Marten, what is this?"

"A way to cover our tracks."

I looked at him in question. How could a piece of costume jewelry make a difference?

He moved closer and met my eye. "Listen carefully. When the time comes, I'll send word. You are to go to Greenburgh, where you'll be met by Peter Bottoms."

I drew back as though he'd bit me. "Peter Bottoms? Why him?" Peter was our local tavern owner, and a creature as foul as the Horseman himself. The man wore a permanent scowl and had his fingers in a lot of pies. Most, inedible.

Marten pressed a finger to my lips to quiet me.

I clutched his hand. "Marten, no. Not Peter. I'd rather have dealings with Satan."

"It has to be Peter," he argued. "Once we're away, I'll explain."

"Explain now."

He loosened my grip on his hand. "There's no time. Just listen. From Greenburgh, Peter will take you to Sawpit. There will be a small boat waiting. The man piloting that boat will ferry you to my ship. As payment for delivering you, you're to give Peter this bracelet. Understood?"

Not really. "But this is simple costume jewelry. Why would he want it?"

"Believe me, Katrina, he does."

I examined it, running my finger over each clay rose. Intricate, but not delicate. "If he wants it so badly, then what's to stop him from simply nabbing it and abandoning me on the road?"

Marten hesitated, his eyes heavy, then said, "Because I'll be waiting with the rest of the payment. The only way he can get it is to comply."

I twirled the bracelet on my wrist, thinking of the complexity of this scheme. "It feels like I'm being smuggled."

"Would you rather risk pursuit from your father?"

I shook my head. My heart beat fast as I thought of what was to come. "Marten, are we doing the right thing?"

He gazed at me like I'd lost my mind. "Katrina, there is more at stake here than living your life tied to this farm. The Hollow has become far too dangerous."

"For everyone."

He drew close and whispered, "I cannot save everyone, but I can save you."

Though my mind whirled with questions, I quietly nodded.

He stood, looking down at me sharply. "Weigh your thoughts and decide now. Because once I sail away from Sleepy Hollow, I will never return."

* * *

When I stepped inside, Simon was walking toward the door. "I was just coming out to find you, Miss Katrina. Your father's asking for you."

I hurried to his study.

"Oh, good," he said, rising. "There are some inconsistencies on these export registers. I need a fresh pair of eyes to look them over."

My eyes were anything but fresh, and in no way would I be able to concentrate. "Can it wait until this evening? Ichabod's coming and I must prepare."

"Ichabod won't be coming." He tapped the ledger and went on as though that statement needed no explanation. "I feel there is some miscalculation in the tobacco column, but it could very well —"

"What do you mean he's not coming? It's Wednesday. He's expected."

Father kept his gaze on the numbers. "Not anymore." He ran his finger down one of the columns as though rechecking the figures, but I knew he was simply waiting for my response.

There could only be one explanation. I exhaled, determined to stay calm. "Why have you put a stop to it?"

Father exhaled his own sigh, more from impatience than surrender. "Because he did not use discretion." His finger grew white as he pressed it to the ledger. "He made me look weak before the Council."

Father? Weak? Not when his money set the rules. "I can assure you, Ichabod told no one." He would never jeopardize all he'd contended.

"We'd agreed he'd teach my slaves, yet there were others from neighboring farms."

"That was not his doing."

Father jerked his head up. "Then whose?"

I froze, mum. I couldn't name Leta. "Perhaps you should've rationalized it to the Council instead of giving in."

His face flushed as his eyes bored through me. "I did not give in! I simply came to realize the ridiculousness of it."

I returned his glare. "It's not ridiculous."

"You're right. It's not ridiculous, it's preposterous. I should've never agreed."

"But he only means well," I argued.

"Are you so sure?"

Without a doubt.

"Katrina, the Council is starting to question whether Crane is a teacher or a troublemaker. He's allowing the children too much freedom and filling their heads with unorthodox thought. One child reported that he had them spend the afternoon studying ants!"

Had I not been so angry I might've smiled.

"We're keeping a close eye on him."

"Perhaps the Council should worry more about the Horseman, and less about Ichabod."

He jabbed his finger down on the page again. "Perhaps you should stop arguing and come help me as I asked!"

I stood stock still, considering my options. I turned and swept to the door.

"Where are you going?" he called.

"Out," I said, glancing back. "I will find the numerical problem when I return."

He lifted his finger from the ledger and pointed it as straight as a pistol. "You are not to leave this house."

"Why? Because of the danger? You're forgetting, Father, the Horseman only rises at night. Or are you more afraid I might encounter Ichabod?"

Before he could protest further, I hurried down the hall.

* * *

I spurred Dewdrop into a gallop—riding hard, the sting of the cool wind on my face. My intention had been to get away. To taste a little freedom. To breathe. But after a few minutes, I changed course, and didn't slow until the schoolhouse came into sight.

The school day had ended, but Gunpowder was still tethered in front. *Good.* I hitched Dewdrop, then smoothed down my windblown hair. I touched my palms to my face. How must I look after that fierce ride? *Rosy nose? Mottled cheeks?*

I pushed through the door. "Ichabod?" The room was empty. I peeked out at Gunpowder…then I remembered.

There's a comfortable patch of clover near the water. An excellent spot to think.

Of course.

I hurried through the schoolyard to the old birch by the brook. Ichabod sat against it, journal and pencil in hand. His eyes were fixed to his notebook. He wrote intensely, like the words might evaporate before he could get them onto the page. I watched for a moment…then two. I could've watched for an hour, but secretly observing him felt a bit lewd.

"Ichabod," I whispered.

He started as I brought him out of his trance. "Katrina."

Quickly rising, he tucked the journal and pencil into his vest pocket. How beautifully handsome he was. I touched my cheek again, worrying that I looked like a smallpox victim.

He stepped closer. "You seem upset. Has something else happened?"

I dropped my hand from my face. "I just heard that Father has ceased the Wednesday lessons."

He shrugged a shoulder. "I gave it my best. Maybe after the Horseman is dealt with, he'll reconsider."

"Father? Don't count on it. And don't make excuses for him. "

"Relax, Katrina. Progress takes time."

I studied those vibrant green eyes. "How can you always be so carefree and optimistic?"

His lips softened. "Because I prefer it to the alternative."

I swept a windblown lock of hair from my face as I stepped a little closer. "I wish I could be as mild tempered. I'm always one heartbeat away from strangling someone."

"Well then," he said, holding out his hand, "I'll show you

something that'll settle your murderous rage." When I reached over, he quickly drew his hand back. "If it's safe."

I playfully swatted at his arm. You *make me cheerful.* Then, gently taking my hand, he led me to a white ash tree just yards from the rippling water. There, on the ground, was a large cluster of black and gray rocks. I peered down at them, confused. But after a moment, the grouping took shape. "Oh! It's a dragonfly."

"Yes." He beamed. "It's a mosaic."

I knelt and ran my fingers over the smooth stones. "It's beautiful."

He knelt too. "After all the children have faced this week, I thought it would be uplifting to resume classes in a more enjoyable way."

I thought of the Council and their watchful eye. "What exactly did this teach them?"

He gave me a heart-melting smile. "Mathematics."

I stepped back, admiring it. "It's utterly amazing."

"Katrina, you should have seen them working. They completely engineered it themselves. I had no hand in either the design or the building of it." I'd never heard anyone speak with such pride.

"Please don't let Father or the Council see this. They already think your methods unconventional."

"I know. They feel all learning should be written or read. But if they find this grounds for dismissal"—He threw up his hands—"then good luck finding a replacement."

I laughed. "Yes, you do have *some* leverage."

He helped me to rise, then stepped intimately closer. As close as we'd been in the cellar. Tingles danced along my skin as I drew in his scent.

"What about you?" he asked. "How do you feel about my methods?" He waited, like my reply was the only thing that mattered.

"I think you're absolutely wonderful." *Did I just say* you're? "Methods. I think your *methods* are wonderful." His presence was like nectar, and every part of me wanted a taste. I needed that kiss—the one that had been interrupted several days ago.

After a few seconds of anticipation, I finally took a step back. "It's getting cooler." I rubbed at the nonexistent chill on my arms. "Maybe I should let you get back to your"—I circled my finger toward his pocket, indicating his small notebook—"story."

I turned to go.

"Katrina."

When I turned back, he pulled me into his arms, and in an instant, his lips were on mine.

With plans in place to sail away, I should've pulled back. Why do this to myself? To him? Instead, I wrapped my arms around his neck and drank the nectar.

We kissed at length, and with passion—as though our very existence depended on it. When we finally parted, he whispered, "Had I spent another second without holding you, I might've gone mad." He pulled me in for another kiss, and I melted into it.

My fingers played through his hair as I consumed every eager moment. My heart raced, and my breath came quick and shallow. I'd never known a joy like this.

We kissed again and again among the solemn sounds of the rolling brook. But just as I'd lost myself completely, an eerie chill swept through me, as it had that Sunday night. I broke our embrace and glanced around.

"What is it?" he asked, suddenly on guard.

"I don't know. It feels like someone's watching."

He drew me close as he scoured the area. "Unless you count the birds and insects, there are no eyes upon us."

"But the Horseman has no eyes," I whispered.

Sensing my apprehension, he placed his arm around me. "We should get inside."

The sun had tilted in the sky and our shadows fell before us. Though leaving Ichabod would be difficult, I needed to get home straight away. Dealing with Father would be easier if I returned well before dusk.

As we approached the school, Ichabod slowed his pace. His brows dipped and his eyes narrowed. "Did you leave the door open?"

"No." Yet it stood opened all the way.

"Stay here," he said quietly. Then cautiously, he took the steps and went inside.

I waited, biting a fingernail and straining to see in. After a few moments, I couldn't wait anymore. I hurried inside and... "Dear God!" It looked as though a cyclone had found its way in. Overturned desks. Copybooks ripped, pages scattered to the floor. The water basin shattered. And fireplace ash was smeared across the floor, windows, and walls. Even some of Ichabod's personal books, including Aesop, had fallen victim to this rage.

He stood limp, assessing the damage—a mixture of hurt and awe on his face.

"Oh, Ichabod!" I knelt, scooping up papers and quills.

"No, Katrina. Leave it." He bent to help me stand, but I continued whisking up all that I could hold.

"Katrina," he urged.

"Who would do this?" I asked, slipping pages into their covers.

"Don't worry."

I couldn't help but worry while I gathered more and more. As I reached for a page of scripture lying under a tumbled bench, my bracelet caught on a loose nail. Instinctively, I jerked back, snapping the thin chain. The tiny roses clicked to the floor, bouncing and rolling in various directions.

"No!" I dropped everything, sweeping it all aside. I quickly plucked up three of the beads that hadn't strayed far.

Ichabod knelt to help me. "Here." He took my hand and dropped two more into my palm.

Five. Only five. "There's one more. I have to find it."

I ran my hand across the filthy floor. "It has to be here." Peter's payment. *What have I done?*

"I don't see it," he said.

"Search!"

Ichabod lifted me to my feet and wrapped me into his arms. "Katrina, relax. It is here, somewhere among the clutter. I'll find it. I promise."

I gently pulled away from him. "I need to find it now."

"Believe me, it will turn up when things are put back in place."

My eyes roamed over the devastation that had been his orderly school. "That'll take hours."

"On the contrary," he said, placing his hand to my cheek. "Tomorrow I'll bring a pocket watch, and my students will have a lesson in ingenuity and time management." Then he whispered in my ear, "I bet your father would approve."

I forced a smile.

He retrieved a handkerchief from his pocket, then, loosening my cupped hand, he placed the five clay roses and chain within it. "Can you have it repaired?"

"I need the sixth one."

"I assure you, it's here somewhere." Then his lips touched mine, comforting me with a kiss. I again fell victim to his affection.

He ran his thumb along my jaw. "Come. I'll accompany you home."

"No," I said, "you have much to do here."

"But I would feel better if –"

"Really, I'll be fine." I couldn't risk Father seeing us together. "Just promise me you'll be back at Van Ripper's before dark."

"I promise."

He helped me around the clutter, then rested his forehead against mine. "Remember, Katrina, nothing can undo the happiness you brought me today."

Before leaving, I tucked the handkerchief into my bodice. I couldn't risk losing the rest.

Ichabod smiled, his eyes soft. "I'll find the other and return it Saturday."

"Saturday?"

He winked. "When you bring me more sausages and beer."

* * *

I had intended to ride back to the stables, but as I neared the house I saw Brom on the piazza, leaning against a column, arms crossed. I hitched Dewdrop in front.

His eyes narrowed as I approached. "So how was your visit with the schoolmaster?"

Without hesitation, I drew back and slapped him hard across the face. "You're such a child!"

His eyes widened as his hand flew up, touching the sting.

I stormed into the house.

"Katrina," he called, following. He reached out and latched onto my arm.

"Let go of me." I jerked free, glaring.

Father came out of his study. "What the devil is going on here?"

"Katrina, stop!" Brom barked.

I continued walking until Father stepped in front of me. "What is this nonsense?"

I took a deep breath to compose myself. "How you can

employ such a monster is beyond me."

"What has *he* done?" Father asked, implying that I'd done plenty.

I glanced back at Brom, who stood firmly, his cheek crimson from the slap.

"He's cost you money for new copybooks."

"Katrina—" Brom said.

I stepped around Father before he could further intervene. "Tell Simon I'll take dinner in my room."

* * *

I waited all evening for a tirade from Father, but no reprimand came. *Did Brom have a hand in that?*

I spent the better part of the evening conflicted. I wanted more than anything to be with Ichabod, even at the risk of my "someday." But would Father allow it? Never. Not after Ichabod had *shamed* him before the Council…a body far more important than me.

On Saturday, I sneaked a hamper into my cabriolet and secretly rode back to the schoolhouse, praying that Ichabod had found the missing rose. If the bracelet was that valuable to Peter, I had to make sure all six were returned to Marten.

I was surprised to see Isaiah there, loading flagstones from the wagon into a handcart. With the teaching exchange off, it didn't make sense. I didn't see Ichabod around, but assumed he was working in the cellar.

Isaiah stopped as I approached.

"I didn't expect to see you here," I said.

"Mr. Brom insisted I be here every week until the floor is done."

This was before he destroyed the schoolroom, I presume. "Did he mention why?"

"No, ma'am. He just tells me what, not why."

Has Brom suddenly grown a conscience? "Well, I'm sure Ichabod appreciates your hard work."

A trace of a smile crossed his lips. "He's a good man, Miss Katrina."

I remembered then that Isaiah was the father of three children, one being the adorably rambunctious Elijah.

I patted his shoulder. "Come help me with the hamper."

As we were spreading a quilt, Ichabod popped up from the cellar. "Do I smell food?" His wool shirt hung loose, the collar undone, and his hair was wildly rumpled. Even in a disheveled state he was beautiful.

I sat down next to the basket. "I have brought nourishment."

He washed his face and hands and joined us.

He'd barely sat before I blurted, "Did you find it? My rose?"

His expression dropped. "I'm so sorry, Katrina. We searched everywhere. *Every*where. We turned the hunt into a game, and I even offered a reward to the student who could produce it. It simply wasn't there."

"That makes no sense. You saw it break loose. It couldn't just vanish."

"And somehow it has." His eyes glimmered with empathy. "Can you order a replacement?'

"I'm afraid not." How's Marten going to take this news?

Ichabod reached over and touched my hand, sending delightful sparks through my flesh. "I'll continue to look. This cabin is old. Some of the boards are loose. It could've fallen through."

"That would be like finding a pea in a pumpkin patch."

His lips curved into a smile. "I happen to be a proficient pea-picker. But now"—he snapped away the cloth covering the hamper—"let's celebrate what we do have."

I turned to Isaiah. "Has he been this cheerful all day?"

"Mr. Crane is always agreeable. But he only gets cheery when you show up." Quickly adding, "It must be this great food you bring us."

Ichabod winked.

We laid out the spread, then spent our time eating, laughing, and discussing how the weather had taken pity and stayed dry. Once we'd had our fill, Isaiah said, "I'll unload those stones into the cellar." He heaved away, going back to his chore.

"Is there much left to—" Before I could finish, Ichabod drew me into a kiss. It tasted of salt and seasoning and was absolutely delectable. When I worried my passion might overtake my good sense, I broke away and tamped down my emotional fire with a swig of beer. "As I was about to say, is there much left to do?"

"It seems I've barely started." He stretched out and laid his head on my lap. "Before I can put in the planks, I have to lay a stone foundation. That's what I've been doing all morning." He groaned.

I brushed back some of his black curls, which were damp from perspiration. "I could help you."

He chuckled.

I didn't.

His eyes narrowed and his smile disappeared. "You're serious?"

I twisted a clump of his hair and pulled.

"Ow." He laughed again. "Katrina, masonry is not woman's work."

"I guess I misjudged you, *Mr. Crane*." I pushed his head off my lap. "I thought you were a freethinker. For your information, any task that I'm capable of performing is woman's work. And I can certainly lug a few rocks."

He rubbed his head where I'd tugged. "Yes, I keep

forgetting that you're no ordinary woman."

I patted down the lock of hair. "Just don't let it happen again."

"Yes, ma'am." He pulled me into another long, delicious kiss then said, "Let's get to work."

We packed away the remains of the meal and went to the cellar. Several lamps were lit, the flames bringing life to the room. Along the right-hand wall, flagstones were fitted about eighteen inches off the dirt floor—a drum of mortar beside them.

I noted how the stones were cut and assembled to conform. "Your own mosaic."

"You might say that. Only mine will be hidden by wooden planks."

I ran my fingers across the rugged rock. "I'll know it's there."

I helped Isaiah carry down more. After a while my palms reddened and stung. Of course, I'd never let on to Ichabod.

He stayed fixed, working the trowel. Occasionally he'd raise his arm to wipe his face with his sleeve. I found that I lingered more and more, just to watch him work. He took his time, fitting each stone just so.

After a bit, Isaiah stopped. "We've unloaded 'em all. I'm going up to chisel more."

Ichabod finally rose.

Once Isaiah had gone, I reached for him, wanting another kiss.

He took a step back, palms raised. "I'm filthy."

"That won't stop me." I put my arms around his neck, and our lips met in a sultry kiss.

After a few more, I leaned back and cocked my head. "I'm keeping you from your work."

He pulled me in and whispered, "An enticing distraction."

It was then that we heard the gallop of an approaching horse.

Ichabod looked up. "Who could that be?"

Please don't be Father. Or worse, Brom, looking for trouble.

As the horse neared, an eerie chill shrouded me. That foul breath rolled down the back of my neck. "Ichabod!"

I'd barely spoken his name when a strong, searing wind shot through, slamming the cellar doors and extinguishing the lamps. We were instantly thrown into darkness.

My heart drummed as I clutched Ichabod close.

"Careful," he said, his voice soft and soothing. "It's only the wind. I'll help you out of here."

He led me through the blackness till we reached the cellar stairs. Just as we'd managed two of the steps, we heard it—the grinding sound of metal scraping wood. We both stumbled back down as the heat of burning kindle struck us.

"Someone's burning the doors," I said, quivering.

Ichabod held me. "Shhhhhh. Stay still."

Suddenly the grating stopped, leaving only the severe odor of fiery embers.

Are we trapped?

Shadows passed over the doors, and ribbons of smoke curled through the cracks.

My heart rose to my throat. "Ichabod."

He laid his fingers on my lips, staying perfectly still.

The sound of the horse's hooves—heavy on the earth—faded, leaving us in that blackened void.

"Let's go," Ichabod urged, hurrying me up the steps.

We burst through the cellar doors into the cool air. I held him close as we surveyed the area. Tendrils of smoke rose from where the hooves had branded the grass. Several small fires remained. The wall of the school had been burned as well.

Ichabod let go and went to the doors. He closed one then the other, revealing a long black slash seared into the wood. I recognized it immediately.

"Oh my God!" It was the same as the mark scored into Garritt's window.

Ichabod studied it for a moment, then turned, panicked. "Isaiah."

We dashed around to where he'd been working.

"Isaiah!" I screamed, when I saw the work area empty. "Isaiah!" *Please let him be safe.*

Then we heard rustling within the woods. He approached, eyes wide, lit with fear. The chisel was still gripped in his hand. "I'm here."

"Did you see him?" Ichabod asked.

Isaiah trembled. "Yes, sir. It was like the devil himself rode in—all dressed in black, swinging that sickle. I hid in those trees."

Ichabod exhaled relief. "Thank God you weren't harmed."

Isaiah rested the chisel on one of the stones. "What brought 'im here? He never rides in broad daylight."

"He's right," I said to Ichabod, my skin crawling like ants. "The Horseman's never been seen during the day."

Ichabod's eyes searched as though looking for an answer. Or maybe he was trying to rationalize what had happened. Until this moment, he'd only heard rumors of the ghost. This was proof that the Horseman was real.

He placed a shaky hand on Isaiah's shoulder. "Let's assess the damage."

Cautiously, we went back to the cellar. The small fires had died, leaving patches of withered grass. It looked as though the Horseman had circled twice or more before finally riding away. And the blackened gash he'd sliced into the doors extended right to left, moving upward. His scythe had also connected with the schoolhouse wall, leaving a scoring there as well.

My hand flew to my mouth as realization struck. "Ichabod, he has marked you."

His face paled as his eyes coursed over the slash. "Isaiah, take Katrina home."

"What? No! I won't leave you here all alone!"

"Take her," he ordered, his gaze trained on the mark.

"I won't go."

Isaiah looked conflicted, then he faced me. "Come, Miss Katrina. Mr. Van Tassel will have my hide if I let you come to harm."

"Come with us, Ichabod," I cried. "Do not stay here."

He gently reached out and pulled me into a hug. "I'll leave shortly for Van Ripper's."

I buried my face on his shoulder. "Promise me you'll stay safe. Please."

"I promise. Now go."

Reluctantly, I left him and returned to the farm.

* * *

Father rose from his chair when he saw the state of my condition. "What's happened?"

"The Horseman," I said, still quivering in fear. "He's laid claim to Ichabod."

"What?" His eyes cut to Isaiah.

Isaiah nodded. "Yes, sir. What she's telling is true."

"And you saw the monster?"

Isaiah nodded again.

"Father, it's Ichabod he's after. He marked the school in the same manner he'd marked Garritt's window." I continued, blurting the entire story of helping Ichabod in the cellar.

Father's face reddened with outrage as I relayed the event. If the situation weren't so dire, I'd be facing retribution.

"I'll assemble the Council." He pointed a rigid finger in my face. "And *you* will stay inside."

"But I must go to Ichabod. I have to know that he's safe."

"Have you lost your mind?" he thundered. "You'll do nothing of the sort!"

"He's in danger!"

"And now so are you. I forbid you to leave this house." He pushed around me and rushed out the backdoor. Minutes later, he rode off.

I flinched as Isaiah reached to help me remove my cloak. His hand popped back like he'd touched fire. We were both on edge.

"I'm sorry," I said, realizing what I'd done. Poor Isaiah had seen the demon up close. "How are you feeling? Will you be all right?"

Distress still outlined his face. "That's a sight I won't ever forget."

I unwrapped the cloak myself and draped it over my arm. "And one I hope you'll never have to see again."

"Either of us," he said.

After that, he hesitated, not sure what to do.

"Thank you for everything, Isaiah. Now go find your children and give them a hug."

His face softened. "Yes, ma'am." He started to turn, then said, "Miss Katrina, don't worry too much about Mr. Crane. He's a right smart man."

"I know." *But can he outsmart a brutal ghost?*

* * *

Hours later, Father still hadn't returned. In that time, I'd paced a hole in the floor, bitten all my nails, and was close to banging my head against the wall. I sat at the dinner table, slashing marks into my yams.

Simon refilled the one sip of water I'd taken from my glass. "Eat something, Miss Katrina. Starving yourself won't do no good."

"I can't." I glanced at the clock. "Why is Father not back yet?"

"I'm sure he'll be here soon. And he'll have answers."

As much as I wanted to believe that, I knew it wasn't true.

The slashes I'd scored in my yams grew deeper. I was seconds away from risking a ride out to Van Ripper's myself. Then I heard Father's horse on the road. I scraped back my chair and rushed to meet him at the door. I was still holding my fork, which were crusted with yam bits.

"What'd you learn?" I spouted before he could step inside.

I hadn't realized I was aiming my fork at him until he reached out and pushed it away. "I should be the one asking the questions."

He will not do this to me. I wanted answers. "What of Ichabod?"

Father's nostrils flared as he countered my question with his own. "Why in God's name were you at the schoolhouse today? And alone with him in the cellar?"

"Is that really more important than Ichabod's head?"

"To me. Yes." He bore around me, removing his coat. "The whole blasted village knows of this now. Our good name will be ruined."

Not as long as our money fills the veins of this town.

I followed him into the dining room, my fork clenched tight in my fist.

He whipped back his chair and took his usual seat at the head of the table.

"Father, how is Ichabod?"

"Safe at Van Ripper's for now. We're keeping a watch over him. Though he's not agreeable to being kept under guard. The young fool."

I quietly sighed relief, knowing he was being looked after.

But he must've loathed every second of it. Even though I was on shaky ground, I sat down and continued to badger. "What will the Council do now? Did they work out a plan? Maybe it's time to make a list of suspicious citizens who might be controlling The Horse —"

His rigid finger was again in my face. "Maybe it's time for you to stay quiet and consider your defiant behavior." Then he glared down at the empty space before him. "Where the hell is my dinner?" Instead of waiting for Simon, he reached over and snatched my plate of uneaten food. He didn't seem to mind the rutted yams as he jabbed his fork into them and ate.

* * *

The next morning, parishioners packed the church. Father was right. The whole village knew of yesterday's incident. I wanted so badly to speak with Ichabod, but didn't dare. And besides, he was surrounded by grim-faced men who were nodding their heads and stroking their chins. Our eyes met briefly and his widened in a "help me!" plea. If I'd had a way to rescue him from the old codgers, I would've.

I'd barely taken three steps toward the pews when Henny and a throng of other women stopped me. They must have been lying in wait.

"Horrendous," Henny boomed, taking my hand. "You must have been one scared little duckling."

I had no wish to discuss this with her, but she was accompanied by most every busybody in the village, so I couldn't resist filling their ears. "It was terribly frightening." I fanned my face like recalling it might cause me to swoon.

"There, there," Henny said. "You are safe here in church."

I'd have felt safer if I weren't being suffocated by these prattlepusses.

She patted my hand like I was a small child. "We have been going round and round with this and cannot come up with a reasonable explanation as to why Ichabod has made an enemy of the Horseman."

Everyone gawked, eyes immense.

I cocked my head, tossing her a questioning look. "And you think *I* would know?"

"Of course not," Henny said in a *tsk, tsk* manner. "But you were there with him at the time."

I breathed in, lifting my chin. "Yes, I was. But that doesn't mean I'd know why the Horseman appeared."

"I understand, my dear," Henny patronized. "You were probably too preoccupied in that cellar to even give it a thought."

Sheer delight crossed the ladies' faces.

"Yes," I said, pulling my hand away. "Those doors weren't the only things smoldering."

A dozen jaws dropped.

I smiled sweetly. "Now if you'll excuse me." I proudly pushed through them to where Father sat.

Reverend Bushnell took to the pulpit. He led us in an opening prayer, asking God not only for an end to this unholy affliction, but to also keep safe our beloved schoolmaster, who especially needed His benevolent hand. I didn't know where Ichabod sat, but I imagined he wanted to crawl under the pew.

The reverend continued, preaching a sermon on enticing evil. He read to us from Psalm 59: *Deliver me from mine enemies, O my God: defend me from them that rise up against me.*

Only when we bowed our heads did I not feel judgmental eyes on me. But I read the scriptures and sang the hymns as though it were any other Sunday. I listened for Ichabod's voice, but could not hear it. He must've felt it best not to drown out Mrs. Twiggs on this particular morning.

Service finally ended, and I was able to turn and look. That was when I saw Elise. Knowing how she felt about Ichabod, I had to explain.

I caught up to her. "Elise, I'm sorry."

"No need to apologize." She stood stiff and straight and spat the words like they were poison.

"Please, I want you to understand."

"I do," she said, her eyes narrowed. "You're Katrina Van Tassel. The daughter of the wealthiest man in Sleepy Hollow. You always get what you want. You always have."

"You know that's not true."

"Isn't it?" Her mouth curled into a false smile. "Perhaps I should loan you that book of Persian tales. There's an intriguing story of a man named Ali Baba. A fable filled with theft and deceit. I'm sure you'd enjoy it very much."

Before I could comment, she whisked away. But what else could I have said? I had failed her.

After many parting pleasantries, the parishioners began to filter out. My father stood in one corner, speaking with the Council. Ichabod was among them. I casually wandered over—yes, to eavesdrop, but also for a chance to be close to him. I stayed in the shadows behind the pew, thumbing through my Bible, trying not to look obvious.

"We'll resume at my home this evening," Father said to the men. "And I suggest you arrive in groups—safety in numbers."

They all nodded and mumbled, then broke their circle.

Once they'd disassembled, Ichabod walked by me, slipping a folded piece of paper onto my Bible as he passed. After making sure no one saw, I opened it. It contained one sentence: *When and where can we meet?*

The when and where I knew. But how could I tell him? Especially now that he was across the room, between two men.

Just as I looked up, he said something to one of them, and then came back to retrieve his Bible lying on the windowsill. He sauntered over to where I stood.

"Three o'clock. Our stables," I whispered. "But Ichabod, should you risk it?"

He kept his voice low. "Katrina, they even escort me to the privy. I've got to get away."

The misery weighed on his face.

"Then three o'clock if you can manage it."

"I won't be a second late."

* * *

Keeping to his word, Ichabod rode up on a splendid roan. I met him just inside the stable doors, holding Dewdrop's reins. "Thank God they gave you another horse. Do you think it can outrun the Horseman?"

He rubbed its neck. "You'd be amazed at how fast a frightened horse can gallop."

"Then let's go quickly before we're caught."

I spurred Dewdrop into action. Ichabod followed closely at my side. Our horses raced at a full gallop—crossing fields and orchards—carrying us to my sacred haven. Not only would we have the privacy to talk, but I also longed for Ichabod to see it.

When we reached the hilltop, we did not immediately dismount, but instead cast our gaze over the beauty of the countryside and the quiet, rolling waters of the Hudson. I could tell by his expression that he was breathing in every wondrous detail.

I climbed off my horse and stepped to the edge, drawing my cloak around me. Ichabod joined me and we stood together, overlooking the tranquil domain.

"This is my sanctuary. I call it Bliss," I said.

"Bliss," he murmured.

"I played here often as a child."

He continued to look on in awe. "I've never seen anything like it."

"Ichabod…I must apologize."

He turned to me, brows furrowed. "What for?"

"For everything. For everyone. The Council brought you here under false pretenses, and never warned you afterward. You're in danger because of them."

He ran his fingers along my cheek. "Katrina, you shouldn't apologize for them. Especially since you were the only one who was honest with me."

"But the Council—"

"We should be thanking them for bringing us together."

"But now they're keeping us apart."

There was a sudden rustling nearby. "Come," I said, "we should go inside."

He raised an eyebrow. "Inside?"

I led him around to the old weather-beaten granary. As I pushed open the door, we were met with the golden scent of scattered grain.

We climbed the stairs to the very top, and stopped at a small, crusted window that overlooked the beds of wild asters. "I spent my best hours here," I said, unfastening my cloak and setting it aside.

An old patchwork quilt lay in the corner, next to a wooden stick pony and a tangled marionette. I unfolded the quilt, shook out the grain dust, and settled it onto the floor. Then I sat down, bringing him with me.

"Ichabod, what are we going to do?"

He wrapped me into his arms. "We're going to find a solution."

"Can we?"

He gazed out the window, thoughts circulating behind his eyes. "There's obviously more to the Horseman's killing than random choice. He murdered the previous schoolmaster and now he's marked me. Why does the position of teacher incite him?"

"It's not just that. What about Garritt? He was an apprentice to his father. He had nothing to do with teaching or education."

"That's another part of the puzzle that I can't place." He heaved a frustrated sigh. "It makes no sense. In life the man was a Hessian. A mercenary. He killed for profit. What does killing gain him now?"

"Perhaps he kills for the thrill of carnage."

"Then why pick and choose his victims? Bloodlust is blind. It controls the slayer. This ghost has a purpose."

"Have you told any of this to the Council?" I asked.

He laughed. "They're looking for ways to exorcise a demon, not put it under a microscope...as they have made clear to me twice now. They insist it's my radical behavior and modern teaching methods that's attracted him."

"That's absurd."

He tilted his eyes toward me. "Remember, we're talking about the Council. I was surprised the word *modern* was even in their vocabulary."

Nothing surprised me when it came to those men. "What about the belief that someone controls the Horseman?"

"That still doesn't explain how the victims are chosen."

I stroked a finger across his cheek. "Surely they'll find a solution. They must feel some responsibility."

"I've heard no apologies from them. And anyway, it's not really my head they're worried about. Should the Horseman take it, then more citizens of Sleepy Hollow could fall victim. As long as I'm marked, everyone else is safe. That's all that really matters to them. They look after their own."

A fact I've known my entire life. "Right now, yours is the only head I'm concerned about."

He gave me a gentle squeeze. "We have so little time here. Let's not waste it talking of this."

I arched a brow. "What shall we waste it on?"

He lifted his hand, noting our surroundings. "I'm quite curious how you spent your best hours here."

I kept my brow lifted. "Would you like me to show you?"

"Absolutely."

"It's very girly," I warned.

"I will admit, it's your girlishness that I noticed first."

I tickled him and he chuckled. *God, I love that laugh.* I then took out my small basket of miniature delft teacups and tiny silver spoons.

Ichabod held up one of the wee cups for inspection. "Oh, now I see. Were your party guests of the imaginary sort?"

"I had a lot of dolls back then. And Elise was here with me sometimes."

He set the cup down and rocked back, resting his arm on his knee. "I can envision it now. You...innocent-eyed. Lace bonnet. Pink apron."

"That's not too far off. But of all the toys I brought here, nothing compared to these." Moving the crate that I'd used as a table, I pulled out a blue silk pouch I'd hidden underneath. I turned away, holding it to my breast. "Do you, Ichabod Crane, solemnly promise not to laugh at what's in here?"

He moved behind me, resting his chin on my shoulder. "So help me God."

I paused a moment, then unclasped the silken pouch and removed the contents.

"Paper dolls!" he said, intrigued.

"I cut them from issues of *The Lady's Magazine* that I sneaked out of my mother's bureau. That's why they're such a secret."

"Why did your mother not share her fashion papers with you?"

"Are you familiar with that publication?"

He sighed dramatically. "Sadly, I let my subscription expire."

I reached back and tickled his side again.

He buckled, laughing. "I should never have shared that particular weakness with you."

"I'm glad you did. Now I'll always have an advantage."

He nodded back toward the dolls. "You were saying?"

"Mother never shared her fashion papers because some of the articles and stories were not suitable for children."

His lips twisted into a grin. "And yet you read every one."

"Of course," I said with a giggle.

Ichabod brushed my hair aside, his fingers skimming my cheek. "You've never spoken of your mother."

"She died of a fever when I was twelve." Six years had passed, yet at times, I still feel her about.

"I'm so sorry," he said.

I gazed down at the paper dolls. "You would've liked her. She was kind and giving, and always smiled. Always. Even as she lay dying she had a smile for us. I can't recall a single moment when she was cross. Father says I favor her. And there are times when I look in the mirror and can see it." How different life would be had she lived.

Ichabod looked at me with loving eyes. "Then she must've been very beautiful."

I turned and gave him a kiss.

He rested his chin back upon my shoulder and pointed to the paper dolls. "So, how many lovely ladies do you have there?"

I spread them on the quilt. Only three had survived my hours of play, and they were creased and dark and worn. But the beautiful details of their fashions had not faded. Elegant wigs. Wide-brimmed hats. Low-cut bodices and grand hoop skirts. All adorned with ruffles, lace, and flowers. Gloves, parasols, and fans.

"Quite a parade," he said.

"They still make me happy."

"Tell me, do these refined ladies have names?"

I blushed. "Yes, but those will remain secret."

"I'll bet they have grand names like Dorothy and Ester and Florence."

"I tend to prefer floral names."

"Then Peony and Iris and Rose."

"You got one right."

As I placed them back into the pouch, Ichabod curled his arms around my waist, laying soft kisses on my neck. Tingles prickled my skin. He brushed aside my hair, making his way around to the nape. I closed my eyes, shutting out all senses but this.

We lay back on the quilt, reveling in our closeness—our kisses. But there was still one thing between us.

"Ichabod," I said, grazing his cheekbone with my thumb, "tell me about Connecticut. Why did you leave?"

He rolled onto his back and gazed somberly at the beamed ceiling. "Katrina, let's not do this now."

"I want no secrets between us."

There was anguish on his face. Whatever the reason, it was something he couldn't bear to relive. Yet now, more than ever, I had to know.

"Tell me…please."

Then, closing his eyes, he did.

"Just after finishing my studies at the university, I worked as an aide to one of the professors. My two closest friends were still students. One evening, the three of us were at a tavern. A young woman happened to be there. Until she struck up a conversation, we hadn't even noticed her. We talked, had a few drinks, then she left.

"Several days later, I began thinking about her…a lot. And with each day, more and more. No matter what I was doing, she was there, invading my thoughts. Eventually, she was all I could think about. I wanted badly to see her again, but I had no idea where she lived. So it became my mission to find her."

"And you did?" I asked.

He opened his eyes, but kept them to the ceiling. "Believe me, it wasn't easy. Hartford had completely swallowed her up. But just when I was giving up hope, she came back to the tavern. I hadn't remembered how beautiful she was. Breathtaking. By the end of the evening I was completely in love."

As I'd feared. He'd come to escape a broken heart. "What happened then?" I asked, hoping he couldn't detect how those last words stung.

"I became obsessed," he answered. "I spent every second I could with her—leaving work unfinished, papers ungraded, and neglecting my friends as well. She was the oxygen I breathed, and my only purpose for living."

My blood rose with jealousy, yet I still needed to hear.

"My two friends tried to intervene, but I threatened them. Even fought one of them. I'd let no one come between us.

"As weeks passed, I'd lost myself completely. I no longer read or wrote. My job was hanging by a thread, and my friends had abandoned me."

He finally turned to look at me. "Then one day she came to the university, crying and begging me for help. Before she could explain, two constables marched in and arrested her."

"Arrested her? Why?"

"At the time I didn't know, or even care the reason. I rushed them, swinging and clawing. The more she wept and reached for me, the more it fueled my rage. They were going to arrest me too, but my professor intervened and vouched for me. I'm indebted to him to this day."

I searched Ichabod's face, trying to imagine this gentle man expressing any kind of anger.

"I quickly learned," he went on, "that she'd been accused of witchcraft."

"Oh, Ichabod."

"Supposed evidence was found by her servant, who presented several small pouches of bristle and bone. The servant also claimed to have seen her conjure fire. Two merchants came forward as well, alleging to have witnessed her manipulating the weather and seas. Particularly in the case of export ships."

Her servant? Obviously her place in society was greater than I thought. "Did you see her do any of this?"

"No. All I ever saw was her."

My teeth clenched, but I reminded myself *You are here with him, not her.*

"Nevertheless," he continued, "I was outraged. I spent the next several days outside her cell, refusing to eat or sleep or even bathe. By that third day, I looked like one of the beggars who slept in the streets."

Dear God.

"But her trial was swift, and she was sentenced to hang." He raked his fingers through his hair, misery in his eyes. "On the day of her hanging, I became a pure madman—screaming and gnashing. My friends seized me and locked me in a closet. But I was like a diseased animal, literally growling and charging the door. Finally, I grew so sick and tired, I just curled up, wanting to die."

"Ichabod," I whispered, wanting to take him into my arms and soothe away his past.

His eyes softened as he gazed into mine. "But then, instantly, everything changed. I knew the exact moment she was hanged—the very second that she died. Because at that moment, every feeling I'd held for her fled. Every one. I no longer felt love. Or hate. Like or dislike. I had no more concern for her than I would a stranger I'd passed on the street. That was when I saw the truth."

"She'd bewitched you."

"And nearly ruined me."

My heart ached as I soothed his brow with my fingers.

"The professor, understanding the situation, took me back. But it was never the same. I'd lost my standing within the community. Then I saw Baltus's advertisement and a chance for a new start."

"Is this why you study that book of witchcraft?" I asked.

"Yes. I feel a need to understand." He brushed my hair back, searching my face. "I hope this doesn't change anything between us."

I put my hands to his cheeks and kissed him. I'd never let her win.

He relaxed into the kiss, relieved. But there was one other thing I needed to know. "Ichabod, what was her name?"

He shook his head. "No. Forget her."

"Please, tell me."

He sighed and spoke it softly. "Victoria. Her name was Victoria."

Victoria. Now I knew whom to loathe.

We lay silently for a moment, and then he pulled me close. "Katrina, I'm ashamed of what took place in Hartford, but I'm not the least bit sorry. Had it not happened, I wouldn't be here with you."

I curled up next to him, my head on his shoulder, my hand upon his chest. I could never imagine this gentle person as a brutal beast.

We held and caressed each other for a time, then Ichabod

said those dreaded words, "We should get back. Surely, they'll be looking for us."

I knew he was right, but I was not ready to face the harsh realities outside the granary walls.

"It's safe in here," I whispered. "Out there the Horseman waits."

"We'll find an answer," he said. "I promise."

We rode back under a violet sky, the sun already beneath the trees. Before leaving the stables, he drew me in for one more treasured kiss. "And now, I must face the Council."

I groaned. "Which is nearly as bad as the Horseman himself."

* * *

Brom was standing out back as we neared the house, like it'd been his duty to wait.

"Ichabod," he said, his voice scathing and sharp. "I thought you were under watch."

Ichabod walked ahead, wearing a smile. "I managed a prison break." He opened the back door and stood aside for us to pass.

Brom placed his hand on the small of my back, guiding me forward. Though his touch was light, I could feel the tension wound inside him. Within a few steps, he leaned slightly and inhaled.

He smells Ichabod on me. I could practically hear his teeth grinding.

As we entered, Brom stopped in front of Ichabod, their faces mere inches apart. "Where were you?"

Ichabod leaned even closer. "Hiding from the Horseman," he whispered. Then, patting Brom's shoulder, he ducked around and walked off.

Brom turned every shade of red as his chest heaved with anger. He whipped around, stabbed me with a glare, and stalked out. I sighed relief, thankful that it hadn't turned into a more serious confrontation.

A short time later, dinner was served. I sat toward the end of the table, where I could eat in silence and not interfere with Council business. Archaic, I know, but thankfully, it meant I was seated away from Brom. Notary de Graff sat next to me. The man looked older and frailer every time I saw him.

Father snapped his napkin and placed it in his lap. "Now that you're actually here, Crane, maybe you have some input that'll help us resolve this matter. It is your neck on the line, after all." Judging by Father's tone, the Horseman might've been the least of Ichabod's worries. But to my relief, I saw no indication that Father knew he and I had just been alone together.

Ichabod kept his chin high. "I didn't mean to worry anyone. I just don't take well to being leashed. Even for one day."

"Well that leash won't hold if you're missing your head." Father tore into his pheasant and cast his eyes from man to man. "Speak up, gentlemen. How are we going to end this?"

Magistrate Harding turned to the reverend. "I keep saying some type of exorcism is in order."

"And I keep repeating," the reverend countered, "I wouldn't even know how to go about that."

Exorcise a ghost? I thought that was a practice for demon possession.

"I say we get to the source," Caspar Jansen suggested. "There's still talk of witchcraft."

"There's always talk of witchcraft," Father said. "We need evidence."

I expected some discomfort on Ichabod's part, but he kept his composure. "Witches usually control the living, not the dead."

"You have some experience in the matter?" the reverend asked. He seemed eager for an answer, as though Ichabod could educate him on a subject that he should already know front to back.

Ichabod shifted in his chair. "Only what I've read."

He was not an expert liar, but the men didn't seem to notice.

I glanced over at Brom, who glowered at his boiled potatoes as he diced them into small bits with his knife. It was evident he was seeing more than a helpless lump of food as his victim.

Go ahead and murder your dinner, if that puts you in control.

"Those accounts won't help us," Father said to Ichabod.

"Then what will?" Caspar asked. "We can't kill what's already dead."

The magistrate drummed his fingers. "Think about it, gentlemen. This is merely another haunting. Not the first we've had."

"I know," Father said. "It's like there's a contagion in the air that sweeps through Sleepy Hollow, bringing with it all manner of spirits and specters."

Goosebumps sprouted on my arms. *Why is our village haunted?*

Van Ripper nodded, pheasant broth glistening on his chin. "The Woman in White. 'Member her?"

They all grunted acknowledgement.

"All her shrieking got your skin to crawling, it did."

"I hadn't heard about her," Ichabod said, lifting his glass of port.

Van Ripper's lip curled, as though the subject were bitter swill. "Lost her way searching for her children in a snowstorm. Screamed and yelled for them till her vocal cords went numb.

They found her clinging to a tree, froze harder than a January pond. After that, her ghost screeched every time a storm was due."

Ichabod's eyes gleamed like a child's as he absorbed the eerie tale. "Really? There are many stories throughout New England of the so-called Wailing Woman. Though the accounts are different, she's become a popular legend."

Van Ripper swiped his chin with his sleeve. "Are you saying you don't believe us?"

"No, I'm merely stating that it's a common form of haunting."

"Common or not," Father said, "she plagued us for years. We finally put a stop to it."

Ichabod's face was widely curious. "How did you accomplish it?"

"We all knew her," Father answered. "It was Dora Hindricks. Turns out her children weren't really lost—they'd found their own way home. Poor Dora died in vain. Her husband, Augustus, was so distraught over his wife's death, he packed up the children and moved to Raven Rock."

The magistrate let out a brisk sigh. "Didn't seem fair that we had to put up with her moaning instead of him."

"What'd you do?" Ichabod asked.

"Someone had the good sense to suggest we find her children," Father answered. "A couple of the townsmen rode out to Raven Rock and brought them here. They were grown by then. The daughter had a child of her own. We escorted them out to the tree where Dora had died. They each one told her not to cry—that they were well and fine, and that was it. Not a sound out of her since."

"Which was kind of a shame," Caspar added. "She was the best weather forecaster in the vicinity."

The men broke into laughter, including Ichabod.

Brom didn't join in. He sat, hunkered, face pinched, still threatening his now mutilated meal.

The magistrate took a healthy gulp of his wine. "Shame the old Hessian doesn't have children we could send for."

"The reverend paused, his eyes fixed on a thought. "Well, when you consider it, Dora was searching. The Hessian is searching too."

"For Crane," Father pointed out.

The reverend looked at Ichabod, his brows furrowed. "What about Hartford? Did you bring something with you that the Horseman might be wanting to take away?"

"Besides my head?"

The reverend faltered. "I'm just saying that sometimes evil is attracted to certain elements...like a particular sin or a black spot on your soul."

Notary de Graff, who had stayed mum all this time, slammed his glass down, sending a splash of port over the side. "How dare you? My son was a good, sinless boy. There was no black spot on his soul. And for you to suggest otherwise..." There was a momentary lapse as he choked back a sob.

"I'm so sorry, Garth. I didn't mean to imply that Garritt was in any way sinful."

"But you implied that I was," Ichabod stated. "I've done nothing to attract the vengeance of a demon."

"No man is without sin," the reverend mumbled.

"Including you," Ichabod tossed back.

Brom sat up straighter. "I have an idea."

Everyone turned and looked his way.

He glared at Ichabod. "You could leave town."

Ichabod met him eye to eye. "Is that your suggestion? Because you might keep in mind that as long as I'm marked, you aren't prey. Nor is anyone else." He nodded slightly toward me, sending Brom the obvious message.

Brom gripped his knife. "Who knows? If you leave, the Horseman may follow."

Ichabod shook his head. "Doubtful. He is a ghost of the Hollow. His purpose lies here."

And believe me, Brom, if Ichabod leaves, it is I who will follow.

Van Ripper guzzled his wine with a shaky hand. "Well, I ain't gonna lie to you, boy. Having you under my roof is making me mighty nervous. First Devenpeck. Now you."

Casper's face crooked into a grin. "Look out, Hans. If your tenants keep dying, folks might start blaming you."

"Bull dung!" Van Ripper swore.

"There's a lady present," Father warned.

Van Ripper squinted an eye. "I just don't want to lose my head because I happened to be standing in between Crane and that savage ghost. The Horseman could come stalkin' 'em at my place the way he did at de Graff's."

The notary propped an elbow and placed his head in his hand. My heart broke for him. Did they really think he, of all people, could offer a solution?

"Look," Ichabod said, "if it's a problem, I'll find another place to stay."

Father waved him off. "Don't worry about it. That port isn't the first drink Hans has had this evening. He's just talking out the top of his head."

"And I hope to hang on to it to talk out of," Van Ripper grumbled.

Ichabod turned to Father and spoke low. "I could move into the schoolhouse."

Father's chin tucked as his eyes grew wide. "You'll do nothing of the sort. Now please, everyone, let's get back to the purpose of this dinner?"

The magistrate nodded. "We had hoped that by putting our

heads together—pardon the expression—we would find a solution tonight."

"I have a suggestion," I said, my voice a bit shakier than I'd intended.

They all stared at me like I'd just confessed murder. Father razed me with his stare.

But Ichabod looked on me softly. "If it'll save my life, Katrina, I'd like to hear it."

Their eyes were all on me, waiting.

"I think he haunts the Hollow because he's buried here. If we were to dig up his grave and —"

"What?" Reverend Bushnell erupted. "Are you mad?"

"But if we were to send his bones away."

The reverend shot me a look that could melt iron. "We will *not* desecrate a grave."

"It wasn't a Christian burial," I argued.

"He's still interred in the church cemetery," the magistrate reminded.

"By whom? Perhaps we could find this person—"

Father slammed his fist to the table. "We've heard enough of this prattle. Disturbing his grave would only bring his wrath down on the entire Hollow. It's neither an option nor a good suggestion."

I sat back, pretending to resume my meal.

Ichabod shrugged. "I don't know. Any suggestion to keep me breathing sounds pretty good right now."

"Not that one," Father barked.

How can they know that for sure?

Ichabod looked around, his face questioning. "So what now?"

Father peered at each of them too. "Well?"

They all wore blank faces.

Father huffed a sigh. "Gentlemen, if we don't come up

with something soon, we'll be looking for a new schoolmaster. And considering the demise of the first two, I doubt a third would be willing to take up the position."

"Speaking of which," Ichabod said, "what about the children?"

The magistrate lifted his brow. "What about them?"

"Their lessons have already been interrupted once."

Casper jolted and turned. "Now hold up there, young man. If you think I'm going to send my sons back to you for instruction, you're completely out of your mind. I'm not going to risk their lives."

"I wasn't implying that I should teach them directly. But I could prepare the lessons and someone else could teach them."

"We're all concerned for the children," Father said, "but there's no one —"

"I'll do it," I interrupted.

Brom's fork screeched across his plate.

Father's lip quivered. "Katrina—"

He was interrupted again when the magistrate bellowed a laugh. "Dear girl, what qualifies you?"

My grip on my napkin tightened, but I pledged to myself I'd remain calm. "What qualifies me? I can read and write. I have a keen aptitude for mathematics. I love children. And if Ichabod is volunteering to put together the lessons, then I volunteer to administer them."

"Preposterous," the magistrate said. "Even if it was a good idea, there is no meeting place. The schoolhouse is out of the question."

"What about the church?"

The reverend popped his head up. "I don't know, Katrina."

"Why?" I asked. "Do you think the good Lord would object?"

Ichabod sputtered a chuckle that he quickly covered with a

cough.

The men again gazed one to the other, then the magistrate said, "It's entirely up to you, Baltus. If you think your daughter is qualified."

Now Father found himself in a quandary. I could see it all over his face. On the one hand, allowing me to teach would be granting me permission to leave the house. On the other hand, not allowing me would be admitting that his offspring was inferior and not up to the task. He wouldn't want to again look weak before the Council. "She's *more* than qualified. If anyone could make a success of it, it would be her. And she'd be safe in the church." He directed a scornful glare toward me. "But someone other than Crane will deliver the lessons."

Sigh. I had won one battle but lost another.

He then continued his lecture at Ichabod. "And you will put together traditional assignments. She won't be filling the children's heads with a lot of hogwash. Is that understood?"

Ichabod shrugged as though doing it otherwise would never cross his mind. "Completely."

"Then it's settled," the magistrate announced. "We'll alert the parents. Katrina, you'll start on Tuesday."

It took every ounce of me not to let out a cheer. The notary reached over and patted my hand.

"Meal is done," Father said. "Let's continue this conversation in the parlor."

I was sure that suggestion was to guarantee no further interruptions from me.

I only caught bits and pieces of what the men were saying as they swirled their brandies and nodded their heads. There was talk of Garritt—the mark on his window compared to that at the school. They pressed Ichabod for more information about his endeavors with the cellar. From what I could discern, no solution was brought forth.

At the end of the evening, Father called me in. "Katrina, help retrieve the overcoats."

I hurried to the coat closet and assisted Simon as he took them down.

"Keep a watch on Crane," Father told the men. "Take turns if you have to."

Ichabod sighed. "My horse is in the stable. Who is going to *guard* me as I retrieve it?"

"No one," Father said. "Brom, bring Ichabod's horse around."

Brom opened his mouth then snapped it shut. How could he protest? Though his expression was icy, he practically spat fire as he turned and tramped off.

Even though Ichabod had no overcoat, I went over to him. "You have something stuck to your sleeve." I took his right hand in my left and lifted his arm, pretending to brush away imaginary lint. He curled his fingers around my hand, giving it a loving squeeze. I ached to kiss him.

"Thank you," he said. "I hadn't noticed."

A few minutes later Brom brought the horse around and the men walked out. Father and I followed.

Ichabod took the reins and looked back. "I must admit, I do miss Gunpowder."

"Just get on your horse, Crane," Van Ripper complained, clambering onto his.

Ichabod glanced at me with one last smile. For a fleeting moment, I considered leaping upon the horse with him and spurring it off, taking us away for good. How easy it would be. But I simply smiled back and, too soon, they rode away.

Father whirled, ready to lash into me, for speaking out of place, I was sure. But he caught sight of Brom, who stood back in the shadows of the piazza. Father glanced at me, then him, then turned and went inside.

I intended to follow. Whatever reprimand Father would mete out was more desirable than hearing Brom's pompous tantrum. But before I had a chance to retreat, he strode over and clutched my arm, leading me once again to the side of the house.

He narrowed his fiery eyes at me. "Katrina, for God's sake, what have you done?"

I pulled my arm free of his grip. "I don't know what you mean."

His breathing was ragged and rough. "You were gone for hours."

"Were you holding a vigil?"

"Should I bring up yesterday's event in the cellar too?"

I had no patience for this. "Brom, where I go and what I do is my concern, not yours."

"I have a right to know where you were."

"And who granted you that right? Father? Or was this a self-appointment?"

He pointed his finger in my face. "We *are* to be married. That gives me every right."

I knocked his finger away. "I'm not your property, Brom. Or your servant. I don't heel at your command. And I'm most certainly *not* going to marry you."

His face reddened and he struggled to maintain patience. "I'm going to ask you one more time, where were you and what were you doing?"

"What was I doing?" I clenched my fists, my heart racing with rage. "Are you honestly accusing me of—"

The blacks of his eyes shrunk to pinpoints. "Have you given me a reason?"

I wanted so badly to slap his face raw, but that would serve as an answer. He didn't deserve one. I put my finger to his face. "What I do, immoral or not, is none of your damn business."

He grabbed my hand and twisted. "But it's your father's. Suppose I tell him what you were up to?"

I drew close, my face nearly touching his. "Do not attempt to control me with threats. If Father saw how you were treating me right now he'd discharge you in an instant."

"You really think that? Baltus loves his money more than he loves you. He's not going to dismiss an excellent overseer because of his daughter's stubbornness."

His words cut deeper than his hold on my wrist, but I refused to believe them. "Shall we test it?" I nodded toward my hand, now turning white within his grip. "Drag me inside right now. Tell him what a naughty girl I've been."

He pushed my hand away, but kept his eyes adhered to mine. "Let's test it a different way. I'll quit and leave you to run the farm. I'm sure you'll enjoy waking up before dawn, mucking the stables, slopping the hogs. By day's end you'd be praying to have me back."

I stepped away, shaking my head. "Enough of this nonsense. I'm going inside."

"You won't think it's nonsense when your farm starts losing profit."

I sighed and turned to go. "Goodnight, Brom."

As I reached the door he said, "Goodbye, Katrina."

* * *

Brom's goodbye was goodbye. He was absent the next morning, and his cabin was empty of his things. Father cornered me in the library where I was reading through a book that I considered using with the next day's assignments.

"What did you say to him?" he railed.

I looked at him in question.

"What did you say to Brom? You were the last to speak to him."

"Nothing." I couldn't tell him the truth without confessing

that I'd been alone with Ichabod.

His eyes narrowed. "He gave no indication he was leaving?"

I snapped the book shut. "You saw him at dinner last night. He was clearly unhappy. And he always has been irresponsible with his romping about and frequenting the tavern. As far as we know, he could've run off with some hussy he'd met there."

"But he was never irresponsible about work." Father paced a few seconds, thinking. "Until I find a new overseer, I'll be needing your help."

Oh God, will I really be mucking the stables and slopping hogs?

"Without Brom, I'll need to be away from the house much of the week. We have grain shipments scheduled. That means you'll be responsible for all the accounting."

I'd rather slop the hogs. "Father, there are plenty of men who would take the overseer job."

"Yet none that I trust."

"But"—Don't sound whiny—"I'm to start teaching tomorrow."

Father looked down his nose and huffed. "That's hardly an option now."

"Then what's to be done about the children? They need to be educated."

He waved it off. "Their parents can teach them to read and write."

"What of the Council?" I chanced. "How will it look to them that you've changed your mind?"

He cut me with an impatient glare. A moment later, he closed his eyes and pinched the bridge of his nose. After two deep breaths, he said, "Fine, Katrina. Do what you will."

My heart dipped as I realized how selfish this was. After all, it *was* my fault Brom had left.

As he walked away, I called, "Father." He paused without turning. "I promise to give my full attention to the ledgers every evening when I get home."

He stood with his back to me a few seconds more, then hurried off without a response.

* * *

The next morning, Simon poured my tea. "Let me know when you want to leave, Miss Katrina."

"Don't worry," I told him, adding sugar to the cup. "I'll hitch the cabriolet myself."

"No, ma'am, I got the carriage all ready and waiting."

I paused my stirring. "The carriage?"

"Yes, ma'am." He tilted his head, seeing my confusion. "Didn't your father tell you? He don't want you going alone, so I'm taking you to and from."

"Oh…" Of course he'd have me escorted. "I'll be ready shortly." I gobbled down my breakfast and gathered my things. The sooner I got to the church, the sooner I could feel some independence.

* * *

Reverend Bushnell had made some effort to accommodate me. A table and chair had been set up facing the pews. The table held a goose quill, ink, paper…and a leather satchel. My heart trilled as I unbuckled it. I took out the instructions, all written in Ichabod's hand. The top page read: *Katrina, I thought we would start the morning with a lesson on measurements. **I** have enclosed the necessary tools. Most importantly, remember **L**iters, **O**unces, **V**olume, **E**stimation. **You** understand?*

Perfectly!

And at the end of the day, please send back a report on how the lessons progressed and **what you feel** could be done for improvement. I treasure **your vision** and **contemplate a** successful balance in this **unique partnership**.—Ichabod

There could not have been a more beautifully concealed love letter.

I emptied the tools he'd supplied. Cups, spoons, a measuring compass, a protractor, and a ruler. This appeared to be a lesson both complicated and messy. I sorted through the instructions. He'd written every one with minute detail, including the estimated time it would take for the project, as well as how to simplify or complicate it for individual students.

I was still going over them when the children arrived. Only nine. Half of the usual attendance. They plodded and bounced in, with no respect for their surroundings.

Elise's brothers, Dirk and Devlin, dropped down next to each other on a pew.

"Oh no." I guided Devlin by the arm and settled him one row up across the aisle. I'd known these two all my life and to call them hellions would be doing them justice.

Dirk kicked the underside of his seat with his heel. "Not fair."

"Dirk, you're forgetting that you're in church."

"No, I'm not. I'm at school."

"But it's still the house of the Lord."

He kicked the pew again. "It's only the house of the Lord during worship."

"And where do you suppose He dwells the rest of the time?"

A tiny boy named Carver spoke up. "Amsterdam?"

I sighed.

"Grandmother said when she goes to live with the Lord, she wants to be buried in Amsterdam."

This was clearly not how I expected the morning to begin. I could imagine the playful smirk on Ichabod's face were he here watching.

"Whether the Lord is absent or not, it is time to begin the lessons."

"This is stupid," Dirk called out. "You're just a silly girl. You're not a teacher."

I should've anticipated this. "I am today."

"Oh?" he taunted. "And what are you going to teach us?"

I took up the ruler and whacked his knuckles. "Manners."

"Ow!" He shook his hand briskly. "Mr. Crane never hit us."

"You probably never gave him reason." Had I really told the Council that I loved children?

"My sister said you're rotten. I can't believe it took her this long to figure it out."

I knew that Dirk was just being Dirk. He had always been the annoying little brother, full of mischief and pluck. But those words had stung as badly as the rapping I'd given his fingers. I guessed we were even.

"Though Mr. Crane is not present, your lessons still come from him. I will do my best to make them as interesting and engaging as he would. And if you refuse to take part, it will be reported back to him and he shall deal with you when he returns. Is that understood?"

Nine blank faces gaped.

I managed to get through the lessons with Dirk calling me a ninny just once. And I was never happier than to see the heels of their little shoes as they scampered out the door.

I dropped down at the table to write my report.

Lessons went well, considering. Perhaps tomorrow you can include instruction on how you managed them without harnesses. **I** did eventually discover that the proper ingredients for discipline are **L**eadership, **O**rder, **V**eneration, and **E**xample. I assume **you** used these elements **too**.

I have included detailed notes on each of the lesson pages

you sent. I look forward to a time when we can discuss these matters face to face.—Katrina

I slipped everything into the satchel, buckled it, and left it on the table to be returned.

I walked out, pausing on the church's doorstep. The day had gone gray, but there was no scent of rain in the air. Only a mild chill. I stared off, far across the cemetery. I could not see the Horseman's grave, but the untended weeds towered within view.

"How do I get rid of you, you savage fiend?"

I stood for a full minute or more, pondering.

"You should not dwell on it," came a voice from behind me.

"Aih!" I started, clutching my hand to my heart. "Reverend, do not sneak up."

"I was plenty loud. Your mind was on that abomination that mocks us." I then noticed that he had collected the satchel. "So how was your first day?"

"It would have gone more smoothly if the Lord had not been in Amsterdam."

His face twisted. "Pardon?"

"Never mind," I said with a weary smile. "Thank you so much for the use of the church. Hopefully the need will be of short duration."

"Indeed," he said. "Well, I must deliver this. Do be careful on your way home."

"I shall."

Moments later, Simon arrived to escort me home.

* * *

By the time Friday arrived I had a new respect for Ichabod. I imagined there was little squabbling and strife in his classroom, and he managed twice as many students as I.

What kept me motivated were those wonderful little notes

we shared. It was a delightful challenge creating clever ways to express my feelings. But my heart ached for him. I wanted to whisper my endearments in his ear. To show my affection through touch. And more than anything I wanted to hold him.

When the students arrived they were especially full of vigor. Most likely because they were only a few hours away from the weekend.

"When is Mr. Crane coming back?" Devlin crowed, arms crossed.

I refused to let them wear me down so early. "Mr. Crane is ill. He'll return when he's better."

"That's not true," Dirk argued. "My sister said he's been marked by the Horseman."

"Then find a way to rid us of the Horseman and you can have him back."

I walked over to the table to retrieve the lessons when a girl named Rachael said, "Sage."

I turned back. "Excuse me?"

She looked at me with bright eyes. "My mother sprinkles sage on the windowsills at night to keep the ghosts out. Perhaps we could sprinkle sage everywhere."

"Sage is a wonderful idea," I said, "but sprinkle it throughout the Hollow? It would be in short supply."

Another rascal about town, Finn, spouted, "Maybe we could get it to *rain* sage."

At this children blurted laughter, causing Rachael to shrink in her seat.

Then Carver put in, "I would drop a cannonball on his grave to hold him down."

Dirk jerked around, facing him. "Carver, you half-wit, a cannonball on his grave won't stop him."

I intervened. "While I appreciate all the suggestions, we need to begin class."

Vincent, the blacksmith's son, rose, raised his fists and proclaimed, "I'm not afraid of the Horseman. I'd wrestle him right off that giant steed and snatch his sabre away. I'd thrash it back and forth, until I frightened him back into his grave. Then I'd thrust the sword deep into the dirt, sealing him in forever." These words were accompanied by great drama on his part.

There was a moment of awed silence before Dirk burst into laughter. "The Horseman would lop off your head before you could even touch his boot."

It was time to take control. The mischief-makers were frightening many of the students, who cowered with wide eyes.

"Enough of this now—"

Vincent cut me off. "You don't know anything, Dirk. The only way to rid the town of a ghost is by sealing it into its grave. Just ask my father. He once sealed the specter of a fur trapper by stabbing the grave with the dirty swine's own skinning knife."

I held up the papers. "Enough, Vincent. If we finish our lessons on time, perhaps then you could share that tale."

His brow crinkled. "I just did. Weren't you listening?"

"Then let me put it this way. If we finish our lessons quickly, you may be dismissed early. But I will keep you all here until they are done."

You could've heard a pin drop.

When class ended, I sat at the table, writing my report. I wrote no comments about the children's daily rebellion. Nor did I include hidden messages expressing my love. I simply ended the correspondence with: *Thank you so much for guiding me with these excellent lesson plans. They have been invaluable to me. I look forward to seeing you in church on Sunday. Until then I send my sincerest regards.—Katrina*

I slipped everything in and buckled the satchel. Sunday. I longed for it. For him.

Reverend Bushnell appeared at the door. "And what are you smiling about, my fair Katrina?"

"That the school week has ended," I answered.

"I would imagine this first week was an adjustment."

"Adjustment? More of a reformation."

He laughed. "Well, Simon is waiting. Time you head home and recuperate."

"I won't argue with that."

He took up the satchel, and I walked out with him.

"I'll see you at worship on Sunday," he said.

I nodded.

Just as we'd descended the last step, I asked, "Reverend, have you ever heard of sealing a spirit into its grave?"

"Yes," he answered. "And from what I've heard, it's an effective practice."

"Have you ever carried out such an act?"

"I've never had the occasion."

"But would you, should the occasion arise?"

His brow dipped and his eyes narrowed. "Katrina, it's already been suggested. You're forgetting, we have no personal effects of the Horseman with which to seal him."

I sighed. "Of course. Good day, Reverend."

"God be with you, dear."

* * *

I chatted with a few parishioners on Sunday morning, my eyes occasionally glancing toward the door. Mostly, I was asked about my first week as teacher, how I found the children's behavior, and if I was looking forward to the new week. In other words, they were forcing me to lie in church. I waited for a lightning bolt.

I was not watching the door, but I knew when he'd come in. There a scuffle of feet as several men pushed in together. I turned to find him crowded next to Van Ripper and the magistrate. He didn't bother to lower his voice as he shrugged them away. "Gentlemen, I am in church. I doubt the Horseman will follow me in."

The two backed off, letting a new swarm of people overtake him. I casually made my way over.

Our eyes met, and he did not hold back his smile. Just as I reached him, Elise stepped beside me.

"Ichabod, I've been so worried about you," she fawned. "I hope you are being well taken care of."

"Too well," he replied. It came out as a jest, but I knew how miserable he'd been. He was much too free-spirited to be kept under lock and key.

"You're definitely safe for now," she continued. "Father is working diligently with the Council to find a solution. The children need their schoolmaster back."

Ichabod nodded politely. "I hope for a speedy return as well."

Still batting her flaxen lashes, she said, "My brothers are absolutely miserable. And so are the other students, I hear. They don't seem to be gaining what's needed for their education."

How could so much venom be hidden in such a sugary tone?

Ichabod lifted a hand. "I assure you, Elise, their lessons are prepared by me. And I'll always see that they get the proper assignments."

Elise sighed. "It's just a shame that you're not there to instruct them fittingly."

And she claims I'm rotten?

"I've seen their progress," he said. "They're doing quite well."

Before she opened her mouth again, he turned to me. "Which reminds me, Katrina, I need to speak with you about some of the lessons I'm preparing for next week. Is there a place where we can talk?"

"Of course." Then to Elise, "Excuse us."

Her eyes turned to ice as I led him away.

We settled into a pew, facing each other, yet keeping a respectable distance. Father was making no effort to hide his disapproving glances.

"This is excruciating," Ichabod said, his voice low.

"What is?"

"Not touching you." His eyes gleamed with affection, and a yearning for him rippled through me.

"It's agonizing for me too."

He risked leaning a bit closer. "In case I don't get a chance to say it later…I love you."

Hearing him speak it lifted me to the rafters. "I love you too. More than I could ever express."

I looked back at the magistrate, then to Ichabod. "They seem to value you as much as I."

He sputtered a laugh. "Katrina, they care nothing for me. It's only themselves they're worried about. And the other citizens of Sleepy Hollow. Remember, as long as I am marked, the Horseman will leave the rest of the Hollow alone."

"You owe them nothing, Ichabod. At the first opportunity, hop on your horse and flee. Go back to Connecticut. I'll sneak away and meet you there."

"Believe me, nothing sounds more enticing, but what if I don't make it? Didn't your friend, Garritt, try to escape too?"

Garritt. Had the Horseman known of his plans to run?

I sank back against the pew, disheartened. "If someone doesn't find a solution soon, I'll go insane."

"That makes two of us."

It was then that the parishioners began taking their seats. Though it had always been my custom to sit with Father, I did not make an effort to move. Instead, Ichabod and I pushed in a little closer and faced forward. We had just over an hour to be together. And even though we could not touch, the warmth of his closeness filled my senses.

Eyes were on us, but I didn't care. The sphere of the church extended no farther than the small space we shared.

Reverend Bushnell took to the pulpit, his Bible open and flapping like a bird. Whenever we rose for song, I always sat back down just an inch closer to Ichabod. I ached to touch him.

After the last prayer had been uttered, the Council descended upon us. There would be no private goodbye.

Van Ripper clapped Ichabod on the back. "Come on, Crane. Baked ham and gooseberry pudding await."

Ichabod took my hand in his. "Katrina, I just want to tell you again, you're doing a wonderful job in my absence. The children are blessed to have you."

"Thank you, Ichabod," I said cordially. My heart broke when he released me and walked out of the church.

* * *

The usual students entered class the next morning. But their disheveled hair, yawns, and grimaces indicated I should start easy. The beginning of a work week is always an unfavorable time, and having read over Ichabod's lessons, I could see that he had taken this into account. Experience is everything.

We were starting with something Ichabod felt was both educational and stimulating. I was to read a vocabulary word, and ask the students if they could tell me something they'd heard, seen, or experienced that would put that word into place. The first one was *attempt*.

"Any form of the word," I instructed.

After a moment, two children raised their hands.

I called on Devlin, who related something about attempting to eat a worm on a dare. I only heard a bit of what he said because the word, *attempt*, sparked a flurry of thoughts.

When he finished I gazed down at the next word, *batch*, but I barely saw it. I hadn't realized the long silence until Carver said, "Miss Van Tassel? What's the next word?"

I snapped to. "Oh, it's…" My eyes blurred on the word, then, "Never mind this. I've a better idea." I set the word sheet aside. "Vincent, tell us about your Father sealing in the trapper's ghost."

His brows dipped as confusion clouded his face.

"And expound," I added.

"Expound?"

"Give us details."

His mouth twitched and he shrugged. I could see this would take some goading. "Why was the trapper troubling your father?"

"'Cause Papa had made some leg traps for him, and when they found the trapper dead, he was caught in one of them. I guess he wasn't able to open it before he bled out. He must've thought Papa made a faulty trap."

His father, Clive Van Helt, was our local blacksmith. He was never known to make anything faulty.

"Did you see the ghost?" I asked.

"No, but Papa did a bunch of times. He said the old coot meant to skin him alive."

By now the class was filled with wide eyes and slack jaws.

"How did your father go about sealing him in? How did he get the trapper's knife?"

"Papa had made the knife too. He got it back along with the other traps."

That certainly made it easy. "And was the trapper buried here in the Hollow?"

"They buried him in the mountains, next to his camp. No one barely knew him anyway."

"And your father trekked there to seal him in?'

Vincent's mouth twitched again. "That's the only way he could do it."

"Did he relay any details?" I had to know.

His mind seemed to be churning, and I hoped any fabrication of the story would be part of his father's telling, not his.

"When Papa set out for that camp, he carried the leg trap with him, hidden under a blanket. The old banshee figured out that Papa aimed to seal him in, and he came at him like a wild-eyed wolf. So Papa threw back that cover and showed him the trap. That was like showing him a key to hell. That trapper stayed clear of Papa the rest of the journey."

If that part were true, it was most intriguing. "So the very thing that killed the trapper is what kept him at bay?"

"That's what Papa said."

If only I had that fatal cannonball. "Then what happened?'

Another shrug. "He took the trapper's knife and stabbed it in the grave. And he dug it in real deep so the rain wouldn't wash it away."

"And he's not been plagued by the spirit since?" I asked.

Vincent shook his head. "Nope."

I relaxed, placing my hands in my lap. "Thank you, Vincent. That was an intriguing story." *Quite intriguing.*

Dirk crossed his arms and clucked. "But I didn't hear a single vocabulary word in the whole thing."

The children broke into laughter. For once I wanted to hug Dirk for bringing us all back around to our lessons.

* * *

On the carriage ride home, my mind churned.

"The only way to rid the town of a ghost is by sealing it into its grave."

"...it is an effective practice."

"We have no personal effects with which to seal his grave."
But what if we did?

* * *

At dinner that night, Father sat like a rock, moving slowly as he took small bites. He reminded me of a clock winding down to its final minutes. His weariness weighed on my guilt, even though I had kept all the accounting up to date. But I now had plans to rid us of the Horseman, which would leave Father with only the worries of the farm.

"Tell me," I started, knowing I had to tread carefully, "how is the search for a new overseer?"

He turned his eyes to me like he'd only just realized I was in the room. "Done. And coming to us next week from Chappaqua." He slurped a sip of wine. "Though I did have to offer a higher wage."

I couldn't help but wonder where Brom, who'd lived here all his life, had gone. Wherever he was, he, no doubt, was having a good laugh.

"I hope he works out well," I said.

Father shuffled his diced potatoes before spearing them with his fork. "How was your day with the children?"

That caught me by surprise. In all this time, he'd never once asked. "Better. But it'll still take some adjusting."

He snorted. "You know as well as I that nothing comes easy."

Too well.

I was careful in selecting my next words. "It'll be nice when they can meet at the school again. Proper desks and all." *Tread carefully.* "And hopefully that cellar can still be converted into a shelter."

Father scowled as he chewed his beef. "Put that cellar out of your mind."

"It's just a shame," I said. *Tread carefully.* "Now it will never be anything more than a root cellar."

"A marked root cellar," he reminded.

"Better a marked root cellar than a weapons repository, I guess."

His face actually brightened at that remark. There was even a trace of a smile. "Old Smedt wasn't storing turnips down there, that's for sure."

I feigned a chuckle. "Whatever happened to all those weapons, anyway?"

He shrugged. "Most were sold at public auction."

My heart sank. "And the rest?"

He ran his napkin across his mouth. "Stored them in the courthouse basement, I believe." He paused, thoughtful. "I should remind the magistrate of it. If there's any decent metal left, it could be forged into something useful."

That, I had not accounted for. It was imperative that I didn't waste time. So as not to cast suspicion, I made a few comments about the farm then said, "If you'll excuse me, I think I'll retire. I must be mindful and alert each morning."

"Teaching," he huffed. "I don't know how you do it."

I looked on him softly. "Believe me, Father, I'm only doing what needs to be done."

* * *

There is no other feeling like the anxiety of waiting alone in the dark. Among the shadows you have only your thoughts to occupy you. And it is then that you learn who you are, what you're capable of…and to what extreme.

While it was true that I have done a few immoral things in my life, tonight's endeavor would be illegal.

Who would be hurt?

No one.

Who would be saved?

Everyone.

This is what I'd become. Someone capable of going to the extreme.

I waited until Father turned in—till all was still and quiet—then, with only the waxing moon for light, I slipped down the stairs and crept to the stables.

My heart nearly drummed out of my chest, but I forced myself on. I quietly saddled Dewdrop and, petting her soft gray muzzle, led her out. "Shhh." It was only after guiding her to the road that I mounted.

I glanced over my shoulder toward the hill, expecting the Horseman to be waiting. Tonight it stood empty.

Where are you hiding?

At first I was inclined to spur my horse on, race toward town. But a clandestine endeavor such as this required silence. And no one would likely be roused by the gentle clip-clomp of Dewdrop's hoofbeats. With my cloak and hood to conceal me, I pressed on.

The magistrate's court sat squarely in the middle of town, but I skirted around the main road to avoid the River Song. Though fear of the Horseman had most town folk shut in, the tavern dwellers would always take risk for a drink.

Save for a few lighted windows, the streets were dark and vacant. I dismounted and led Dewdrop to a foul-smelling neglected alley between the butcher shop and the courthouse. An overgrowth of walnut trees blocked the moonlight, and though I stumbled in the darkness, I was thankful for the cloak of blackness to shield me.

I tried the backdoor—*please open*—and of course it was locked. My only other option was to climb through a window. Fortune was with me as one in the back slid easily open. Checking left and right, I clambered up and slipped inside.

The room in which I found myself was spacious and wide. An elaborate oak desk with block and shell carving sat in the center, surrounded by three walls of shelves. With trembling hands, I lit one of the candles on the desk. Holding it high, I circled, then came to the realization that this highly wrought office could only belong to one person…the magistrate. And that meant somewhere within that desk would be a precious set of keys. I combed through two of the drawers before I found them. With the candle to guide me, I stepped out and into the court chamber. I then took the short stairwell that led to the basement.

It descended into a corridor with three doors. Three doors and seven keys.

Quickly.

My heart sounded in my ears as I chose the smallest door under the stairs. And after trying two of the keys, the lock quietly clicked open.

I stepped inside and—*Dear God!* This room had surely been forgotten. Dust. Cobwebs. Clutter. A graveyard of broken furniture, rusted lanterns, and trunks. *What a mess!*

I scratched my nose, stifling a sneeze.

Tracing through the maze of disorder, I spotted a large pine box against a wall. It had no lock, but several crates were stored on top.

Please let them be moveable.

I managed two, but the other was like lugging a stubborn mule. I shifted it back and forth. It inched closer and closer to the edge, then dropped off with a thud. My chest heaved from the effort, and I took a moment to catch my breath—which was already shallow from fear.

The pine box had no hinges, so I shoved the top off. Then lifting the candle, I peered inside. There they were—the remaining weapons—broken, rusted or taken apart. Among them were a few muskets and pistols. Some bayonets. The swords had settled to the bottom. When I lifted one of the guns the entire mass shifted, sending a racket of clanking iron echoing through the room.

I scrabbled back and froze, holding in a yelp. Surely the entire Hollow had heard that. I waited, hand to my heart. Somewhere in the distance a dog barked, but there was no other noise.

No one heard. Now hurry.

I removed sword after sword, laying them out for inspection. Some were still sheathed in their scabbards. Most appeared to be standard military swords, used by the patriots who fought and died here. There were daggers, cutlasses, sabers. This was idiocy. Even if the Hessian's sword were here, how would I know which was his?

But then...

I gingerly took out one incomparable to the rest. A grim sword with a single-edge jagged blade. The hilt looked carved from an antler. The yellowed grip was worn and speckled, but it was the pommel I found most repulsive. On each side, were the carved faces of tortured men, their mouths frozen in silent shrieks.

This was his.

On further inspection, I noticed the grip felt too dense and smooth to have been shaped from an antler. Realization seized me. *Holy God in heaven!* This hilt was crafted from bone.

Human bone.

Bile rose to my throat, and I took gasping breaths to suppress it.

I loathed the thought of touching this evil weapon, but... *This is why you came.* With quaking hands, I sheathed it in one of the scabbards, then replaced everything as best I could—except the heavy box I couldn't lift. I tucked the sword under my cloak and cautiously crept out, locking the basement tight. I exited through the back door, mounted Dewdrop, and wasted not a second fleeing the scene of my crime.

My heart thundered as I bolted home.

Is he waiting? Wanting? I'm carrying what is rightfully his.

The closer I got to our farm, the more anxious I became.

So close. So close.

When I made the final turn onto our road, my eyes cut to the hillock. Empty. The Horseman was not there. *Thank God.* I rode straight to the stables and quietly led Dewdrop to her stall.

I hid the sword under a bed of hay—*I will not have it foul my room*—and then slipped into the house, tiptoed upstairs, and readied myself for bed.

With only the sound of my breathing, I waited through the cold, dark hours.

* * *

Rising before dawn, I slinked out of bed, prepared, and hurried downstairs.

With no hearth fire lit, the empty kitchen was like a frigid tomb. And while every part of me quaked, I needed that biting chill to keep me moving.

I had no stomach for food, but I took an apple for later and grabbed a small bag of sage from our herb cabinet—for extra measure. Trying to steady my hand, I wrote a simple note to Simon. Though he could read a little, I felt the note itself would serve its purpose.

Have gone alone. Do not tell Father.

I left it in the tea bin, where only he would find it. Then sweeping on my cloak, I set out.

The predawn air spiked me, and a light morning frost clung to my hem as my skirts brushed over the crisp brown grass.

After reaching the stables, I raked back the hay, retrieving the sword. No phantom had come in the night to reclaim it. I tugged on my gloves, assuring the vile thing would not touch my flesh, then, hiding it under my cloak again, I rode.

The moon had set and all but a few stars had faded. Claret rays of the eastern sun now lined the horizon. Dewdrop galloped with haste as we rode amid gray and blue shadows…all the way to the cemetery.

There was little light, but enough to see my way. The towering weeds were dry and brittle, easily drawn back and trampled. I walked slowly, careful that no burrowing rodents scurried under my skirt.

I expected the grave to be a dense patch of packed earth, but thanks to the ants, gophers, and moles, there were many runners and mounds that loosened the dirt.

Fortune is on my side.

But my heart drummed with each step as I conjured images of a bony hand bursting through the soil, clutching my ankle, and dragging me under.

Concentrate.

Inhaling all my fears, I raggedly exhaled them away. Then, unsheathing the sword, I gripped the hilt with both fists, braced my arms, and brought the blade down, stabbing it into the grave.

Almost.

It'd only gone halfway.

Blast!

With gritted teeth, I bore down on the hilt—thrusting and straining and driving it until it sank the rest of the way in.

I stumbled back, sweeping loose strands of hair from my face. Still heaving, I opened the sage and sprinkled it on the dirt.

"Try rising now, devil."

Feeling confident that I'd completed the job, I spat on the grave and left.

The sun was finally making an appearance when I reached the empty church. It was still quite early, most of the Hollow just rising. Exhausted and drained, I sank onto the chair at the table, and laid my head upon my crossed arms.

It is done.

I'd rest a short time—until the reverend arrived with the satchel. Just close my eyes…for a bit.

I didn't know if I'd lolled there minutes or hours. Time was lost. But I became aware of footfall behind me. The stalk of someone's boots. I held my breath, keeping my eyes clamped tight. I did not need sight to know who was lurking.

How have you risen?

I remained dead still, worried that my banging heart might give me away. *Flee,* I told myself. *Go! Now!* But my body was leaden. Some metaphysical bond held me.

How could this be? I was in church. Nothing evil should befall me here. Yet the coldness threatened, as though God really had forsaken me and retired to Amsterdam.

The footsteps halted. He stood directly behind me…over me. Next, I felt the cutting chill of a steel tip pressed lightly against my neck.

Heaven help me. Instead of sealing him in, I'd given him back his sword.

Now it was I who was sealed. Pinned. If I attempted to rise, the blade would thrust through my throat, skewering me like a roasting hen.

How long did he mean to restrain me? Until all the blood drained from my limbs? Until my body cramped and screamed with pain? It was evident that he knew my weakness. Confinement. This was more than just retribution for my attempt to seal him. *This is a game of torture.*

He held me there for an eternity. My arms tingled, my neck pinched, and my resting cheek grew weary. Then, just when the pain reached its agonizing peak, he dragged the tip of the blade to my jaw. Stepping closer, he took up a lock of my hair, and with the swish of a swift stroke, he sliced it from my scalp. It ripped more than cut, leaving a burning sting behind my ear. That was when I did scream—a piercing shrill that echoed through the church.

He gripped my shoulder, squeezing hard.

"Miss Katrina."

I screamed again.

"Miss Katrina!"

My eyes flew open and I started, nearly tumbling from the chair.

Simon grabbed my arm to keep me upright. "Whoa there, Miss Katrina."

I jerked about, checking my surroundings.

"Calm down now," he soothed. "It was just a bad dream."

"Of course," I said, my limbs tingling as the circulation returned. "I must've nodded off."

Or had I? I still felt the chill of the Horseman skulking nearby.

Simon waited until I'd composed myself before saying, "Miss Katrina, you had me worried sick, running off like that."

"I'm sorry, Simon. I didn't mean to put you in such an awkward position."

"Just please don't do it again. Mr. Baltus would string me up."

I considered all that I'd gone through last night. "I won't." But I avoided making it a promise.

"The reverend asked me to bring this in." He placed the satchel on the table.

I took a moment to clear my head, then glanced at it. The remedy for all my aches and fears lay inside. Surely Ichabod had sent me another written reminder of this affection.

Simon patted my shoulder. "If everything's all right, I'll be heading back."

"Everything's fine."

He nodded, satisfied with that. "But I *will* be here to fetch you this afternoon."

I smiled up. "Of course."

Once he'd gone, my senses revived. I eagerly reached out for the satchel. That was when I noticed my fist was clenched. Inside was a large wad of my hair.

* * *

I spent the better part of the school day sitting behind the table. Not only because I was exhausted, but in an attempt to hide the hem of my skirt—rimmed with mud from dragging it through dirt and dew. As it turned out, I was kept awake and alert by the children, who always tested my patience. And my mind churned as I wondered how to tell Ichabod exactly what I'd done.

We had always proceeded carefully in case the reverend or another of the Council felt a need to review our correspondence. But that afternoon I took a chance.

Ichabod, I have spent a long, weary night securing your safety. Everyone's safety. Among the swords that had been confiscated from Smedt's hoard, I found the Hessian's. I braved the dangers (for you are more than worth it) to imprison him with his own blade. He is now sealed in his grave.

My immediate dilemma is how to confess this to the Council. Not only did I do this in secrecy, but I obtained the sword illegally from the magistrate's court. It could be they'd forgive me on virtuous effort, but they are a stern group of men, not accepting of decisions and deeds carried out by one such as I. My lack of masculinity proves me inferior by their standards.

I am looking to you for a solution. Soon all will be revealed and you shall be free.

With love, Katrina.

I tucked the letter between the return assignments, knowing that Ichabod reviewed them right away.

On Wednesday morning I found a simple note among the lessons.

Sacrifice is the ultimate form of love. And though I find your lack of masculinity superior (and enticing), I shall handle things from here.

* * *

The Horseman was sealed. Ichabod would be freed. I should've been filled with jubilation. But there was still one loose thread to my happy ending. Elise. I'd lost my closest friend, and wanted so badly to make things right. While sitting at Father's desk that afternoon, I wrote her a simple letter.

My dearest Elise,

My heart is broken. Please understand that I never meant to hurt you. What came to pass between Ichabod and me was pure chance. There was no deceit on my part. Say you'll come next candle day. I cherish your friendship and miss you greatly.

Forever your companion,

Kat

I sealed it, then hurried out to the slave quarters, where I found Leta shelling peas. I put the letter into her hand. "I need you to deliver this to Elise Jansen."

She dropped a long pea pod back into the heaping bowl. "Yes, ma'am."

"Go straight away," I urged.

She hopped up. "Yes, ma'am."

"And, Leta, do not return without a reply."

"Yes, ma'am." She brought the letter to her nose, sniffed it, then slipped it into her apron pocket. And with a spirited smile, she dashed off across the field.

I went back to the house and waited.

A short time later, Simon found me in the study. "Miss Katrina, there is someone at the front door asking for you."

I looked up, puzzled. "Who?"

He shrugged. "Don't know. He's a stranger to me."

He?

A scruffy boy in frayed green breeches and a tattered shirt stood on our piazza. He smelled heavily of fish guts and bilge water. In one hand he held his knit cap, in the other a small piece of paper. "I'm supposed to deliver this to Katrina Van Tassel."

"I'm Katrina," I said, taking it.

The paper was folded into six small squares. Once opened, it read: *It is here. I'll come by soon.* Even though I recognized the scratchy handwriting, I asked the boy, "Who gave you this?"

He gazed up with round eyes. "Marten Piers."

I looked back at the message, tapping the paper...thinking. Marten had told me to weigh my thoughts and decide. My decision was made. "Can you take me to him?"

The boy tugged his cap on slantwise and nodded.

"Wait here." I hurried up to my room and placed the broken bracelet and beads into my pocket. *How will Marten feel about the one lost rose?* Then, taking my shawl from the peg, I made sure no one was watching as I slipped out.

When we reached the pier, the boy pointed out Marten's ship. I stood, gaping. Maybe ship was the wrong word. This two-masted schooner of about sixty feet was patched, faded, and worn. As I watched it bob drunkenly within the river wash, I could only assume the barnacles held it together.

I shielded my eyes with my hand, looking up. "Marten?"

No answer.

"Marten," I called a little louder.

I tested the gangplank, then scurried aboard. Though I could've never imagined it, the topside was even worse. Its brittle wood—intercrossed with patchwork—creaked at every step. I tiptoed, afraid it would crack and send me plunging through to whatever lay beneath.

"Marten?"

There was no cabin, just a hatch to the ship's hold. Just as I reached for it, it flew open, nearly whacking me in the face. Marten's head popped up with it.

"Katrina, no." He hopped out, frantic. "You should not be here."

"But I have something to tell you."

"Not now," he said, practically dragging me back toward the gangplank.

We'd only made it halfway when someone else emerged from the hold. "Look who's come to visit."

My blood chilled. Peter Bottoms. The beads in my pocket suddenly felt leaden.

His eyes crawled over me as he asked, "To what do we owe this pleasure?"

I looked to Marten, but his face was ashen and his lips pressed tight.

"I simply wanted to see Marten's ship," I offered. "I didn't know he'd have company."

Peter snorted back phlegm. "Wasn't the plan that you stay hidden?" He cut his eyes to Marten.

"Yes," Marten answered. Then he turned to me. "Katrina, you took a great risk coming here." I felt there was more to that statement than me being seen. I was caught like a rabbit in a snare. What would happen if I told the truth? That I no longer intended to leave?

Peter drew closer. "I think this one is a bit of a risk-taker. Isn't that right, sweetheart?"

Marten held my arm again. "Peter, she made a mistake. And now she's leaving."

Peter glanced at my wrist. The beads in my pocket were on fire. *Why does he want them so badly?*

"Yes," I agreed. "It was a mistake. I'm so sorry."

"What's done is done," Peter said, advancing. "Now that you're here, you might as well come below and have a drink with us. I brought my best rum from the tavern."

Marten took a step in front of me. "There is still water and debris down there. It's not fit for a lady."

Peter grinned, revealing a mouthful of stubby yellow teeth. "It'll be fit soon enough. And I bet he'll have your bunk smelling like roses."

Marten gripped my arm tighter and urged me away. I hurried down the gangplank without looking back.

* * *

Once home, I went straight to my wardrobe. Then tearing away two stitches, I tucked the roses and chain into the hem of a blue summer gown. Why they were valuable I didn't know, but until I returned them to Marten, I couldn't risk another being lost.

When I went down, Leta was in the kitchen, helping Simon with dinner. "Did you deliver the letter?" I asked.

She leaned close to me and sniffed.

"Yes, I know. I smell like a wharf rat. Did you present the note?"

"Well," she began, "when I arrived, Miss Elise wasn't there. Her ma said she'd gone to Mr. Van Ripper's."

"Van Ripper's? Why would she go there?" Though I could guess.

Leta's eyes widened. "That's what I asked."

"And...what did her mother say?"

"She said if it was any of my business she would've told Henny."

"Leta," I prodded, "what happened next?"

"I told her that I had a note for Miss Elise, and that I was to deliver it straight into her hands."

"Did you?" I asked, growing impatient.

"Yes, ma'am. I shot like a bullet to Mr. Van Ripper's farm."

She said this with a fair amount of pride.

"And was Elise there?"

"I found her on the road, coming back. She was prancing and grinning like someone had just gave her a shiny new coin."

No doubt she'd seen Ichabod.

"Did you give her the note?"

"Yes, ma'am."

I waited. "Leta! Was there a reply?"

She pulled open her pocket, peeped in, then gazed up at me with doleful eyes. "Just this." She scooped out small bits of ripped paper and dropped them into my hands. I stared down at the mass that had once been my letter.

"Thank you, Leta. That will be all." I let the pieces flutter into the bin and dusted the spite from my hands. There are some wars that are never won.

* * *

The one good thing about not having an overseer is that it kept Father away from the house. That meant there was no one to oversee me when I left for the schoolhouse the next afternoon. I needed to find that bead. And I'd pull the place apart if that was what it took.

I rode quietly under a sky of gray drizzle. As far as I knew, no one had been to the schoolhouse since the Horseman marked it. As I approached the schoolyard, Dewdrop halted, refusing to take another step—much like the day I visited Garritt.

Were there still traces of evil here?

I snapped the reins. "He is bound in his tomb, you silly nag." Fruitless. She wouldn't budge an inch. But then it occurred to me, did I really want my horse hitched out front? Only Ichabod and I knew there was no further danger. If Father or the Council found out I was here, I'd have no fitting excuse.

I led Dewdrop into the woods and tethered her to a limb.

"Pray that I find it." Then, creeping through the trees, I treaded across the damp ground. I found myself glancing left and right, worried someone might spot me. I swear, I'd done more sneaking in the past week than I had my entire life. It was becoming second nature. But still, my blood chilled and my heart raced as I drew closer to the school.

I took the longer path, avoiding the marked cellar. I wanted no fresh image of it haunting me.

The porch had not been swept in all that time and was covered with leaves and twigs. A scattering of molted feathers had collected under the door. I double-checked for watchers, pushed my way in and—*Dear God!* It had to be at least ten degrees colder inside. Had the closed windows contained the previous night's chill? My body quivered, but it was a discomfort I'd have to endure.

On hands and knees, I searched, starting with the farthest side of the room first. That was where the bracelet had broken. And while I knew that Ichabod and the students had swept the area more than once, I couldn't leave a single stone unturned.

I hunted for at least ten minutes. As remarkable as that rose was, it could not up and vanish on its own. It was here. *Somewhere.*

I ran my hands along the cleft between the wall and the floor. I checked the cracks in the benches. The crevices in the desks. My fingers brushed any surface with a dimple. *Guh! Where is it!* I was nearly ready to throw something when I heard approaching footsteps outside.

I froze, the blood draining from my face. I darted under Ichabod's desk, holding my breath and hugging my knees.

Within moments there was footfall on the porch...then the creaking of the door. I closed my eyes, shivering. Who other than I would chance coming here? Had I failed in my attempt to seal the Horseman? And if I had, would he dismount and seek me on foot?

Go away, go away, go away.

Whoever had come in stepped softly. He seemed to be wandering rather than stalking.

My heart hammered as he approached the desk. I was trapped with no way out and no weapon to defend myself. But then, what weapon would I use against a ghost?

Then he stopped. I could feel him standing close, sensing me. The stranger sniffed the air, drew in a deep breath, and said, "Katrina?"

Oh my! I scrambled out. "Ichabod!"

With two strides he was there, sweeping me into his arms. "At last," he murmured as he pressed his lips to mine. I was ravenous for his touch.

When we finally parted I gazed up at him, then stepped back, bewildered. "How did you know it was me?"

His mouth creased into a grin. "Your perfume gave you away."

I must remember that next time I need to skulk about. "But how is it that *you're* here? The Council simply released you?"

He sat against the edge of his desk. "After I convinced them that I'd sealed the Horseman into his grave."

"I'm amazed they believed you."

"Oh, trust me, they were skeptical. But after I confessed to sneaking out, robbing the repository, and driving in the blade, I took them to the cemetery and showed them the sword. I have to admit, I put on a pretty good act." He circled his finger around his nose. "Most people can read this boyish face like a book."

Of course, that brought about a smile. I turned and leaned against the desk too. "You'd think they'd be awarding you a medal."

His eyes widened. "Ha! You should've seen the magistrate. He was furious! I honestly thought he might arrest me for robbery." He mashed his chin to his neck and rumbled, "You should've discussed it with us first, Crane."

I covered my laugh with my hand. "What about the sword? How did they determine it was the right one?"

"By examining the hilt. Even I could see it was the weapon of a madman." A look of pure admiration then crossed his face. "Katrina, that must've taken great strength."

"But the outcome was more than worth it." I brought my lips to his for another glorious kiss.

His eyes slowly opened as I withdrew. "I have more good news."

I couldn't begin to guess what it was.

"After some persuading, they agreed that if I'm still in possession of my head on Monday, I can go back to teaching...in the church, of course. And only traditional assignments." The last part was said in another deep-voiced imitation of the magistrate.

Relief swept over me. "That's not good news, Ichabod, that's great news. Teaching is not something I'm cut out for."

He quirked an eyebrow. "I love the way you're cut out."

He wrapped me into his arms, warming me from the harsh chill. Which reminded me, "Ichabod, why did you even come here?"

He glanced around the room. "Because there are still so many unanswered questions. I can't stop wondering why the Horseman chose me? Why Devenpeck?"

"Does it even matter now?"

He tilted his head. "Probably not. But still...what's his connection to school teachers?"

"Ichabod, you're forgetting Garritt. He was educated at home. I don't think he'd ever set foot in this school. And as far as I know, he barely knew Nikolass."

"I'll always be curious." Then he looked at me quizzically. "Now it's your turn. Why are you here?"

That brought me back to the bitter truth. "I was searching for my tiny rose."

"Of course. I'd forgotten. Where have you looked?"

I held my palms up. "Everywhere." Then, sighing, I asked, "Do you think one of the children could've kept it?"

"No. To them, the money I offered was more valuable than the rose. Not to mention the extra points I promised for their grade. Trust me, they not only cleaned up the mess that day, they rooted through everything."

My heart ached. "I can't leave till I find it."

"Then we'll find it. But let me light a fire first. This cold is making your nose red." He kissed the tip of it.

As he started for the fireplace, I grabbed his arm. "Wait! I haven't thoroughly searched there." I hurried over, knelt, and shoved aside some of the logs. Then I ran my hand along the cobbled floor. There was an unusual amount of debris— snapped twigs, dirt clods, bird feathers. I'd never seen so much fall through a chimney. As I skimmed across it something pricked my finger. "Ow!" I quickly withdrew my hand and examined it. A large splinter had pierced the skin, the wound already livid.

Ichabod pulled a handkerchief from his pocket. "Hold still."

"That's going to be extremely difficult," I said, quaking from the cold.

"Yes, it'd be easier to remove the sliver if my hands weren't shaking too. I'll light a fire first."

Drops of blood were beginning to form, so I wound his handkerchief around my finger.

Once the fire was lit, Ichabod brought over a basin of

water. He took my hand, cradling it in his. "And now, my fair patient..."

I bit my lip as he slid the splinter free. The burning pain was nothing compared to the blood that freely streamed. He dipped the handkerchief in the water and pressed it to the puncture.

"Ay! That water's freezing."

He tied it on tight. "Good. It will stop the bleeding faster."

I looked down at the bulky wet bandage. "Thank you, doctor." Just when we were leaning in for a kiss, we noticed the air had gone thick and gray. Puffs of dark smoke billowed from the fireplace.

Ichabod waved his hand in front of his face. "The chimney's clogged."

I remembered the twigs and feathers. "I think there were birds nesting in there." I covered my mouth, coughing.

Our eyes watered as he went for the broom. Staying clear of the flames, he thrust the handle up into the flue. "There's something blocking it." He prodded and poked, shielding his nose with his crooked arm.

"Ichabod, I can barely breathe. Let's extinguish—"

Right then, a welter of dead birds and dried sprigs crashed down from the chimney. Ichabod jumped back as the heap struck the hearth. Debris rolled toward us, bringing flaming embers with it.

I shot back, keeping my hem raised.

While the smoke now rose upward, the room was still filled with a stinging haze. Ichabod stomped out some of the cinders. But I reacted quickly, picking up the basin, pitching the water, and dousing the fire.

We both stood back, agape.

"What in God's name?" I muttered.

There were at least a dozen dead blackbirds cluttering the

floor, sticks and vines entangled in their wings.

"Now we know what caused the blockage," he said, fanning the musky air.

"But how? Why?" I looked to him, still astounded. "Was this the work of the Horseman?"

He put his arm around me, drawing me close. "No. This was a manmade nest."

"Who would do such a thing?"

"I don't know," he answered, "but I think we'd better leave."

As much as I longed to find that bead, I knew he was right.

We made our way through the smoky room and stepped out into the misty air. I inhaled, clearing the smoke from my lungs.

He nodded toward my hand. "How is your finger?"

My finger. I'd nearly forgotten. I untied the handkerchief to examine it. "Swollen." It still bled.

He turned the handkerchief over and retied it. "It needs a poultice to prevent infection."

"I'll take care of it when I get home."

Placing his hands on my cheeks, he leaned down and kissed me. The medicine I truly needed.

"I love you, Katrina."

"I love you too."

He gazed on me, his eyes soft. "When can we meet again?"

"After the school day tomorrow. The granary at Bliss."

He cocked a brow. "The naming of that property was great foresight on your part."

Then we were intertwined again, kissing with passion. I eventually gained my senses and whispered, "Ichabod, though it hurts me to leave you, I may well bleed to death."

He relaxed into a smile. "Go take care of your finger. I'll see you tomorrow."

And with one last kiss, we parted.

* * *

Father never said a word about Ichabod at dinner. And I certainly didn't press. I'm sure in some roundabout way, he felt sealing the Horseman was yet another attempt by Ichabod to make him look incompetent. He hurriedly chewed his food, then, throwing his napkin upon the table, he finally looked my way. "Katrina, I'll need you to take care of all the arrangements for the party."

My jaw dropped. "We're still having our harvest party?"

"Of course," he bellowed, eyes wide. "We have much to celebrate."

My dinner became all the tastier.

* * *

The next day dawned as frigid and damp, yet reminders of icy rooms and tumbled birds could not erase my joy.

I reached the granary early, spread out the quilt, and waited. A short time later, I heard Ichabod's footsteps on the stairs.

His dark hair glistened from the mist and his vibrant eyes glimmered—sending a wave of tingles throughout me. He knelt and inspected my bandaged finger. "Is it better?"

"Much better, though the children taunted me, saying I sliced it on my sharp tongue."

"Ah, yes." He nodded. "I've heard that you are a most cruel schoolmistress."

I huffed. "I certainly can't have them taking advantage of me."

"Of course not," he said, drawing me close. "That's my job."

We kissed for a time, holding, touching, caressing. It was as though nothing existed outside the granary walls. But still, there was something gnawing at me.

"Ichabod?"

"Umm-hmm?" he answered, nibbling my ear.

"Did Elise come to see you?"

He sat back. "Yes, she came bearing strudel."

"And?"

He shrugged a shoulder. "She told me she was pleased with what I'd done, complimented me on my bravery, and said she looked forward to when I could dine with her family again."

She'll never give up.

"That was it?"

"That was it."

I stretched my legs in front of me and scoffed. "At least her father informed her of your release."

Ichabod teasingly pursed his lips. "I'm beginning to think Baltus doesn't like me."

"Only because he's stubborn, old-fashioned, and can't accept change."

His eyes softened as they met mine. "Perhaps that is why he keeps you so close."

The thought lingered. Father's dominance toward me had started just after Mother died. Did he really fear losing me? "Regardless, he'd never allow us to be together. Not as long as we remain in the Hollow."

He rolled a lock of my hair in his fingers. "Then let's not remain."

I snapped my eyes to him. "You want to leave?"

His never flickered. "Don't you?"

I felt so light, I feared I might float away. I placed my hands on his face and drew him into a deep kiss. But within the passion, my mind churned, remembering Marten's scheme. "Ichabod, we need to plan our departure."

He smiled, still drunk from the kiss…and the thought of us leaving, I guess. "We could go now if you'd like. This second. What's to stop us?"

"Plenty. Father's money goes a long way. He'll stop at nothing to bring me back."

He sat a little taller, his face taut. "Katrina, don't. We can go halfway around the world if that eases your mind, but I won't spend the rest of my life constantly looking over my shoulder."

"But I will." I rolled onto my knees. "I'd always be wondering what bounty Father had set."

He wrapped his arms around me and pulled me close. "If it'll make you feel safer, then we'll come up with a plan."

I laid my head on his shoulder and closed my eyes. "I already know a way."

He waited, listening.

"I have a friend who's recently purchased a ship…"

* * *

The days leading up to the party were spent in preparation. Our home was overrun with servants, who aired linens, buffed wood, and polished silver. The new overseer had arrived, yet Father still spent time away from the house.

I kept my nose to the ledgers, budgeting for the affair and seeing to every detail. Father was right. There was much to celebrate.

Now, more than ever, I couldn't be seen near Marten's ship. If Father thought I'd escaped with Ichabod, Marten would have nothing to fear. And thank God we no longer needed Peter Bottoms.

On the evening of the party, Leta fastened me into a rose taffeta gown. Once my tresses were securely pinned, I powdered my face and bosom and stepped into white brocade slippers. I swept into our great room to check that everything was in place. The fragrance of alabaster roses filled the air. Amber and cream ribbons wound up our banister. And every wall shimmered with flickering candlelight. As always, it was like stepping into a fairy tale.

Soon came the first knock at the door.

Father and I stood together, greeting the guests as they arrived. As usual, Reverend Bushnell was the first. He spouted pleasantries and praised the Lord for delivering us from our recent nightmare.

Reverend, I did the delivering. You should be praising me.

He was followed by a few members of the Council. Even Notary de Graff came, though he was still dressed in mourning clothes. His hand trembled when I took it to thank him for coming.

I'd barely finished greeting him when I heard a saucy voice say, "We got our real schoolteacher back." Dirk Jansen. He glared up at me, his arms firmly crossed over his chest.

The little oaf.

"Believe me, Dirk. No one is happier about that than I."

"I doubt that," he countered. He poked out his tongue, then motioned for his brother, Devlin. They pushed past me, tracking their way to the table of sweets.

Was it wrong that I'd hoped the pastries would rot his little teeth?

As I turned back, Elise stood before me in an ice-blue gown dripping with lace. Her golden hair, pinned up in curls, was adorned with gossamer butterflies. And the glass beads of her necklace twinkled their way down to a delicate jay-feather pendant. My breath caught at the sight of her.

"Elise, you're dazzling." How could she afford such splendor?

Her smile was as cold as her eyes. "Thank you. You look quite lovely tonight too."

"Please," I whispered. "Let's resolve this."

She turned her nose and walked in, ignoring my plea.

How regal will she feel when she hears Ichabod and I have

run away?

A few more villagers arrived, offering compliments and bits of banter. The music had already begun, and laughter floated from our great room. I felt light and uplifted...then along came Peter Bottoms. Just the sight of him caused my stomach to shrivel. He took my hand and leered with yellow eyes. "Why, Katrina, you look good enough to eat."

Hot bile rose to my throat. I was tempted to spit it into his face. *Thank God, this will be the last I'll see of him.* "Believe me, Peter, you'd find me quite sour."

He leaned close, clicking his mouth. "I'd still like a taste."

Before I could react, he laughed and walked away.

I promptly wiped my hand on my skirt and turned to the next guest.

Three more families passed, then Ichabod approached. I was absolutely agog. His black silk suit and ivory waistcoat fit flawlessly—every fold of lace on his neckcloth perfect. There was a bluish tinge to his raven-wing hair, and his emerald eyes sparkled. My breath hitched at the thought that this delicious creature was all mine.

He greeted us with a smile as warm as our hearth.

Father's face pinched. "Well, Crane, you're still in one piece. That risky endeavor paid off for you."

"More preservation than risk," Ichabod said. "And, as I see it, it paid off for everyone."

Father's expression held firm. "Curious, though. I'd never have thought to look in Smedt's store, even after Katrina questioned me." He peered down at me, his eyes dark slits.

Ichabod came to my defense. "I'd asked her through our correspondence if she knew what had become of the confiscated weapons. I'm just grateful the sword was there."

"All in all," Father said, "I hope you've learned your lesson."

A vein in Ichabod's jaw pulsed. "And which lesson would that be?"

"You can't mock God with all this progressive thought. It leads to no good end." Father bit each word as it rolled from his mouth.

Ichabod clapped him on the back. "Sound advice, Baltus. I'll advise President Washington." Knowing we were leaving had made him beyond brave.

Now it was Father's jaw that tightened. Ichabod quickly stepped forward and took my hand. "Katrina, you are absolutely radiant this evening."

"Thank you, Ichabod," I said, a thousand tingles feathering through me. "That was most kind of you to say."

He discreetly winked before walking away.

Over the next several minutes we welcomed more guests. The display of wigs, plumes, blossoms, and jewels made for a colorful parade. But my eyes kept straying, catching glimpses of Ichabod. It was during one of those musing moments when I heard, "Katrina." Marten stood before me. He looked charming in a crimson tailcoat and black breeches—a contrast to his usual sweaty clothes. Every sun-kissed strand of hair was combed, and he smelled of toilet water.

"Marten, I'm so glad you've come." Then, in a near whisper, I said, "We must speak."

His eyebrows dipped and his eyes lit, warning me to stay quiet. "You know I wouldn't miss it." Then, with a smile, he added, "I'll see you inside."

A few more villagers followed, then I went about my hostess duties. My eye was continually on the spread of luscious pastries across the room. When I finally made it to the table, I was weighed with a major decision. *Cranberry or lemon tart?* An arm reached around, offering me a glass of brandy punch. "It appears our ship's captain is in attendance," Ichabod said softly in my ear.

"Shhh." I took the glass. "I'll speak with him later, when everyone's too tipsy to notice." I took a sip of the tangy drink.

"Good." Then Ichabod quirked a brow. "What happens if *you* become too tipsy?"

"Believe me, you do not want to witness that."

He snorted a laugh.

I nudged him with my elbow. "What?"

"Nothing." His crooked smile was both devilish and adorable. "I was just wondering if you become a stumbling drunk or a besotted braggart."

"Neither." I took another small sip. "I recite naughty limericks and talk to the curtains."

He sputtered the drink in his mouth. "Now there's the Katrina I *really* want to see."

I held up my glass. "Just promise you'll stop me when I start slurring my words."

We were interrupted when Clive Van Helt, Vincent's father, staggered over. He appeared to have started celebrating before his arrival. He reached out and poked my arm with his callused finger. "I thought you'd like to know that Vincent enjoyed having you as his teacher. He spoke about you a lot."

That caught me by surprise. I was truly flattered. "Thank you. That's very kind. He is an industrious student." *And one I'm extremely grateful to.*

Clive then cut his eyes to Ichabod. "Well, Crane, seems we've had similar undertakings."

"Oh yes," Ichabod said. "I'd heard about that. The ghost of the old trapper."

Clive poked Ichabod's arm too. "You should've come to me for some advice. You could've bungled the whole thing."

Ichabod remained calm. "I apologize. The next time I need to seal a ghost, I'll certainly consult with you first."

Clive took a swig from a whiskey bottle that didn't come from our store. "You young folk think you're so smart. Think you know everything about everything."

Now I knew where Vincent got his gall.

Ichabod whispered to me from the corner of his mouth, "Please tell me you don't become like this."

"What'cha saying there?" Van Helt wheezed.

"Nothing. I'm just thankful that it all worked out in the end."

He poked Ichabod's arm again. "I should probably go out to that grave for an inspection."

"And while you're there"—Ichabod poked him back— "feel free to redo it." He then drew my hand to his lips and kissed it. "Katrina, it's so lovely to see you. Now if you'll excuse me, I'm sure there are other parents waiting to reprimand me."

I motioned to the table. "Please, Mr. Van Helt, help yourself." I dodged around him and wandered away.

I spotted Elise across the room, standing with her mother. *This may be a mistake, but…* I weaved my way through to them. I first addressed Mrs. Jansen—an older, more worn version of Elise. "I hope you're enjoying yourself."

She gave me a broad smile. "Katrina, these parties are always so lovely."

At least her mother hadn't turned on me.

Then to Elise, "And you?"

She shifted, causing her dress to glimmer like a spring pool. "It's nice. Though I've noticed that you're short a guest."

"Oh?" I skimmed the room.

"Brom. I haven't seen Brom tonight." She dallied with her feather pendant. "He never misses your parties."

"I'm sure you've heard that Brom is no longer our overseer."

"And no longer seen," she snipped. "I wonder what's

driven him away?"

I gently gripped her arm and took her aside. "Let's not play these ridiculous games."

She glared at me, her eyes blue fire. "I'm playing games? You snake. You knew how I felt about Ichabod and you tromped right over me."

"I did nothing of the sort."

Her nostrils flared. "He was sweet and good to me. But then there you were, all over him—kissing out in the open where anyone could see."

How dare she? "I've never kissed Ichabod in public."

"I didn't say in public, you ass. I said in the open. By the brook." Her teeth ground deep. "Did you not think for a second that someone might see you?"

I stepped back, aghast, as it all became clear. "It was you. You're the one who destroyed the schoolhouse that day."

"Can you blame me? I went there with word from my father. He was going to lend Ichabod equipment for the cellar floor. Your horse was there,"—she poked her finger to my shoulder—"but you were not. It enraged me when I saw the two of you together."

I shoved her hand away. "Then you should have confronted me instead of turning into a spoilt child. You ruined pottery and schoolbooks and furniture. What on earth were you thinking?"

"That it was your hair I was ripping instead of pages."

In turn, I poked a finger into her shoulder. "And I suppose it was you who clogged the chimney with dead birds."

She stepped back, her mouth open. "You know about the birds?"

"Only after a fire was lit. Was burning down the schoolhouse part of your revenge as well?"

She rose a little taller, finding composure. "Hardly. I did

that after the school was marked."

After? "Elise, that's madness."

She threw up her hands. "No, Kat, not madness...love. If you'd paid attention, you would've seen bird feathers lining the doorway and windowsills too."

I did remember seeing them as I'd entered. "I still don't understand. Why?"

"To remove the Horseman's mark. I love Ichabod. I only meant to keep him safe."

I couldn't fault her for that. "And you risked going to the schoolhouse alone?"

"Oh forget it," she spat. "You probably think it's superstition."

"No, I think it's witchcraft."

"At least I took measures. What have you done to ensure his safety?"

Broke into the courthouse. Stole from the weapons store. And risked a trip to the Horseman's grave to seal him with his own sword.

I burned with anger. "You have deluded yourself into thinking that there's something romantic between Ichabod and yourself. That has never been the case."

"But it might've been had you not interfered, you spiteful minx."

"And now you resort to name-calling." I wanted to fling my brandy right into her face. "I am truly at a loss, Elise. I don't know what you expect me to do."

"Spin your treasured globe, point to a destination, and *leave*."

Before I could counter, she turned and stormed away.

Tears filled my eyes, and I was helpless to control them. I hurried to the staircase, meaning to hide in my room to regain composure. But I had the misfortune of passing Henny, who was captivating a small crowd with one of her tales.

"Oh, Katrina!" she called as I tried to slip through. "Come, come."

I sniffled back tears. "Henny, I—"

"We were just discussing our wonderful schoolmaster. That young man is the embodiment of bravery."

"Yes, he's quite noble. Now if you'll excuse—"

"Noble?" She slapped her meaty hand to her chest. "Positively fearless!"

There was a great nodding of heads following that statement.

Henny pursed her lips. "Did he tell you of his encounter with the Horseman?"

Oh dear. "No," I said, blinking away the tears in my eyes. "I don't recall him relaying that story."

"What?" Her face opened in astonishment. "Why, I would not be surprised if he wrote about it for publication. A tale far more enthralling than any fiction."

And yet I knew what I was about to hear would be fiction indeed.

"You see," she began, "he came to know of the Hessian's sword by way of a dream."

"A dream, you say?" I found that a bit of a compliment considering I was that dream.

"Yes, it was relayed to me that he dreamt of the sword as a glowing hot blade, shining brighter than the sun."

I mocked surprise. "It's a wonder he didn't have to shield his eyes."

She clucked. "Remember, Katrina, it was a dream."

"Of course."

"Knowing that Smedt had pilfered that sword, Ichabod devised a plan to save us all from that abominable spirit."

"Well, he is quite cunning."

"Oh, more than that!" Henny praised. "He not only managed to recover the sword, but chose the witching hour to carry out his task."

I twitched my mouth as though curious. "Interesting that he didn't wait till the safety of dawn."

"Not our courageous Ichabod! He set out to finish that demon once and for all." Henny took a deep breath, most likely to spew the rest of the story in one uninterrupted exhale. "He stood by that grave and waited. In a matter of minutes, the Hessian was there. It was a vicious battle. But in the end, our fearless Ichabod prevailed, slicing through the Horseman with the fiend's own sword, then driving the blade into the grave, he sealed him in forever. Bless him and his immeasurable courage."

"Yes, we are blessed to have him."

It was then that Ichabod sauntered over, no doubt to rescue me. "Ladies."

"Oh, Mr. Crane!" Henny said, crossing her hands to her heart. "We are indebted to you for your daring deed."

"Well…" He shrugged. "It was a deed that needed doing."

"Indeed!"

"Katrina," he said, taking my hand. "Would you honor me with a dance?"

"Of course." At last, I was freed.

He nodded toward Henny's assembly. "If you'll excuse us." We took to the middle of the floor.

We'd barely danced two steps when he said, "Something's upset you."

I shook my head. "It's nothing."

"No, it's something." He peered into my eyes.

"Really, forget it."

"Forgotten." He spun me around and brought me back. "So what will it take to make you smile?"

I chewed at my lip as though contemplating. "It's hard to say. Especially since I'm not ticklish."

His warm breath brushed me when he let out a sigh. "You'll always hold that over me, won't you?"

"You can count on it." I broke into the smile he was longing to see.

"That's better." He leaned closer. "This is a party, Katrina." He spun me again. "Have fun."

I didn't hesitate to heed his advice.

As the night progressed, the spirits flowed. The more drink consumed, the more everyone enjoyed themselves. There were all manner of circle and folk dances. We partook in several parlor games, and I played a couple of songs on the pianoforte, accompanied by the quartet of musicians.

Near midnight—the witching hour, as Henny would call it—the festivities had not ceased. The fiddlers sawed the strings, and the music stayed wonderfully fast and uplifting.

Twice I'd looked for Marten, but he was always within a crowd or drinking with Peter. But I could not let the night end without speaking to him. I brazenly grabbed his hand and pulled him onto the floor. "Dance with me."

He'd never cared for dancing, but he was inebriated enough not to object.

"Marten," I said, once we were amid the stumbling mass, "how much longer?"

His kept his voice low. "So you haven't changed your mind?"

"No, I haven't, but there is a new…hitch."

"No, Katrina. Everything must go as originally planned." He glanced at Peter, who'd cornered a young woman against the wall.

"Forget about Peter," I said. "We won't need him."

Marten's face darkened as he clutched my arm. "Katrina,

listen to me. Terms are set. We cannot change them."

"But Marten, you don't understand."

His grip tightened. "No, you don't underst—"

That was when the window exploded with a thunderous crash. Shards of glass showered as a flaming log burst through, landing at our feet.

"Marten!"

He wrapped his arms around me and jerked me away.

There were yelps and gasps from the crowd. People scattered. The musicians leapt from their chairs.

Three men pitched forward to stomp it out, but it was still kindling when another log shattered the next window and hit the floor.

"What the devil?" Father roared.

As more men rushed over to beat out the flames, a shovelful of hot cinders flew in, skittering next to them.

The shrieking and howling of guests pierced the room. Caspar Jansen peered out the window, then stumbled back. "It's the Horseman! He's returned!"

My heart thrummed. *That's not possible.*

"What should we do?" someone shouted.

Marten kept a tight hold on me, attempting to block me from danger. Heat and smoke choked the air.

Another window smashed as more burning wood and coals flew in.

The crowd grew chaotic—wailing, crying and shouting. Some rushed the stairs seeking refuge, but a fireball blasted through, hitting the steps and setting the decorative trim ablaze.

Burning cinders skittered under Gertie Marris's skirt as she cradled her infant son. Her hem ignited, blue flame gobbling her dress. She held her child out to the frantic crowd. "Take my baby! Please! Please! Someone take my baby!" Ichabod was among the many who came forward to help.

People cowered in corners and under tables. Some scattered to the inner parts of our home.

Efforts were made to extinguish the flames, but as soon as one fire was snuffed, the Horseman would launch another blazing missile.

"Someone do something!" the magistrate ordered.

Father turned to him, disgruntled. "A bloody suggestion would be nice!"

Peter Bottoms stumbled forward, a fierce glower in his eyes. "We all know what he wants." Then he shifted his gaze to Ichabod, who was beating hot coals with his silk coat.

"It's true!" Caspar Jansen shouted. "He wants Crane."

The Horseman made another pass, his outline visible among the torches.

"Deliver him," Clive Van Helt cried, "before the Hessian takes us all."

"No!" I screamed, struggling to break Marten's grip.

Caspar ground a cinder with his heel. "Send him out."

Then the lynching began.

A crowd descended upon Ichabod, grabbing his arms and legs. He flailed and fought, but there were too many.

I shoved my way out of Marten's hold. "No!"

Father slammed his fist to the wall. "Are you all mad? We cannot offer this man up as a sacrifice."

But the drunken villagers were heedless.

I rushed them, pounding and kicking. "Let him go! Let him go!"

They pushed toward the front door, dragging and shoving Ichabod as the Horseman still cast cinders inside.

The magistrate stomped his foot. "Order! Let there be order!" No one complied.

Father scrambled to block the way, but was shoved upon the hearth. His head thwacked against the brick, splitting his scalp and sending sheets of blood streaming down his face. "Father!" I ran to his aid, cradling him as he bled onto my dress.

The magistrate, now in a frenzy, shouted, "How is sending this man to his death going to help us? What guarantee do we have that the Horseman will be appeased?"

But those determined to have Ichabod butchered would not hear a word.

Notary de Graff hurried over to me with napkins in his hands. "Katrina," he said, pressing one of them to Father's head. "Don't let them do this."

I grabbed the fireplace fork and charged, swinging, pounding, and thrusting. One man, named Dathan, pulled it from me and shoved me to the ground.

Marten ran to assist me, then, with one solid blow, bloodied the man's nose.

The brawl continued as many of Ichabod's defenders stormed forward to barricade the door. But I feared the mob were too many. I looked around for something...anything!

Elise huddled behind a table, whimpering.

"Please, Elise, please! Help me!"

"I cannot." She sobbed, her gown clutched within her fists. "I cannot go against my father."

I raced back into the revolt, pulling and tugging. Ichabod still struggled, teeth gritted. Our eyes met and he cried, "Katrina!"

Dear God!

Caspar, who clutched one of Ichabod's sleeves, yelled to me, "Move out of the way!"

"We won't let you through," the magistrate held.

"Then we'll toss him out the window!"

They shifted direction, traversing the room.

I flew to the kitchen in search of a weapon, my heart slamming against my chest.

Simon, as though by accident, knocked a large cleaver off the sideboard close to my feet. I snatched it up and ran back.

They continued to trudge, dragging Ichabod through the cinders and glass. But I streamed around them, standing at the window with the cleaver held high. "Let him go or I'll chop all your heads off myself!"

"Move out of the way, Katrina," Peter Bottoms ordered in a drunken slur. He grabbed for me, but I brought the razor-sharp blade down on his shoulder. I wasn't strong enough to sink it, but it sliced through his shirt, sending a spray of blood from the slash. He buckled, then reached for the cleaver, trying to wrest it from my hands.

No! No!

The reverend pressed in, holding up a Bible. "Stop this ungodly behavior now!" But they struck him and shoved him aside.

Peter continued battling for the cleaver. Though I held strong, it finally popped from my grip, sending me stumbling back, nearly toppling out the window. They would've tossed Ichabod right on top of me, leaving both our fates to the Horseman.

Just when I thought there was no hope, Father stepped up, a rag tied to his head and a musket aimed at the crowd. "Stop! I will not stand for this in my home. Release him at once."

The room went silent. The lynching ceased. No one wanted to chance a bullet.

Ichabod shoved out of their hold. He slumped against a wall, panting. His hair was disheveled, his shirtsleeve ripped. The top button was missing from his waistcoat and the second one dangled from its thread.

The reverend rose from the floor. "He's gone."

We all turned to the window.

"The Horseman is gone," he repeated.

I rushed to Ichabod, throwing my arms around him, both of us trembling.

The magistrate took charge. "Now, let's see if we can manage some decorum." He held up a finger, glancing around. "Baltus, how badly are you hurt?"

Father wavered and sat. He still clutched the musket tight. "I'm fine, Harding. But check on Peter there."

I had sliced deeper into Peter's shoulder than I'd thought. He held his coat to the wound, but blood still splattered onto the floor. His eyes bled hatred as he narrowed them toward me.

I looked around for Marten, but he seemed to have disappeared.

Marten, where have you gone?

Doctor Goodwine examined Peter's wound. "He will require stitches. I'll need sewing notions."

Father called for Simon to fetch them. "And show Gertie to my room to find a dress among my wife's things. Get some salve for her legs."

Gertie, dressed in a table cloth and clutching her child, sobbed as he led her away.

The magistrate turned back to Father. "This is your home, Baltus—what do you intend we do?"

Father looked around at the whimpering wives and children. "We'll gather in the common room."

Most of the throng had now dispersed, looking guilty and shamefaced. Once we settled back, the Council, without Caspar, took charge of the situation.

"It is quite evident," the magistrate said, "that Crane failed in his task to seal the Horseman."

"Or likely, he used the wrong sword," the reverend added.

I buried my face on Ichabod's shoulder. All this was because of me. I had risked everyone's lives.

"Either case," the magistrate continued, "it is my duty to

insure the safety of the Hollow. Nobody leaves this house before dawn."

No one argued.

"Come morning, we'll place Crane in a secure spot. It's apparent that the Horseman has a grievance with him."

I snapped my head toward him. "Grievance? You make it sound like they simply quarreled."

"Hush, Katrina," Father warned. He was too weak and weary to bark.

Ichabod laced his fingers through mine to calm me.

The magistrate shook his head. "This much we know—as long as Ichabod is safe, so are we. The Horseman has marked *him*. The ghost will not take vengeance on any of us until he's taken Crane's head. That's why it's in our best interest to keep this man alive."

"And where will you take him?" the notary asked.

"Don't worry," the magistrate answered, "There is one place where the Horseman can't reach him." He waved us off after that, concluding, "Now, I recommend we spend these next few hours making peace amongst ourselves. It's the only way we'll survive."

I reached up and stroked Ichabod's face. "I have never been so terrified in my life."

"Nor I." There was still fear within his eyes. "I should've taken my chances with the Horseman."

"Ichabod," I whispered, "what are we going to do?"

He worried the dangling button. "I don't know. But for now, I'm trapped. These men will never let me leave."

* * *

At first cockcrow, there was a stirring. Everyone gathered their things. The reverend held up his hand for attention. "Church services will still be held, but moved until two this afternoon. I suggest you all attend."

The guests left in groups. Little was said. No goodbyes or expressions of gratitude. And the few apologies uttered were to the Council, not Ichabod.

When most everyone had gone, the magistrate said, "Come on, Crane. Let's get you to safety."

Ichabod made no attempt to resist.

"Where are you taking him?" I asked.

"For the sake of the Hollow, it's best we not divulge that."

"But this is wrong. You can't make him a prisoner again."

Father managed to step in, his face haggard and gray. The bloodstained bandages were peeling, revealing the severity of his wound. It was stomach-clenching. "Katrina, you will not stand in the way of the magistrate."

I threw my arms around Ichabod's neck and whispered, "I will find you. I promise."

He closed his eyes, breathing in my voice.

I watched, helpless, as they escorted him out. He walked like a man condemned. When he mounted his horse I thought, *Ride away, Ichabod. Ride away now.*

But no matter how much I willed it, I knew that he would not.

* * *

The dawn shed its light on the disaster that was our home. We were accustomed to the clutter and mess that followed our yearly parties, but what I laid eyes upon looked more like the aftermath of war. Scorched planks. Shattered glass. And the russet stains of blood. All encased within a fetid stench of smoke, like that caught in the schoolhouse by the barrier of dead birds.

The windows, now gaping mouths of broken teeth, breathed the outside frost. I welcomed the chill as a reminder that I could still feel something. Carefully stepping through the debris, I closed the remaining curtains. It was our only defense against exposure until the slaves brought boards and nails.

Every inch of me ached as I trudged to my room.

Will this dark cloud ever disperse?

Exhaustion finally overcame me, and I fell into a dead sleep.

* * *

Over the next two days, I budgeted for repairs while Father saw to the farm. Our newly arrived overseer had fled back to Chappaqua. Who could blame him?

I worried for Father. His ghastly wound was now a livid lump, the color of egg yolks and chicken livers. The gash within it had crusted over with a prickly maroon scab. It turned my stomach every time I doctored it. And it was causing him headaches, I could tell.

And, of course, my mind was continually on Ichabod. What place in the Hollow was safe from the Horseman's reach?

I considered having Leta deliver a note to Henny, the one person who may have wrangled the information, but that would prove too risky. I was sure she had already concocted stories of a lurid affair between Ichabod and me. The query would only add kindling to the fire. I'd have to figure another way.

My first real hope came on Thursday. Reverend Bushnell had been invited to dinner. He knew where Ichabod was being kept, and I'd find a way to wring it out of him.

After grace, Father picked up his spoon. "Reverend, I again offer my humblest apology for the chaos last Saturday."

The reverend lifted a hand. "No need, Baltus. It was no fault of yours."

"But had I known the Horseman was not restrained, I would never have..." His words trailed off as though he no longer had the strength to speak them.

"Do not concern yourself. As it is, we are now somewhat skeptical of the whole business."

"Which business?" Father asked, his spoon trembling in his hand.

Reverend Bushnell cast his eyes to me. "How Crane was able to slip away undetected and carry out the sealing process. There was no real proof that it was the correct sword. We now think it was just a ploy of desperation. A way to free himself from those whose only motive was to protect him."

I met his gaze, chin high. "Reverend, how would you like being kept under lock and key?"

"Oh, don't misjudge my remarks, Katrina. The inconvenience of his circumstance has not been taken lightly."

Father blew steam from his stew. "So you think Crane took some random sword as a ruse to mislead us?"

"No," the reverend answered, keeping his eyes on me. "He most likely believed it was the true sword. After all, it certainly looked like the weapon of a bloodthirsty Hessian. No, I think there was more at play here."

I was onto his roundabout accusations and met his challenge. "What more could be at play?"

His lips curled into a sly smile. "Perhaps you can tell me? You were corresponding with him during that time. Did he not tell you of his plan?"

He knows. "Did you not read our correspondence yourself? Surely the Council was keeping a close watch."

He sank his spoon into his bowl. "Admittedly, I did go over the exchanged lessons. But only in the interest of the children."

"Since you saw what was exchanged between Ichabod and me, you know that *he* relayed no plan to *me* of sealing the Horseman in."

The reverend chased a pea around in his stew. "Regardless, it was a good plan. I remember you asking me if such a thing would work."

"And I remember you affirming that it would. What a shame that it was not the real sword. Especially since it looked like, as you put it, the weapon of a bloodthirsty Hessian."

He nodded. "But there are so many swords in that stockpile. How could one possibly know the difference?"

"Well, perhaps we should stab them *all* into the grave. That should finish him."

Father kept his faded eyes on his bowl. "A valid suggestion."

"And," I added, "Ichabod should be the one to drive them in. After all, his head is the one at stake here."

The reverend waved it off. "There is no proof that the Hessian's sword is even there."

"And no proof that it isn't. Who was it that bothered burying the German devil?"

The reverend's agitation grew. "Katrina, you were but a babe during the Revolution. You have no idea the anguish and bedlam that took place."

"Oh, trust me, I know a great deal about anguish."

"At any rate, we will never know who dug that grave. But it was most assuredly someone who abhorred the British and their tactic of recruiting rogue soldiers. Quite unlikely that it was Smedt."

"Still," I goaded, "the old hermit might have pilfered the sword beforehand."

The reverend's hard huff mingled with steam on his stew. "Katrina, the entire Hollow knows you have a vested interest and are quite anxious to resolve this…as we all are."

Father suddenly found his voice. "Then let's resolve it. Tell the Council we'll meet at the church on Saturday."

"Fine," the reverend said, slurping his meal.

I made no further snaps, but listened closely for any hints as to where they'd hidden Ichabod. When it was time for the reverend to leave, I helped him on with his overcoat.

"Where are they keeping him?" I whispered as he slipped one arm through.

He heaved his other one in. "Katrina, I cannot divulge that information."

"But you know that it was I who attempted to seal the grave, not Ichabod. Therefore you must also know that I am desperate to free him."

He uttered a small laugh. "Oh, yes. It is your desperation that I fear most. What other extremes might you employ?"

"I will do whatever it takes," I assured him.

"Even at the risk of endangering the Hollow?"

"Reverend, there is another way to keep me out of your hair."

He smiled, amused. "Now that's a suggestion I'm anxious to hear."

I moved in close. "Marry me to Ichabod so that I may hide with him."

His eyes bloomed and his jaw dropped. "Without your father's consent? That's preposterous."

"Please. I beg you."

He wrapped his scarf around his neck. "Believe me, Katrina, if I could do it, I would. Crane is just as bullheaded as you. The two of you belong together."

"You'll not even consider it?"

"No," he huffed. "Out of the question."

Had I really expected he would? "Can I at least send a message to him?"

He placed his hands on my shoulders. "It's best that there be no written exchange between you for the time being."

"Then will you deliver a verbal message?"

He sighed, waiting.

"Tell him that I hope he finds at least one *grain* of

happiness in his cruel situation."

He straightened his hat. "That seems harmless enough."

"You're forgetting, Reverend, I'm not the one who means him harm."

* * *

I kept hope that the Council would come to some decision—find some method to blast the Horseman back to hell. When Saturday did arrive, I could barely think. They couldn't possibly adjourn without something substantial.

Simon came into the kitchen after running errands in town. It was far too early for dinner, yet he remained, finding ways to busy himself. And there was a certain restlessness about him.

"How are you today, Miss Katrina?"

I rested my forehead against my fingers. "As well as can be expected."

"Would you like me to make you some tea?"

I peeked up, now curious about his motive to linger. "Yes. That'd be nice."

I watched as he dallied with the kettle.

Sensing he had something to say, I asked, "How were things in town?"

He shrugged in a "so-so" manner. "Just the same, I s'pose. Lots of talk and such. I always hear some of the oddest things when I'm there."

Odd? "Tell me, what did you hear today?"

He set the kettle on the stove. "It's not my place to gossip."

Again there was a bridge of silence, as though he needed permission. "Please, what did you hear?"

He picked up a cloth and began wiping down our spotless sideboard. "Seems there was a brawl at the tavern last night. The fellow that caused it went crazy wild. Tore up the place."

"Has Brom returned?" I scoffed.

"Oh no, ma'am, it wasn't him. I didn't catch the man's name."

I picked up the tea canister and walked next to him. "I hope this nameless man took some of that rage out on Peter Bottoms." *And beat that vulgar sneer off his face.*

"I don't know about that," Simon continued, "but the curious part is they didn't arrest that man. They just sent him on home."

That was curious. "Why didn't they arrest him?"

"That's the oddest part. It turns out there was already somebody in the jail."

"Was there any reason they couldn't have tossed him in with the other prisoner?"

He stopped wiping and gazed past me. "I thought that too. But I heard they wouldn't have none of it." He then turned his deep eyes to mine. "Makes you wonder who's occupyin' that jail, now don't it?"

Our gaze held.

Oh, my sweet, wonderful Simon!

I plopped the canister onto the sideboard. "On second thought, I think I'll wait until later for tea."

His lips curved into a thin crescent. "Yes, ma'am. Is there anything else you need me to do?"

I gave his hand a squeeze. "No, Simon, you've done more than enough."

Sweeping on my cloak, I hastened to my horse. I didn't care who saw me, and to what consequence. I spurred Dewdrop into a winged gallop and did not slow until I'd reached the magistrate's court.

I pushed inside, marching straight to the jail.

The jailer, a rangy lizard named Fallon, stepped in front of me, blocking my entry.

"Move out of my way," I ordered.

He remained stiff. "The prisoner is not allowed visitors."

I slipped off my gloves. "Prisoner? Is that what you're calling him?"

He puffed his chest, as though that should intimidate me. "You have no business here."

"I am going through," I said, "and you won't stop me."

The blacks of his eyes shrunk to beads. "You think I can't?"

I met his glare with equal measure. "I think you're forgetting something extremely important. My name is Katrina *Van Tassel*. My father is Baltus Van Tassel. Our wealth keeps this village alive. And if I'm not mistaken, pays your wages."

He flinched, blinking. "I will have to notify the magistrate about this."

"Go ahead." I nodded toward the door. "He is presently at the church with the other councilmen. I'm sure you can still catch him."

Fallon seethed, practically breathing smoke.

"Now let me through."

"Fine," he said. "But you'll get no key."

"Not yet," I muttered as I hurried past.

Ichabod lay on a cot, his journal and pencil in hand. "Katrina." He flung them aside and rushed to the bars.

We caressed each other as best we could. He kissed my hands and fingers, then reached through the bars, placing his palms to my cheeks. I placed mine on his—the bars too thick for our lips to meet.

His mouth creased into a smile. "What took you so long?"

My heart ached. "Ichabod, what have they done to you?"

He drew his hands in and gestured. "Take a look."

For the first time I saw his cell instead of him. I blinked surprise. They had dressed it up nicely. He was afforded a writing desk, chair, goose quills, a sheaf of paper, basins, quilts, and a large, comfortable featherbed. I then gazed up at the small barred window just under the ceiling—the pane shut tight. "No fresh air?"

"Believe me, it's best closed."

I remembered the ghastly stink of the narrow alley beyond it.

"So," he said, his eyes playful, "what do you think of my new quarters?"

"I'm certainly relieved. I feared they had you in shackles."

His fingers swept across my cheek. "They do."

His touch only deepened my anger at the Council. "Ichabod, this is outrageous."

"Well, they are right about one thing. The Horseman can't touch me here."

"Nor I. Not in the way I wish." The desire gripped me.

He braved a smile. "So our fates are in the collective knowledge of the Council, and yet my optimism isn't raised."

I clutched his hands. "Ichabod, I intend to free you."

"I'd put my faith in you before them, but I don't know how you can. And Fallon would swallow the key before turning it over."

"Perhaps I could slip some type of sleeping draught into his cider."

He chuckled. "He's rarely alone during the day. And at night I'm protected by two guards. I think they'd grow suspicious if you were to show up with a jug."

I squeezed his hands tighter. "Then I'll find some way to stop the Horseman myself."

He rested his forehead against the bars. I placed mine on the other side.

"Katrina," he whispered, his voice grave. "I know how you think. Please don't do anything to endanger yourself."

"If you know how I think, then you know I'll stop at

nothing."

"Just promise me you'll not do anything rash. You've taken a huge risk for me already."

I closed my eyes, feeling his warm breath on my face.

"Katrina…promise me."

I could not. "I can only promise that I will find a way to end this."

He sighed, concern glistening in his eyes. "Whatever will I do with you?"

We held each other as best we could. How unfair—the victim being jailed. And though it was risky for me to linger, I could not tear myself away.

It wasn't long before the courthouse door opened and we heard mumbling through the wall.

We still held hands as magistrate Harding stepped into the jail room. He looked neither angry nor disappointed. He simply gazed, blank-faced. "Does your father know you're here?"

"No," I answered, trying to keep my voice calm. "Are you going to tell him?"

He didn't answer directly, but his expression showed that he would not.

Ichabod leaned against the bars, arms crossed. "I'm assuming by your lax demeanor that the Council is still as baffled as ever?"

The magistrate pointed a finger. "Don't test me, Crane."

Ichabod ignored it. "I'd like to see the minutes of the meeting, being that I am the reason it was called."

"The Horseman is the reason," he countered.

"And?" I urged. "Did you come up with anything?"

He ran the back of his hand across his forehead, then paused and scratched his nose—like delaying the answer would make the question go away. Finally, "There was talk of bringing in more clergy."

"Oh goody," Ichabod said. "More religious wit. Always the answer."

The magistrate scowled. "I should've let the mob toss you."

I stamped my foot. "And they are the ones who should be locked up!"

"Katrina," he barked, "I will not discuss this with you."

"You cannot keep him caged like this."

"I can do whatever is best for the Hollow. Now visitation is up. Go home."

On the magistrate's orders, I had no other choice.

Ichabod brought my hand to his lips, kissing it gently. Then he whispered, "On second thought, bring all of them cider."

I couldn't find the strength to smile. "How can you jest at a time like this?"

His eyes softened. "Because I prefer it to the alternative."

The magistrate motioned for me. "Come, Katrina."

Ichabod hesitantly released my hand. As I trudged away, he called, "Katrina."

The magistrate and I both turned.

He still leaned against the bars, an endearing smile on his face. "I love you."

I returned the smile, though it was weak and thin. "I love you too."

* * *

My thoughts spun as I rode home. There was a simpler way to solve this. I could point a musket at Fallon's face, demand the keys, and kidnap Ichabod, taking him so far from here they would never find him. I smiled, thinking how Ichabod would be enchanted by this plan. But if the magistrate was right, I'd be saving Ichabod, but sentencing everyone else to death. The simpler way would not work.

I remembered the story of Dora Hindricks. How the

Council had used her children to give her peace. But the only peace offering for the Hessian would be his severed head, which was probably picked clean by buzzards and piled in a mass grave somewhere.

There was still one solution that seemed the most logical to me—remove his blasted bones. Yes, the reverend viewed it as desecration, but could it be more unholy than what the ghost had enacted upon us? I would not be so cruel as to inter them in another vicinity. If his ghost did follow his body, then he needed to be buried some place far from human reach or sent washing out to sea.

Washing out to sea.

I could risk it.

There was no sacrilege. No maelstrom. No suffering will follow.

It would take some careful contriving.

I can do this.

A detailed plan of execution.

I've been to his grave once already.

There is no reason I couldn't carry it out.

I lay awake that night, my eyes fixed on the ceiling. *Beware, you old maggot. I'm coming for you.*

* * *

Patience. Something I had little of, but was forced to endure. I could not falter.

But my plan was not failsafe. Even if the ghost were drowned at sea, how could I prove this to the Council? How long would it take them to realize that the Horseman would no longer rise? It was a problem I'd contend with when necessary. And if the Horseman was truly banished, there'd be no pending danger to the villagers should I level Father's musket at the jailer and steal Ichabod away.

I carefully thought out which tools I would need, then

secretly gathered them. The largest cloth bag I could find would in no way carry the intact spine and ribcage of a human skeleton. But this devil had been in his grave for some time. Surely his bones were brittle enough to shatter. I placed a hammer among the shovel, lantern, and knife I'd buried under the hay in Dewdrop's stall. I hid canvas and rope as well.

Completely absorbed with the matter, I could think on nothing else. I relived my previous time at his grave, and what strength it took to drive in the sword. There had been little rainfall since that time, so I could only count on the burrowing field animals to have done more work for me.

By Tuesday, my plan was set. I saw it over and over in my mind, contemplating the worst of situations.

I must keep my head.

When I retired that evening, I did not make down my bed. Instead I sat at my window, watching the skeletal limbs of the trees reaching to each other. Ashen gray clouds sailed lazily across the sky, and my newest worry was that they might hide the glow of the waning moon, which I was counting on for additional light.

Near four in the morning, I dressed, wearing no stays or petticoats to hinder my work. I slipped into a shift then a simple woolen dress. Both could easily be knotted at the hem. I put on two pairs of wool stockings for warmth, and tied my hair back with twine instead of ribbon. My slippers would get me as far as the stables, where I'd placed a pair of Father's sturdy boots. To fit, I'd tucked rolled linen into the toes. My cloaks kept me sufficiently warm, but their hems caught easily on my heels. So I took one of Father's overcoats too.

I lit a small lantern in the stable and quietly saddled my horse. "I am asking much of you, Dewdrop. Forgive me."

I put what I could in a saddle pack then strapped the shovel on. I blew out the lantern, mounted and rode.

As it turned out, those ashen clouds cast a glow, lighting my way. I kept low in the saddle, determined, my heart beating with each pound of Dewdrop's hooves.

The grave looked the same as I'd left it. The sword still buried to the hilt. Again, instinct told me that this was the true sword.

Why has it not kept you down?

I gripped it and tugged. After some heaving and shifting, I managed to raise it and cast it aside.

I removed what I needed, shrugged out of Father's coat, and dug. At first I could only manage the smaller, looser clods. But I soon realized that hopping onto the shoulder of the shovel's blade upturned deeper, larger fills.

The two pairs of gloves I wore were cumbersome, but kept my grip solid. Yet each thrust was a struggle. And though I repeatedly grunted and squawked, I stayed committed.

The one thing lacking was fear. My knees trembled, but from labor, not fright. A few scurries among the weeds startled me, but I gritted my teeth and continued. I had no reason to be afraid.

I am not the one marked.

After a while, my right shoulder ached—a miserable pang that twisted the muscle and pinched my neck. A reminder that I had lived a life of wealth, not labor. A short time later, the ache coursed its way to my wrist. I winced with each jab of the spade.

I had misjudged the depth of the grave. I'd assumed the person who'd dug it had only meant to cover the scoundrel and go. But perhaps the gravedigger had a more personal vendetta, digging with great ferocity. I couldn't imagine that his grievance was greater than mine.

Though the pre-dawn air held a raw cold, my tortured body perspired. I began to wonder if there was anyone buried there at all.

Is that why the sword hadn't worked?

But just when my struggle seemed bleakest, I hit something other than soil. A leather boot.

I stumbled back, letting out a triumphant sigh. *Where there's one, there must be another.* I rooted around with the shovel till I found it. They were the only clothing that had endured the grave. Then, with renewed vigor, I unearthed the skeleton that wore them.

I crawled from the pit, lit the lantern and held it over my find. The Hessian lay face down—or chest down, in this case— likely shoved or booted into the hole.

I slipped back in and crouched. His boots were cracked and crusted and—*ugh*—smelled like dry rot. Instinctively, I covered my nose with my sleeve. After a couple of deep breaths, I carried on.

His right foot was detached, making my task simpler. But when I lifted the left boot, the entire leg bone came up with it. I reached up out of the hole, grabbed the hammer, and—with one fierce thwack—severed it at the ankle.

Logic told me to gather the smaller bones first. After collecting those of his left hand, I reached across for his right. I instantly pulled back, shuddering. The fingers were twisted and coiled like a skeletal claw…in an inviting gesture.

His right hand. *The beckoning hand.*

I did not buckle then, and I would not now. I closed my eyes to calm my breathing, then—*one…two…three*—I gathered my courage and snatched the hand up bit by bit.

The hipbones and upper torso were much larger than I'd expected. And though my muscles twitched and seized, my rage pushed me. By placing my foot on the lower spine, I was able to smash some of the rib bones into manageable fractions. They plinked like raindrops on a clay roof when I dropped them into the sack.

I kicked at the soil with the toe of my boot. When I was sure there was nothing left but my tracks, I pulled myself from the grave.

But there lay his sword, partially covered with the flung dirt.

Leave no part of him.

I picked it up and eased it into the bag.

My lack of sleep and hard labor had caught up with me, so I stopped a moment to breathe. Then wiping back my loose strands of hair, I snuffed the lantern and tugged everything to my horse.

Dewdrop stood patiently as I fumbled, packing her down. I heaved myself on, missing my footing only once. Gripping tightly to the reins, I spurred her off toward the Hudson, focusing solely on my goal and not the abomination that I carried.

After reaching the bank, I tethered her to a low limb. The joints in my fingers had tightened, but I managed to free the bag.

It's time for you to go, monster.

Dragging it across the rocky ground, I made my way to the river's edge.

I waded in and—*Merciful heavens!* Even through wool stockings the freezing water bit my flesh. My limbs trembled and my teeth knocked, sending spiking pains firing through my jaws.

I had chosen this particular area because as a child I was warned not to swim here. The swift undercurrent was strong. But it was that lower tide that I counted on to flush his bones away.

I continued slogging out, shivering like a fevered dog. My boots were now filled with frigid water and the soaked bag lay heavy in my hand.

Just a bit farther.

When the river reached thigh deep, I tried opening the bag. The wet rope had tightened and gripped. I tussled with it as the coursing water drove against my legs, threatening to wash me away. I tensed my muscles against the pull, while Father's boots anchored me to the bottom.

As I managed the sack, the rushing water clutched it, trying to rip it from my hands. I held on, determined.

First, I grappled the sword.

Will the current take it or will it lie on the bottom like a sunken ship?

Seeing no other choice, I pitched it.

I took out the bones, one and two at a time, and flung them as far as I could. But with my loss of strength and benumbed limbs, I could only toss them a few feet. I then removed the Hessian's boots, foot bones within, and sunk them into the current. With no part of him left, I dropped the bag and watched it wash away.

It was done.

Walking back was like trudging through tar. The anchors that were Father's boots now held me. I crossed my shivering arms and pushed forward—my skin prickly, my teeth clicking. Once I reached the shallows, I staggered my way to land.

Just two steps out, I collapsed, gasping for breath.

You cannot stop.

The pain and cold clutched me like I was entombed in ice.

Move, Katrina, move!

My body continued to twitch and quake.

Find warmth or you'll die.

I'd left Father's coat with Dewdrop. Crawling on hands and knees, I urged forward, finally struggling to my feet. I labored, step by step, till I reached the tree where I'd tethered her.

Dewdrop?

The limb had snapped. She was gone. What had startled her away?

I dropped to my knees, helpless. After all that I'd endured, it'd be bitter irony to die now.

I turned my hammering head and gazed down the shoreline. Boats.

Marten.

Self-preservation drove me. How had I not planned for this pain and cutting chill? I pulled myself up and trudged back toward the shoreline where the land was more level.

Dawn was hiding just behind the hills, its amber light splitting the horizon. It felt like I'd walked for hours, stumbling, determined. I finally reached the piers.

The predawn fishermen had sailed, leaving somber gaps in the empty moorings. As the sky grew lighter, I grew nearer, but then...

Dear God! My hand flew to my mouth and tears sprang to my eyes.

Marten.

His battered ship lay tilted, the stern sunk into the silt. One mast had snapped and lay cracked across the bow. Raveled nets hung loose, trapping floating debris. Had I not known it to be his, I would've guessed it a shipwreck washed ashore.

Then I saw it. The Stygian mark of the Horseman, scored deep along the hull.

My breath caught. Panic rippled down my spine. With a hoarse and rasping voice, I cried, "Marten!"

Where is everyone?

"Marten!"

I scrambled forward, blinded by tears.

"Marten!"

There was no gangplank to aid me, yet maybe I could still climb aboard. But the second I touched the ship, I drew my hand back. Though my fingers were already frozen to the bone, that one touch bit my hand the same way it had on Garritt's window.

"Marten! Marten!

"Katrina?"

I cut quickly toward his voice.

"Katrina!"

He was hurrying down the slope, holding bags and boxes, but when he saw my condition, he dropped them and broke into a run. He'd only scrambled a short distance when his gaze caught on his ship. He slowed. His jaw dropped.

That was when I heard it, distant at first—thundering hooves pounding clay. Then *he* came into view—the Horseman—charging straight at Marten.

"Oh God, Marten, run! Run!"

But instead of taking to his heels, he spun around, throwing his arm up to shield his face. The Horseman brought down his scythe, slicing it across Marten's neck, taking his head and arm in a single blow. Marten's head flew from his collapsing body then hit the ground, bouncing and rolling toward me.

"No! No! No!"

I scuttled back, but momentum carried it. And in spite of my panic and attempt to dodge it, his head stopped just inches from my feet, his upturned face frozen in a mask of horror.

The Horseman sat tall, his scythe resting on his shoulder.

I sent you away! I sent you away!

I stared up, afraid to blink. Afraid to breathe.

He popped the reins and trotted toward me.

"No!" I gasped, stumbling back—back into the frigid river.

He stopped at the water's edge.

My heart hammered against my ribs. "I sent you away!"

He remained for only a moment. Then turning, he spurred his horse and raced away from the rising sun.

I plodded out, sobbing, averting my gaze from Marten's face.

Marten.

My wearied body moved by sheer will, my mind numb with shock. Hot saliva filled my mouth and what bits were left in my stomach forced their way out, spilling to the ground.

Marten.

I staggered a little farther, but my senses had now given way. My head swam. The earth blurred. Dark spots bloomed. Then everything went black.

* * *

My eyes blinked open—barely—my vision milky. I tried to swallow, but it felt like hot coals had been poured down my throat. I had a sense that someone had bathed me and put me to bed, yet my hair clung to me, sticky and damp. I moaned.

"Shhh…" The voice belonged to Doctor Goodwine. "Lie still."

I had no other choice. Had someone dropped an anchor on my chest? I moaned again.

He tilted my head and placed a cup to my lips. I gulped the cool water, choking it down.

Once my eyes cleared, he came into view. "Welcome back."

From where?

Father stood just behind him, looking haggard and gray, yet there was a wash of relief upon his face.

The doctor placed a wet cloth to my forehead. "You've suffered a bad fever."

A fever? My thoughts churned, turning over and over. Then the fog parted, and it all came tumbling back. "Marten."

"No, no," the doctor said. "Relax now. Try not to upset

yourself."

Try not to upset myself? All I could see was Marten's severed head at my feet. The silent scream upon his face. How could I ever erase that?

"The Horseman," I whimpered.

He used the cloth to pat my tears. "Katrina, you have suffered a great shock. But right now, we need you to focus on getting well. I know it is difficult, but you must try."

He was asking the impossible.

"Here, have another sip of water." He placed the cup back to my lips.

The next sips went down easier, though my throat still burned. I dropped my head back onto my pillow and whispered, "I have done an evil thing."

"Katrina," Father said, "try not to talk."

But I needed to confess. Reverend Bushnell had been right. Unearthing the Hessian's bones had set a pestilence upon the Hollow. He took Marten—and maybe others for all I know.

"Ichabod?" I tried to sit up, but the pain crushed me.

"He's fine," Father assured me. "Now try to rest." As always with Father, it sounded like a command.

Ichabod. He was probably the only one safe, locked within the jail. But thank God, he *was* safe.

Weakness overcame me and my body melted into the sheets. "Marten is dead because of me."

"No," Doctor Goodwine said. "It was not on your account."

"But—" That was when I saw beyond them to the person standing at my door. Brom. His face was taut, yet blank. Our eyes met only for a second, then he slipped away.

"Brom," I uttered.

Father craned his neck, looking back to the spot where Brom had stood. He studied the emptiness. "There's no one there." He placed a hand to my forehead. "Doctor, are you sure she's out of the woods?

The doctor gave a slight nod. "Oh, yes. But I am worried about you, Baltus. It's time you got some rest."

"I'll rest when I'm ready," Father spat. "I need no medical advice."

"But you've been sitting with her every day with barely a wink of sleep."

Every day? My mind whirled. "What day is it?"

The doctor paused as though he'd spoke out of turn, then answered, "It's Friday."

"Friday?" My breath hitched, leading into a fitful cough. *How can it be Friday?* I had last set out in the predawn hours of Wednesday.

"Like I told you," the doctor said, forcing more water into me, "you have suffered a great shock. And with the fever..."

"What time is it now?" I asked, sputtering water onto my quilt.

He reluctantly consulted his watch. "Just after three."

So many hours lost.

"Settle back," he said. "And rest as best you can. You'll be fine."

Fine? What mockery. I turned my head, shutting my eyes against my tears.

Oh, Katrina, what have you done?

* * *

Though still racked with spasms, by nightfall, I managed a bit of mobility. I could not stand, but with the support of pillows, I could sit up. Simon had placed my dinner tray across me. Boiled liver, collard leaves, and pickled beets—all cut into tiny bites and soaking in a mire of maroon juices. My stomach wrung at the sight of it. I used what strength I had to sip my wine. That, at least, numbed some of the ache.

Father peeked in, then quietly brought a chair to my bedside. The weight of the farm and recent distress carried on his face. He kept his eyes on my tray as he fumbled for words. "You're looking much better."

"I feel like I've been struck by lightning." And even that was a mild description.

"It'll take some time." He fidgeted with his unlit pipe, then drew his eyes to mine. "Katrina, the Council has been asking me about the morning of Marten's death. We need—*I* need to know what happened."

I shook my head, biting my lips. More tears. I turned to face the wall.

He placed his hand on my arm. I couldn't remember the last time he'd touched me so tenderly. "Why were you at the docks? And so early?"

The pink wallpaper roses were a watery blur. I blinked away some tears, yet my chin still trembled. But Father needed an answer. I sniffled, then lied, "Marten was shipping out that morning with no plans to ever return. I couldn't let him leave without saying goodbye."

"Dressed as you were?" His words were a little sterner than he'd probably intended. He softened them when saying, "You were wearing a simple dress and my boots. And your horse returned with one of my overcoats and a shovel."

I had no answer for that. I pushed the tray down and faced him. "I was taking those things to Marten. He needed a few supplies before leaving."

He no more believed me than he would Henny. He examined his pipe for a moment, then said, "Very well. I'll think of something to tell the Council." Heaving up from the chair, he trudged toward the door.

"Father," I said. He turned. "Thank you."

He nodded and walked out.

* * *

I awoke the next morning feeling twice the misery. *Marten.* I wasn't sure which was worse, the pain within my body or that within my heart. I whimpered and sobbed, and cried myself back to sleep. It was much later when someone gently swept my hair from my cheek, rousing me from sleep. "Katrina."

My eyes popped wide, and I gripped his hand. "Ichabod." I drank in the sight of him, then his lips were on mine. This was far more medicinal than the foul plasters and tonics Doctor Goodwine had prescribed. When we parted I smiled weakly and teased, "What took you so long?"

He ran two fingers along my jaw, his eyes rimmed red. He spoke so softly, I almost didn't hear. "Katrina…I have been to the Horseman's grave."

"Oh God. Does anyone else know?"

"Only I." Two of his tears fell onto my cheek. "Why would you take such a risk? If anything had happened to you…" He took my face in his hands and kissed me again.

My own tears ran as well. "I only meant to free you. But I've put everyone in danger instead."

"Sweetheart, do not think your act was selfish. Banishing him would've saved everyone."

"But I didn't banish him."

"But you didn't raise him either. He must've had some reason to strike Marten. You were not the cause."

I thought back on it. Could he have marked Marten before I dug up the bones?

"I need you to listen," he went on. "The Council has turned on me. Since Marten's death, I'm no longer their safeguard. They've terminated my teaching agreement, and asked that I return to Connecticut."

"But you can't go," I cried, holding him close.

"I have no other choice. They've agreed to give me two

weeks to find employment elsewhere. That will give you time to heal, then we can leave this godforsaken place together." He kissed me again with urgency. Pain screamed through me, but I would never let on. Then he looked back toward the door. "Sweetheart, I must go before Baltus returns."

I clutched his lapel. "Will you come back?"

"It may be too risky. Send word to me when you're better."

"Send it where? Are you back at Van Ripper's?"

"At present, they've moved a cot into the filing room.

"But surely they'd intercept any message I sent." If only I could get out of this bed now.

"We will find a way, Katrina. I promise."

He then gave me one last kiss.

* * *

It was another two days before I could rise without feeling like my limbs were being ripped from my body. Though painful, it was a relief to finally move around. Ichabod had given me incentive to heal. But I slept very little. I didn't deserve to flee my guilt so easily. And the nightmares were persistent. How many times would I have to relive Marten's death? Over and over I saw his protruding dead eyes glaring up at me.

I was sitting in the parlor with my tea when Father came in from town. He sat uncomfortably at the edge of the sofa. "Peter Bottoms approached me today."

My stomach roiled at the thought of that vile creature.

"He claims Marten gave you something that's rightfully his, and he'd very much like it back."

My thoughts turned to the beads, tucked inside the hem. "I-I don't know what he's talking about. Marten never gave me anything of Peter's." Nothing Peter earned, anyway.

Father's fingers anxiously twitched. "Well, he's causing quite a stir. I'm refusing to let him speak with you. Especially since he's still boiling over the incident with his shoulder."

"If he's so adamant, then he should come right out and say what it is he wants." *And why. They must be some kind of key to something valuable.*

Father dallied, then asked, "Would this have to do with your morning at the docks?"

For once I could tell the truth. "Not at all." Picking up my teacup, I added, "If Peter thinks Marten had something of his, he should be ransacking the boat, not badgering us."

Father rose. "Someone had already plundered it. Perhaps it was him. Anyway, the ship has been towed and sunk."

Towed and sunk. Marten's dream, rotting on the ocean bed. The thought pricked my heart.

Though he meant to walk away, I quickly stopped him with a question of my own. "Father, will you allow me to go back to church on Sunday?"

His eyes widened like I'd asked to wallow with the pigs. "Certainly not."

"I will only improve with outside stimulation. And I need to move about."

"I can't risk it. You know better than anyone that the Horseman is unpredictable. It's not safe for you to step out of this house."

"But don't you think if the Horseman had wanted my head, he would've left it on the ground next to Marten's?"

Father's cheeks turned a ruddy orange. This was about more than the Horseman. His breath came in quick gasps. "Very well. But under no circumstances are you to leave my sight. Or speak with Henny, or any of those other meddling flibbertigibbets in town. Understood?"

I could only imagine what they were saying. "Understood."

* * *

Father kept his hand protectively on my back as we entered the church. I kept a protective hand on my Bible, holding tightly to what I'd hidden inside it. I'd expected the congregation to descend upon me, batter me with questions, but I was only met with broad stares.

They'd been forewarned.

Elise stood across the room, her eyes filled with venom. No doubt, she blamed me for Marten's death. I turn away so she couldn't see the guilt on my face.

The magistrate and Notary de Graff approached. The notary didn't speak, but his face was filled with sympathy. Maybe he felt we had a common suffering.

The magistrate stood tall—or as tall as a pudgy man about five foot seven was able. "Good morning, Baltus."

"Harding" Father replied. He rarely addressed him by his title.

Then the magistrate's eyes were on me, the pupils pinpricks within a circle of olive green. "I trust you're feeling better, Katrina."

"Yes, sir. Much better."

"Good, then. The Council greatly needs your help."

Why should I help them? "Honestly, magistrate, I'm not sure if I can offer anything substantial."

He held his chin high in order to look down his nose at me. "The Council believes you can. Twice you've had a full encounter with the Horseman. We'd simply like to sit down with you and discuss it."

"Your honor, I don't know that I could contribute—"

Father held up a hand to the magistrate. "Katrina has only just regained her strength."

The magistrate sneered. "And who else will die while we wait for her recovery?"

"Not her," Father countered.

They glared in silent confrontation. Over the last week, one thing had become abundantly clear. Brom had been wrong.

Father did care more for me than his money, his farm, and his position on the Council..

The magistrate turned back to me. "Katrina, we will wait. But the fate of the Hollow could lie with you."

I didn't see how.

"Come, Katrina," Father said, his hand again on the small of my back.

He meant to help me to our usual pew, but when we turned, I bumped right into Ichabod. I was thrilled at the fortunate chance to touch him, but had I known he was behind me, I would've seized this opportunity to carry out my plan.

"Oh dear," he said, holding my arm to steady me. "I apologize."

The warmth of his hand spread through me. "No, I'm sorry, it was I who was inattentive."

He still held me in his grasp. "I've been so worried. But you're looking well."

The magistrate grumbled. He knew better than anyone that it was simply an act.

"Thank you," I said. "I'm feeling much better." *And better still when we can finally be together.*

Father jerked Ichabod's hand off me. "Come along, Katrina."

I nodded to Ichabod, then purposely swept by so that my Bible brushed against his. I used that moment to drop the piece of paper I'd concealed inside mine. I stopped and tapped his shoulder. "Ichabod, you've dropped something."

He kept a blank face as he picked it up, opened it briefly, and closed it again. "Thank you. I tend to write down inspiring prayers and passages. It always uplifts me."

Smiling inside, I said, "Then I'm happy it wasn't lost."

He placed it within his Bible, nodded politely, and went to take his seat.

Father and I took ours. I kept my eyes forward, not once looking Ichabod's way. I prayed that he could interpret the message I'd slipped to him—a single Bible passage: Corinthians 15:37. *And that which thou sowest, thou sowest not that body that shall be, but bare* **grain**. Underneath, in a much smaller hand, I'd written: *Tu. 1.*

* * *

Just before one o'clock on Tuesday, I sneaked away to Bliss. A November wind had blustered through, but I was warmed by the anticipation of Ichabod's arrival.

Please come. Please.

I exhaled my relief—how long had I been holding my breath?—when I heard him enter.

He hurried up the steps and swept me into an embrace.

"How I've missed you," he whispered as he drew my mouth to his.

I melted into him, feeling…tasting…touching. He held me tightly, like I might flitter away. He only let go long enough to say, "Katrina, we must leave."

"How? When?"

"Right now," he urged, his hands cupping my face. "This second. We'll simply get on our horses and go."

Nothing is simple. "And how far do you think we'd get before Father sent a search party? I know my Father. He would find us."

Ichabod sat back, his elbow resting on his knee. "Then we must come up with a plan."

"We can use a byway." I told him about Marten's arrangements for Greenburgh to Sawpit.

He considered it, nodding. "There's no reason we can't do something similar."

"Can we?"

He pulled me back into his arms. "I'll leave in the morning

for one of the ports in Connecticut. I should be able to buy us passage on a merchant ship."

My thoughts rushed like the waters of the Hudson. "To where?"

He shrugged. "To wherever it's sailing. Does it matter?"

I breathed in his wonderful scent. "Not as long as you're there."

I closed my eyes, reveling in these moments, but he stayed tense, his mind on the details of our arrangements. After a bit, he pulled away and held my face close to his. "We'll meet at the school on Friday morning. Since no one ventures there, we won't be detected."

"What time?" I asked.

"Six. Before the village comes to life. Pack only what you need." He drew me in and kissed me deeply, invigorated by our new endeavor. Then he whispered in my ear, "Just two more days, then nothing will keep us apart."

* * *

Two days. Only two days to prepare.

I had more gowns and trimmings than I ever needed, but now I must choose two—one to pack and one to wear. The portmanteau I hid under the bed held so little. Any shoes, shift, stays and hairpins I brought would be the ones I wore. This was a task that required common sense. I rustled through my wardrobe to see what I could fit. Then my hand touched upon the blue gown. *The beads.* Should I take them with me? No. They were only valuable to Peter. And after what he'd done to Ichabod, I'd never hand them over. I dug them out of the hem and placed them into my pocket. I had a better idea. Making sure no one was watching, I crept out to the stables, then rode on to the church.

I roamed through the cemetery, searching out Marten's grave. There was no headstone yet, but it wasn't hard to find. I knew it would be somewhere near Garritt's, with freshly turned sod. The second I spotted it, tears loosened and fell. And those final moments poured into my mind. I trudged forward and knelt.

The day was bitterly cold, and my breath appeared before me. "Marten, I'm so sorry." I sat back on my heels and sobbed. "You wanted to keep me safe, and look what I've done to you. I hope you can find it in your soul to forgive me."

How different life should've been.

It took several moments before I could compose myself, then I wiped my eyes and nose. "You keep these," I whispered, removing my glove. "Better you than Peter." I burrowed a small hole in the soil and, one by one, placed the roses inside. "I'm sorry they're not all here."

Though it was risky to linger, I stayed with him a few minutes more. Then, rising, I rubbed the dirt from my fingers and wrapped my shawl tight. My heart couldn't plunge any deeper. "Goodbye, my sweet Marten. You will always be with me." Quickly turning, I hurried away.

Reverend Bushnell was standing at the church doors as I approached my horse.

"Katrina, my dear," he called. "I couldn't tell if that was your nose or a ripe strawberry. Come in and get warm."

"Thank you, Reverend, but I must be getting back. Father will be worried."

He motioned me forward. "Just tell him you were with me."

I hope to avoid encountering him completely. "I couldn't."

"Girl, you're shivering. Come in. Just for a minute or two."

Sigh. A minute or two.

Stepping into the church was like nestling into a warm quilt. It would be difficult to walk back out.

He hastened to the kettle resting on the iron heater. "Hot

tea will get your blood moving."

"No, thank you, Reverend. Really, I don't have time."

He looked at me for a moment, and then gestured to a pew. "Sit."

I did...reluctantly. He approached with that "sermon" look about him. *I'd rather go home and face Father.*

He dropped down next to me, a smile beaming on his face. "You must be relieved now that Ichabod is free."

"Yes, but for his sake."

"Katrina, you must understand. We did what we had to do."

"I find that a poor excuse, Reverend. Locking Ichabod away proved nothing."

He chewed the inside of his cheek, contemplating. "That's the curious part. Don't you find it strange that the Horseman suddenly transferred his objective?"

"We don't know that it was sudden," I said.

"But you have to admit, it certainly puts a new standpoint on his predictability. We were certain that he had it in for Crane, then suddenly, he murders the Piers boy."

I see. Instead of warming my nose, I was brought in for questioning. "Reverend, are you asking me if I have some theory on all this?"

"Do you?" he asked, as he continued chewing inside his lip.

Why had I agreed to come inside?

"My theory, for what it's worth, is that you kept Ichabod secluded well out of the Horseman's reach. And since the Hessian thrives on carnage, Marten's murder was a form of retaliation." *Not bad for a "pulled from thin air" reply.*

His mouth twitched as he chewed the other side. He'd not met my gaze since we sat down. "That makes the most sense, but if he was retaliating out of anger—and I know this is a harsh assumption—it seems that you would have been a more likely victim."

"That *is* a harsh assumption," I snapped, "but then, I would expect no less during an interrogation." I popped up from the pew. "I must go."

"Oh dear," he said, fumbling upward. "That was not my intent. I just thought your insight could help the Council solve this, that's all."

I clenched my gloved fists. "Then how's this for a theory? The cannonball that took the Horseman's head took his brain as well. He was simply confused."

His eyes finally crossed to mine. "You do not believe that."

"And I also don't believe you invited me in out of sheer courtesy." I pushed by him and went to the door.

"Katrina," he called. I turned. "As your pastor, I feel I should inform you that there is much speculation about your presence at the pier that morning."

"Didn't my father inform the Council that I was merely there to say goodbye?"

He came over, hands clasped behind his back. "Indeed he did."

"If you don't believe that excuse then maybe you should ask Henny. I'm sure she's contrived a wonderful story of my secret tryst with Marten, and how we were going to sail off together."

He regarded me with hooded eyes. "But that story makes no sense either. Were you planning to run away with the boy, you would have at least packed some clothes." He then dared to lean close, whispering, "Or worn something suitable."

The church hadn't warmed me nearly as much as my rising blood. My teeth ground together. "Good day, Reverend."

He stepped back, allowing me space. "Trust me, dear, you would do well to speak with the Council."

I took a calming breath and sighed. "All right. If it's that important, I'll find time next week." *If they can find me.*

"And whose life might be struck down before then?" he asked.

A cold air blast stung us as I opened the door. "Please do not try persuading me with guilt. I do not control the Horseman. For all I know, his next victim could be me."

* * *

On Thursday the sun made a welcome appearance. It warmed the air a little and my heart even more. I hadn't heard from Ichabod, which surely meant he'd secured our means of escape. He'd have sent word, otherwise.

Just one more day.

I checked the portmanteau three times that morning, worried I'd overlooked something. My addled nerves would not let me alone. I checked it again. The clock had never ticked so slowly. But the excitement of being with Ichabod filled me.

I sat at the breakfast table, my gaze fixed on my teacup. I didn't know where my mind was at that moment. Simon came forward and poured some tea.

"You've mended real good, Miss Katrina. It makes me happy to see you so cheerful."

It's that obvious? Was I smiling? "It was the smell of your delicious honey cakes that cheered me."

He placed some dishes in the washing tub. "Don't try to fool old Simon. I've known you since you were no bigger than a lamb. Something's got you lit up. And whatever it is, I'm glad for it." He turned, his eyes glowing with fatherly love. "No matter what, I always want you to be this happy."

God, I'll miss him so much. I crossed over and gave him a big hug. "It's a promise."

A promise I could not keep.

About four that afternoon, Henny rode up in her carriage. I could tell right away she was bringing more than gossip. She hitched her skirts and waddled quickly to our door, wheezing out of breath when I opened it to let in her in.

"Katrina," she gasped. "Oh my dear."

Father came out of his study. "What's going on?"

Henny fanned herself with her hand. "I was just in town and overheard. The Council is on their way here."

Coming here?

"What the devil for?" Father demanded. "And this better not be one of your lies."

"It's no lie, Baltus. They should be here very soon. That's why I must hurry." She placed her palm to her heart, heaving. "Katrina, they're on their way for you."

"For me?"

"Yes," she said, her eyes wide. "They are naming you a witch."

My breath left me and my knees buckled. I grasped the sofa for support. Was this punishment for defying the councilmen?

"That's preposterous," Father bellowed.

"It's the truth," Henny said. "I swear it. And now I must go before they find me here."

Father's fists clenched into hard balls. "Henny, if this is one of your lies, I'll see to it that you're the one tried as a witch."

"Baltus, I do not play you false. And Katrina, my dear, you may do well to hide." She spun and scurried out the door. "God be with you," she called back before shambling away.

My mind reeled and my heart thundered. "Father?"

He peered out the window. "If it's true, they won't set one foot into this house."

"They'll hang me," I murmured, quaking to the bone.

"Nonsense. They will not take *my* daughter."

I rubbed my hands along my arms, trying to piece together thoughts. "What will we do?"

"Stand our ground," he said.

Stand our ground? Against the council?

"Henny's right. I should hide." *Just till morning.*

Father took my chin in his hand and lifted my face to his. "I will straighten this out. They have no grounds to arrest you."

He meant every word, but…could he? Before I could make a decision, I heard their horses tramping into our yard. Then came a fierce rapping at the door—hard and quick, like the knocking of a cane.

It is too late to flee.

The rapping turned into pounding.

Father, keeping a slow pace, opened the door, wearing an air of superiority. "Magistrate, I assume you're here on some legal business?"

What I'd thought was a cane was actually a staff.

"Step back, Baltus. I have an arrest warrant." He held a document up to Father's nose.

Father's jaw tightened as he guarded the door. "You're making a mistake, Harding." He had no choice but to step away as Caspar Jansen and Peter Bottoms pushed their way in.

How had Caspar found his way back onto the Council?

Peter's eyes narrowed to slits when he saw me. His lips curled over his knobby teeth.

The magistrate made a royal entrance, followed by Notary de Graff and Reverend Bushnell. He held the warrant up again so that I might see it closely. "Katrina Van Tassel, you are under arrest for the murders of Garritt de Graff and Marten Piers."

Murder? I still gripped the sofa, but kept my chin high. My time for hiding had passed.

Father strode forward and ripped the warrant from the magistrate's hand. "You have the audacity to come here with these ravings of madness! You've all seen the Horseman. You were here when he ravaged my home. How can you stand there and accuse my daughter of crimes most assuredly committed by this ruthless ghost?"

Harding turned on Father, spittle flying from his lips. "Baltus, she is a witch!"

"How dare you?" Father struck the magistrate with the back of his hand. With the quickness of wild hares, Peter and Caspar lunged at Father, restraining him.

The reverend bustled forward in panic. "Gentleman, let's keep our wits. This does not need to end in a physical altercation."

"Keep your wits?" I cried, no longer able to stand by. "You've obviously lost yours long before you came here. On what grounds are you accusing me?"

The magistrate scowled, his cheek flaming red. "Oh, Katrina,"—a vicious smile spread across his face—"you tend to leave an untidy trail."

"So I'm to assume you have some false evidence to present?" I was sure he could hear the banging of my heart.

He put his hand to the sting of his cheek. "Not false." Then he turned to the notary and motioned him forward.

De Graff raised his weary eyes, then dangled Simon's talisman from his fingers.

How could he betray me this way?

The magistrate tapped his staff. "Did you not give this to the de Graff boy before he was killed?"

I struggled to control my labored breathing. "It was intended as protection."

His beady eyes flattened. "And yet it provided none."

"So you're accusing me of murder because a small charm failed to work?"

The magistrate scoffed. "Do you think we're so ignorant that we'd arrest you on that alone?" He nodded to Peter.

Peter loosened his grip on Father, then opened his fist. "I

believe this belongs to you?"

In the center of his palm was something resembling a burnt seed.

"The other rose. Where did you find it?"

"Inside the hearth at the schoolhouse," the magistrate said. "It was buried under a mass of stiff and stinking birds. Some ritual of yours, I presume."

"That was not me."

"Then who? Who else would create such desecration?"

I dared not betray Elise. Would they even believe me if I did?

Father shrugged away from Caspar and rushed forward. The magistrate held up his staff to prevent being struck again.

"You're all raving mad!" Father spat. "How can intelligent men such as yourselves possibly believe these trinkets are harbingers of magic?"

The reverend intervened, holding up his Bible as though it would calm the room. "Katrina, there is more to this than magical charms and dead birds. It was you who ran that sword into the Horseman's grave."

"For the greater good."

The magistrate blasted a sharp laugh. "The greater good? It was a selfish act to fool us into releasing Crane." His lip twitched. "I should no doubt add fornication to your list of offenses."

Father lunged, but Peter and Caspar clutched his coat and dragged him away from Harding's throat.

"You know it was not witchcraft," I argued. "I only meant to seal the ghost in."

"There is more," the reverend said. "A witness saw you defile the grave."

A chill coursed through me, but I did not waver. "Who?"

The reverend shook his head. "For his own safety we

won't reveal it. But he intends to testify. He watched you shatter and pick at every bone. And he claims you did it with calm determination."

It could only have been the cemetery caretaker.

"You don't understand," I said.

"Katrina," Father barked. "Say nothing more."

The magistrate raised a hand. "It doesn't matter. We saw the condition of the grave. Even before Crane tried to cover it for you."

"He tried to cover it?" *He had not told me.*

"Katrina!" Father ordered. "They're spinning lies."

They weren't. My head swam as the seriousness of my situation overcame me.

Peter rolled my tiny rose between his fingers. "It's easy to control the Horseman when you have his bones. Bring him up from hell to murder Marten."

Father slapped the rose from Peter's hand. "Why would she do that? She cared for the boy. She wished him no harm."

"Unless…" Peter said, dragging the word. "It was the only way she could see fit to release her lover."

"Peter, please," the reverend warned.

But the tavern owner gritted his teeth. "You'd sacrifice anyone to be with the schoolmaster. I bet you'd serve up the bones of your dead mother."

When Father pounced again, Harding struck him with the staff. Then he pounded it twice upon the floor. "We've said enough. Come along, Katrina. Don't force us to bind you."

"You'll have to kill me first," Father said.

Caspar withdrew a small pistol and leveled it at Father's nose. "If need be."

I flung myself forward. "No! I'll go! Please don't hurt him."

Father's breath was quick and ragged. "Do not take her."

"She did what she did," Peter snarled. "Now she has to

face the consequences." He clasped my arms, pulling me away.

"I'm riding in," Father said. "You'll all pay for this."

The magistrate raised his staff. "Do not attempt to interfere, Baltus. If you want to help your daughter, you'll have to seek other means."

"I intend to." Father pointed a threatening finger. "When this trial proceeds, she'll be represented by the best lawyer in New York."

"She going to need him," the magistrate said. He pounded his staff to the floor again. "Let's hasten."

Even though I didn't resist, Peter shoved me out the door. A black carriage waited. He waggled an eyebrow and flashed his tiny teeth. "I'll ride inside with the prisoner."

"No, please," I begged, clutching the reverend.

Reverend Bushnell handed me his Bible. "I'll ride with her. She is in much need of prayer."

Peter narrowed his eyes. "Then perhaps I can comfort her once she's in her cell."

I swayed with fear.

All that is holy, what will become of me now?

* * *

The reverend did pray as we rode to the jail. Silently with his head down. His inability to meet my eye reeked of guilt and shame.

I should've been filled with dread, but we were going to the courthouse. I remembered…

Ichabod resides in the file room. Surely he's returned by now.

When the carriage finally came to a stop, the reverend took one arm while de Graff took the other, guiding me inside. Peter and Caspar followed. As did the magistrate, prodding me with his staff. He wore an air of superiority, probably from smelling my fear.

We pushed through the doors into the sullen courtroom. Fallon waited by the jail, grinning like a bridegroom.

I then lashed out, fighting against them.

"Ichabod!" Is he back? Can he hear me?

"Ichabod!"

The magistrate rammed the staff hard into my back, knocking the wind out of me. "Stop your screeching."

Peter strode up and grabbed my bodice, clutching it so his hand rubbed against my breast. "I've got her."

My flesh crawled with repulsion.

He tugged, practically dragging me out of the men's holds.

Do something. Quickly. I suddenly went limp, wilting within his arms.

"Get up," he spat. When he jerked me upward, I pounced, sinking my teeth into his wounded shoulder.

He yelped like a sick dog, prying me off. "You filthy wench!"

He reached for my throat, but the magistrate struck him with the staff. "You're no longer needed here, Peter. Go tend to your tavern."

Peter leered at me, his eyes brewing with hate. "I'll go gather some sturdy rope." He held his hand to his shoulder as he loped off.

The magistrate handed me over to Fallon. "Lock her up."

"Ichabod! Ichabod!"

"He ain't here," Fallon said, grabbing my arm and twisting it behind my back. I hissed in pain, feeling that it might pop off like a cork.

"Have you seen him at all today?" I moaned between winces.

Fallon tossed me into the cell. "I hadn't seen him in a while." His mouth screwed into a brassy smirk. "I'll wager he's got a mistress somewhere."

He hasn't returned?

"But don't worry. I'm sure he'll turn up after he's done with her." The click of the lock echoed through the chamber, dashing my hopes of escape.

Fallon placed his taut face to the bars. "Mealtime's passed. I'll bring you some bread and water in the morning." Then he paused, his eyes lighting. "Or maybe not. A witch like you could conjure up a hearty feast, I bet."

I curled my lip at him. "If I were a witch, I'd boil up a poison inside your weak bladder, and you'd burn from the inside out."

He sneered like a hungry hound. "Watch yourself, girl, or I'll have Peter serve your meals instead."

He cut away, slinking out of the jail room, locking the door behind him.

I sank back, observing my surroundings. Ichabod's cozy furniture had been removed and I was left with little comfort. The cell held a rickety blue chair, stippled with the wax of guttered candles. The only usable candle left lay on its side, next to a tinderbox. In a corner sat an empty pitcher, veined with gray cracks. Beside it, a tainted chamber pot. And should I tire, I was provided a cornhusk mattress, along with a coarse green blanket, blotched with oily stains.

I was shut off from all heat, and even in summer the crusty barred window would allow no sunshine. The coming night would be brutal. I balanced myself on the wobbly chair and pulled up the window pane. The narrow alley was barely wide enough for a cart and was canopied by overhanging walnut trees. The view stopped some twelve feet away, blocked by the crumbling wall of the butcher's, who'd pitched his carrion there for scavengers to feed. Though most of the meat was picked clean, much of the rot remained, leaving an odor that twisted the gut. I had no doubt it bred rats, which I hoped would not make their way through the cracks in the walls.

I quickly closed the window and sat down on the craggy chair, rubbing my face with my hands.

Ichabod, where are you?

Even if he were here, would he be permitted to enter? Had the Council locked him away as well? My heart bled with fear.

Tears parched my mouth and throat, but the only water was the shallow copper pool at the bottom of the chamber pot. My bleak night would stretch into an eternity.

After a while, the cold seeped into my bones. I had no choice but to wrap myself in the filthy blanket. It reeked of sweat and urine. But after a while, in spite of my chill, my body gave in. I stretched out on the mattress, my head resting against the wall. I fixed my gaze on an ivory chip in the pitcher's handle, and lost myself to the nothingness around me. I don't know how long I was in that daze, but I snapped to when I heard voices just outside the jail room. A moment later a key turned and someone slipped in.

"Father!" I hurried to the bars.

His face opened with shock when he saw my living conditions. "Dear God, this is an outrage."

I reached for him. "Father, help me, please."

"I intend to," he said, "but keep your voice low. The Council doesn't know I'm here and I had to pay that mongrel Fallon a nice sum to let me in."

"Are you sure he'll stay quiet?"

"If he wants the rest of the money I've promised, he will. Now listen to me." He held up a satchel as he spoke. "I leave tonight for the city, and will not return without the best lawyer there." From inside the satchel he removed a napkin. The glorious smell of sweetbread sifted from it.

"I'm too thirsty to eat."

He took out a flask of cider.

I wanted to gulp it all down at once. "Can you get me some water to keep here?"

"I'll try. If we fill Fallon's pockets too deep, he'll not have incentive to turn a blind eye."

He threw a cautious look at the door, then opened a hidden compartment in the satchel. From there, he pulled out a sheaf of paper and a pencil. "Hide these under your mattress." He nodded toward the window above me. "Leta will come every day at noon. She can take any written messages to Doctor Goodwine. He is on our side."

"Doctor Goodwine? What can he do?"

"Whatever you correspond, he'll keep as record. And he'll try to supply medicine if needed." He fastened the satchel. "Now I must go."

Before he could leave, I quickly asked, "Father, have you seen Ichabod?"

He would not meet my eye. "I believe he's gone back to Connecticut."

I was helpless to hold in tears.

Father then looked up. "Do not worry, Katrina. You will be freed." He hurried out, leaving me heartsick and alone.

* * *

Where is Ichabod?

I sat down in the chair, rubbing my arms against the cold. *He'll come. He'll find a way to rescue me.*

My hopes soared when I heard whispers. I rushed to the bars. But the door swung slowly, and Peter Bottoms peeked around.

I stumbled back into the shadows. *Does he have a key?*

He sauntered closer, a loathsome sneer on his lips. "My beautiful Katrina. I'm going to eat your flesh like it was Sunday dinner." He clicked his teeth.

My heart rose to my throat.

"But not yet," he continued. "Not till you give me what's rightfully mine."

"I-I don't know what you mean," I lied, cowering against the wall.

He stepped closer and held up the burnt rose. "Where's the rest of 'em?"

Those beads could be what saved me, but not by handing them over. "I've lost them all."

He rolled the small rose between his thumb and forefinger. "Is that right?"

"You didn't find the others at the schoolhouse?" My cracking voice betrayed me.

He pressed his face to the bars. "Katrina, liars go to hell the same as thieves." He licked his lips. "And old Lucifer keeps the pretty ones for himself."

"I'm not lying to you, Peter. I don't have them." The one truthful statement.

"You've got 'em all right. The bracelet and the necklace."

Necklace? Was that the final portion of the payment Marten had set aside? "I didn't know there was a necklace."

He slammed the heel of his palm against the bar. "Tell me where they are!"

"Oh for God's sake, why are you so eager to have that cheap jewelry?"

"Cheap? Oh, Katrina, you're so naïve." He kept his eyes on me as he placed the blackened bead between his teeth. There was a soft snap as he bit down, shattering it. He spat the crumbs into his hand. "I wouldn't call this cheap." He reached within the fragments and plucked out a gem. Even in the shadows it sparkled.

My mouth dropped. "A sapphire?"

"No, missy." He held it toward the candle flame. "This here's a blue diamond. And there's five more of 'em that were on that bracelet."

Why hadn't Marten told me? I would've been more careful.

"But," Peter said, admiring the jewel, "those are nothing compared to ones in the necklace. Together, almost ten carats."

Ten carats? My mind spun. How had Marten acquired such precious gems?

"Now, as I see it," Peter continued, "those diamonds are rightfully mine. Payment for the money I loaned Marten for his ship. Especially now that the mangled thing's kissing the bottom of the sea."

That explained how Marten got the money for the boat...but the jewels? I turned it over and over in my head. "I don't understand. How did Marten acquire those diamonds?"

Peter considered it for a moment, then threw out a cackle that echoed off the walls. "Oh...poor Katrina. Poor, stupid Katrina. You still thought Marten was a fisherman."

"He was a fisherman."

Peter's face went dead cold. "He was a bloody smuggler, you ignorant dolt. Half the village already knew it. Guess you were too busy counting your money to notice."

I dropped onto the creaky chair and dug my nails into the raw wood. "You're lying."

"I don't care if you believe me," he said. "The truth's the truth. And the truth is, I'm owed about ten carats of blue diamonds. Now tell me where they are."

"Why?" I asked, raising my eyes to his. "Even if I had them, why would I turn them over to you?" He certainly had no means to free me.

He gritted his teeth. "To keep me from ripping your hair out one fist-wad at a time."

I was confident that he didn't have the key, or he would've already been in. "If that would give you satisfaction, then go ahead. But I can't give up something I don't have."

He kicked the bars. "I will find them!" He nodded toward the bloody stain on his shoulder. "And then you'll pay for what you done to me."

He sprang away and slammed out the door.

I settled back, my breath filling my lungs once again. My hands still trembled, but my mind was on preservation. I didn't know how Marten had stolen ten carats of blue diamonds, but if Peter thought I had them, there might be nothing to stop him from making his way into this cell. And how would I defend myself?

I cast my gaze back to the chip on the empty pitcher. One breakable piece could be a sharp enough weapon. I took the pitcher over to the mattress and laid it sideways underneath. With my palms pressed to the wall, I stamped down hard, feeling it give way with a muffled pop. When I raised the mattress, many of the broken pieces came up with it. But they were small and probably wouldn't work their way to the top. I swept the crumbs and shards with the toe of my shoe. Most of the pieces would cut me if I gripped them. But the handle had broken at the chip, causing the end to jut upward into a sloping point. I picked it up, gripping it like a knife. I could easily drive it into his rum-swollen belly.

Brushing the rest of the shards into the corner, I covered them with the edge of the mattress. Then I sat and imagined all the ways my new weapon could protect me.

* * *

I don't know which hour sleep took me. Other than the rasps of my breathing, the room was void of sound. I tried not to think on what this night should've been—me lying awake, heart pulsing, filled with both joy and apprehension. It would've stretched long from my yearning for the hour Ichabod and I would slip away. Not this aching weariness. Not this burdensome dread.

My black mood eventually drew me into slumber. I briefly awoke before daylight and instinctively knew…this was the hour Ichabod and I should be stealing away. Was he awake too?

Where are you?

Eventually I dozed again, only to be awakened by Fallon. "Brought your rations."

He held out a wedge of bread and a half-filled cup of water. The bread had several bites taken from it, and the water most likely contained a dollop of his spit.

"Don't you ever go home?" I asked, contemptuous.

"Of course. I slept like a newborn babe." He placed the cup on the floor then dropped the bread next to it. "And so you'll know, they have two guards on you at night, while I'm gone."

I turned away from him, refusing to pick up the food while he was there.

"Enjoy your meal," he spat. "You only have a few left before you hang."

I ate what I could swallow, avoiding the bits that had been near his diseased mouth. It would be hours yet before Leta would come.

Though my small window was tightly closed, I could hear the noises of the Hollow—carts, crows, villagers passing. Sounds I'd heard all my life, but never as sharply as this.

Just at noon, a walnut sailed up and tapped the window. I climbed onto the chair and opened the pane. Leta stood, head tilted, staring up. She pinched her nose to block out the alley's ghastly smell. "Miss Katrina," she called in a hushed nasally tone.

I gripped the icy-cold bars and peered down. "Do you have news from my father?"

She kept her voice low, shifting her eyes in worry. "Not yet." She tossed up a small pouch. Inside was a hunk of cheese and some cranberries. "I'm sorry it ain't a meat pie."

"No, this is good," I said. "I need to keep up my strength."

"Do you have any messages for me to take?"

Should I have written to the doctor about my visit from Peter? "Not today, Leta."

She bobbed her head up and down. "Then I better go back before they catch me." She was ready to dart away.

"Leta," I called before she disappeared.

"Yes, ma'am."

"Do you know if there's any word from Mr. Crane?"

She shrugged, her shoulders rising nearly to her ears. "I don't know nothing about him."

Did I honestly expect her to? "Then hurry, before you're discovered."

She cupped her hands to her mouth and whispered up, "I'll come back tomorrow."

"Thank you so very much."

Once again, I was all alone. I stood a bit longer, staring at the remote alley. But the frigid air and stench of spoiled meat quickly forced me to shut the window tight.

I set about pacing, pondering my fate. When Fallon came in, I'd find a clever way to interrogate him, to learn what the Council was up to. *An empty head is easily manipulated.*

I also held hope that Father would return soon to procure my release. Though all his wealth might not be enough for the bail that was likely set for me. I'd assuredly be locked in here throughout my trial. Had the magistrate even set a date?

More and more questions plagued me. At times the anxiety was so overpowering, I thought I'd crawl out of my skin. But mid-afternoon, I heard muffled noises outside the jail room. One of those questions was finally answered.

A key clicked and the door slowly opened. I heard the magistrate moan, "One minute. That's all." Then my eyes fell on the one person who could most uplift me during this perilous time.

"Ichabod!"

Tears sprang as I raced to the edge of the cell, extending my arms through the bars. "Ichabod, I've been so worried."

But he didn't rush to hold me. He stayed in the corner, limp and leaning, his gaze cast to the floor. His hands restlessly clenched and unclenched in a gesture of utter despair.

"Ichabod!" I reached as far as I could, but he shied back. "Ichabod, what's wrong?"

Several aching heartbeats later, he brought his face up. There was no mistaking his condition—disheveled hair, crumpled clothes, his mood rueful and despondent.

"Ichabod, what have they done to you?"

His green eyes, now mossy and red, looked upon me with sorrow and gloom. Amid a hopeless sigh, he asked, "Is it true?"

"Is what true?"

He took a long, labored breath. "Their accusations?"

Panic washed over me and I gripped the bars tight. "How can you even ask me that?"

His eyes welled with tears. "How can I not?"

"Ichabod, believe me, our love is genuine." I reached out for him again, but he made no move toward me.

"Katrina…"—he lingered on my name—"I've loved you from the second I saw you. I've thought of little else."

Desperation seized me. "My darling, you must believe me. I'm not a witch."

He slumped against the wall. "The torment of being apart from you…"

"No!" I could not stretch myself any farther. "It's not the same as Hartford. I promise you. You must believe me. I am not a witch." Hot tears rolled to my neck.

"What proof do I have?"

"What proof? *You*. You are the proof!" I clutched the bars in desperation. "Look at yourself. Had I truly bewitched you, you would be the feral beast you'd become before. You would already have stolen the key and opened this cell."

He threw his head back against the wall. There was no mistaking his agony and struggle. He rubbed his eyes with the heels of his hands.

I had to somehow convince him. "Is it really so hard to believe that I'm innocent? That our love is natural?"

"I want to believe it," he murmured.

"Then do. Please, let me touch you."

He took several deep breaths, then stood erect, never once meeting my eye. "I have to go."

"Ichabod! No! You must help me."

He coursed his trembling fingers through his hair. "I need to think."

"There is no time to think. They will hang me."

He turned away, reaching for the door.

"Please, please," I begged, "you must believe me. I am not her." I sank to the floor, sobbing. And though he'd already slipped out, I whispered, "I am not Victoria."

* * *

The glow of the candle cast devils around me. They climbed the walls and crept along the floor. Their glares reflected in the window, and they fed on my despair. I stared at the Stygian shadows, not blinking...waiting for the demons to devour me.

I did not stir when the door opened. Fallon skulked in with bread and water. The creases in his scowl ran deep. "Where's your father?"

Even if I'd known, I didn't have the will to answer.

He kicked the bars, sloshing water from the cup. "He said he'd be back tonight."

I remained still.

"Answer me, witch!"

I finally drew a breath. "Why do you care?"

"I like the toll he pays."

I shifted my eyes to him. "This is why you're such an imbecile. If you had half a brain, you would've already struck a bargain with him for my release. He would've made you a rich man."

His mouth unhinged, but he quickly clapped it shut, grinding his teeth. "I already asked him. He said you wasn't worth it."

"Fallon, you lie about as well as you bathe."

His crusty eyes pierced me. "You ain't smelling so pretty neither. Is that why your schoolmaster chased out of here with his eyes watering?"

Though his words cut me, I refused to show my pain, "It was most likely the misery of seeing how I'm treated here."

"Now who's lying?"

He ripped off a hunk of the bread with his teeth then tossed the rest onto the cell floor. He stirred the water with his finger and placed the mug barely within reach. "Hungry?" he asked, gnawing the bite of bread.

I let out an annoyed sigh.

He placed his face between the bars, his eyes glassy. "Or maybe I should come in there and *comfort* you."

What appetite I had sank like a stone. "Come on in, Fallon. But remember, when the magistrate returns and sees that you've defiled me, he will throw you to the dogs. After all, you do have a sworn duty to uphold the law."

"Eh. Don't matter anyway. You've been fornicating with the devil. No other man could match up."

Especially you. The thought of that rawboned creature crawling on me feathered the hairs on the back of my neck. "Just go away."

He continued to glower. Then he lifted the key, eying it like it was honey. "You better be nice to old Fallon. Cause if I were to swallow this,"—he hovered it over his mouth—"it might be a few days before anyone can retrieve it. And they'd probably make you be the one to dig it out."

"Or," I said, lifting my chin, "should they decide to release me, they'd simply use the magistrate's spare key." *Is there a spare key?* "But go ahead and swallow that one. It's rather large. If you don't choke on it, it'll probably rip open your bowels. I shudder just thinking of the pain."

He dropped his arms to his sides. "You Van Tassels think you're so high and mighty. When Baltus returns, I'll be paying him a visit. His money will be lining my pockets and you'll still hang." He kicked the water cup, sloshing most of it onto the floor. "You got five minutes before I come back and collect what's left."

I turned back to the wall. Once he was gone, I hurried over to the bars and stretched as far as I could to reach the mug. I set it and the bread on the chair, then dragged it close to the bed. If Fallon planned to collect them, he'd have to come inside. I'd burn him with the candle as a distraction, and then smash the chair into his face. All for pure satisfaction. But then I'd have no choice but to flee. What he'd do to me would be far worse than the demons that surrounded me now. I reached under the mattress and touched the cool porcelain of my makeshift lance.

Fallon never returned. The man was nothing but lies.

* * *

I awoke to the sounds of the Hollow, seeming livelier than before. Or perhaps it was my impaired state. If anyone had come to bring me food, I'd slept through it. But last night's bread and water still rested on the chair. Why would they offer more? And why would I care?

Around an hour later—so I guessed—a handful of walnuts blasted against the window. Even though time was lost on me, I knew it was way before noon. I placed the chair under the window and raised the pane. Leta stood in the cold, hopping foot to foot. Her face was screwed into a knot, and tears tracked down her cheeks. "Miss Katrina." Her chalky lips trembled like an injured bird.

I held tight to the window's bars. "Leta, what's wrong?"

She sniffled, continuing to bounce. "That tavern owner came up to the house."

A cold panic swept over me. "Peter Bottoms."

"Yes, ma'am. And he brought out a whole passel of town folk. They was hollerin' and throwing rocks, and yelling that you was a witch, making their hens to stop layin' and their wells dry up."

Peter's turned everyone against me.

"They was demanding for Mr. Van Tassel to pay up for their troubles."

"My father was there?"

"Yes, ma'am." She wiped her nose on her coat sleeve. "He and that lawyer man come back late last night."

"Well, what happened?"

Her face hitched again. "It was the most terrible thing. Even though the door was barred, the tavern owner barged in. He hollered all kinds of nasty things, then he and Mr. Van Tassel started fightin'. They tussled for a bit, then Peter took out a pistol and shot him in the face."

My knees buckled and the chair wobbled beneath me. *Oh, my Lord.* "Is he dead? *Leta*, is he dead?"

Her tears spilled onto her lips. "I don't know. He just laid there at first, but after Peter went to tearing up the house, he started crawling on his elbows toward the kitchen. His whole face looked like an open sore. Simon sent me to fetch the doctor. And I don't know nothing else, 'cause after I got the doctor, I come straight here to tell you." She began bawling again.

The image of Father's blood-soaked face made it impossible to swallow my own tears. How had this all gone so terribly wrong?

The clamor of the village grew stronger. I couldn't allow Leta to remain.

"Listen to me," I said. "It is too dangerous for you to come back here. If you can, ask the doctor to relay word of my father through one of the councilmen."

She rubbed an eye with her fist. "Yes, ma'am."

"And one more thing," I said, quickly. "What happened to the lawyer?"

Her lip quivered. "He hightailed it back to the city after that swarm of people showed up."

I rested my head against the window's cold bars. "Thank you, Leta. Be safe, dear."

She glanced up with wet almond eyes. "Bye, Miss Katrina. I hope you'll be all right."

I sank into a silent sob. No matter what happens, I won't be.

* * *

I stayed at the window long after she'd left, letting the cold air numb my senses. But heavy scuttling and clatter roused me. There were shouts as the echoes of hammers clip-clopped against wood. I pressed my cheek hard to the bars, straining to see. But my only view was the tangle of branches and the butcher's stone wall.

What's happening out there?

I slammed the window and dropped off the chair. Thoughts flooded my mind.

They'll come for me. They'll come for the witch. I paced,

wondering, worrying. Minutes passed like hours. Then the jail room door unclicked. Reverend Bushnell bustled in, short of breath.

I hurried over. "How is Father?"

The reverend held up his Bible as though to ward off my next words. "I'm afraid it's bad news."

"He's dead?" New tears fell as I clutched the bars.

"As you may well be soon," he said, refusing me a moment to grieve.

I snapped my eyes to him. "Don't you think I know that?"

He placed a hand over mine. "The Hollow is in a fever, my dear. Peter Bottoms has incited an uproar. He is preaching against you, blaming you for all the misfortune in Sleepy Hollow. Anyone with failed crops or diseased livestock is crying witch. And now they are taking matters into their own hands, erecting a scaffold."

My mouth went dirt dry. "Where is the magistrate? Is he not trying to stop them?"

The reverend's downcast expression hung loose. "What can he do, Katrina? We are outnumbered."

"Do something! Can I trust that they'll not get in?"

He withdrew his hand, a gesture that spoke volumes. "We're keeping the doors locked and have brought in an extra guard."

"Please, Reverend, let me go. I'll leave the Hollow and never return."

My hopes rose as he considered it, but then he fervently shook his head. "Out of the question."

I slammed the side of my fist against the bars. "And you call yourself a man of God? What are you going to do when they drag me out? Stand in the corner and pray? Will there be any guilt on your part? Any remorse?"

"As much guilt as you feel over the death of Marten Piers."

My body trembled with frustration as I held back a piercing shriek. As much as I wanted to lash out, I knew it would only satisfy him.

Sensing my fury, he took a step back. "I'm sorry, Katrina. I wish I could do more. But here." He offered his Bible through the bars. "Perhaps you'd like to keep this."

I backed away, my chin high. "No, thank you. I find it a useless weapon."

He brought it back, clutching it to his chest. "Yet I fear the lack of it is what put you here. I'll pray for you, Katrina."

"Don't waste your prayers on me, Reverend. Pray for those outside, erecting the gallows. They are the true murderers."

* * *

Once he'd gone, I was left to my thoughts, and the sounds outside the window. The sawing and the hammering were no louder, yet deafening to my ears. And even though my heart had been completely ripped away, I did not want to surrender.

I took my shoes off next to the mattress, then hurried to the bars. "Fallon!" I screamed, banging the chair against them. "Fallon! Come quickly! Hurry!"

The man was incapable of haste. He pranced in, baring his crooked brown teeth. "What you wailing about in here?"

I wrenched my arm through the bars and clutched his sleeve. "I don't want to hang."

His eyes glassed over as though my grip were a sexual gesture. "Don't worry. It'll be quick. You'll drop fast and…" He snapped his fingers.

"I don't want to die. Please, help me."

He plucked my fingers from his sleeve, wallowing in my desperation—something I was counting on greatly. "Know what I did with those coins Baltus gave me?" I waited for whatever snide answer he'd cooked up. "I used them to buy the chance of slipping that noose around your neck myself." He reached through and squeezed my cheeks. "And I'll be kissing them rosy lips just before you drop."

I waited until he released me, then said, "So the money's gone?"

His face twisted. "Not for long. With you and your papa both dead, I'm sure I can find some valuables in that fancy mansion of yours."

"But the villagers may have taken most of it already." I kept the anguish in my eyes. He had to believe I was completely at his mercy. Which, as loathsome as it felt, I was.

"Then maybe I best get out there and pick the place clean." His eyes crawled over me before settling on my breasts. "And while I'm there, is there a particular dress you want me to bring back for you? I think you'd be pretty all laid out in blue." He chuckled and turned to go.

"Wait!" I gripped his sleeve again. "Fallon, you don't understand. My family is far richer than appearances."

His ears and eyebrows perked. I had him.

"A good deal of the Van Tassel money is invested. Father owns piles of bank shares and government bonds. If you get me out of here, I promise, they're yours."

He clutched my hand and squeezed. Raw pain pulsed up my arm. "Supposing that was true, am I to believe you could just legally hand them over?"

I winced against the ache as he crushed harder. "After my mother died, it was I who tallied the ledgers. And since Father was away much of the time, I was left to deal with the money issues as well. My signature is as good as his on any business transaction."

Fallon opened his hand, dropping mine. His mouth twitched as his mind rolled it over. He was buying into my lie.

I lowered my voice to sound more convincing. "We'll go to the city together. Just the two of us. I promise you, every share that was ours will be yours. You'll have wealth like you've never imagined."

He studied my eyes, wanting it to be true. "And what's to keep you from running off after we leave here?"

I tossed him a puzzled look. "You own a pistol, don't you?"

He considered it a moment, then reached through and placed his trigger finger to my temple. "And what's to keep me from firing it into your precious little head?"

"I'll take that risk. I'm dead either way."

He glared a moment, then jangled the keys. "We'll go out the back."

I placed my hands to my chest. "Oh, thank you."

A click. Then the squeak of the iron door. I lifted my skirt, exposing my filthy bare feet. "My shoes." I hurried to the corner. As I'd hoped, Fallon sauntered in.

Kneeling with my back to him, I slipped my shoes on my feet, and the pitcher handle into my hand. I paused, panting, heart thumping. Taking my time. *Careful. Just injure him enough to get away.*

"Let's hurry, woman," he sneered.

"I'm sorry, it's just that"—I pretended to struggle—"conditions here have caused my feet to swell."

"Then just bring 'em along. Once you sign over those bonds, I'll lend you the money to buy new ones." He cackled a laugh that nearly rattled the window.

"I've almost got them."

"Almost ain't good enough." He loped toward me. I spun, ramming the porcelain blade on the inside of his left thigh. His face registered both shock and pain as he stumbled to the floor.

I broke around him, but only made it a few steps before he clutched my skirt, bringing me down.

"You filthy bitch!" He grabbed a huge wad of my hair as he

reached for the handle that protruded just inches from his groin. "To hell with the Hollow, I'll kill you myself!"

Blood coursed as he worked the weapon from his flesh.

I clawed at his hand, trying to free my hair, but he held it too close to my scalp. My eyes fixed on the cell door and the keys still hanging from the lock. If I could only get there, I could lock him in. I squirmed and kicked, but he rolled on top of me, the pitcher handle held high.

I moaned, gripping his wrist to keep him from bringing it down on me.

"Should I take out your eyes first," he sniped, "or just ram it into your throat?" Using his legs, he pushed my knees apart and bucked his pelvis against mine. "Or maybe I should have my way with you first." He ran his wet serpent tongue up my neck.

I closed my eyes, grimacing against the struggle and repulsion. Then his tongue traced the outline of my lips. "Like that, missy?"

He continued pressing his groin against me, but with a slower rhythm. I could feel the heat steaming from his body and taste the spiced pork on his tongue. My stomach curled. Then he brought his mouth down fiercely on mine, trying to burrow his tongue inside. This was my only chance. I opened my mouth to take him and as soon as he crammed his tongue in, I clamped my teeth upon it, refusing to let go.

His eyes popped wide as he fought harder to bring the porcelain weapon down upon me. But I kicked and fought as his coppery blood rolled down my throat. He finally pulled his head upward, somehow freed. I then realized, I still had part of his tongue in my mouth. I spit it into his face.

His eyes darkened with hatred as he rose up, eager to finish me. Blood sheeted down, dropping on me in great gobs. I did not want mine mingled with his. Bringing my foot to his chest, I kicked him off, then rolled onto my hands and knees. But he lunged, grabbing me before I could get away. I turned to fight, amazed that he still had strength.

Grappling for the handle, we fought again, his darkened blood oozing from his mouth. At last, I wrested the weapon from him. When he sprang at me, I brought it up and into the flesh of his neck, just above his collarbone.

We both glared, heaving. I waited for him to drop, but with fingers splayed, he slowly placed his hands to the sides of my face. Then, with the quickness of a deer, he lifted my head and slammed it to the hard floor.

Pain exploded through me as pinpricks of light danced before my eyes. The room blurred. Fallon hovered over me. Then there were two of him. Then darkness closed in.

Within that darkness were fireflies and shooting stars. And rain. *Rain?* Droplets hitting my face. *Blood. Fallon's blood.* The fireflies dimmed. Then the world rolled over and I ceased to exist.

* * *

The fireflies returned, winking upon a sea of blackness. Their number grew greater as their bodies grew larger, becoming the size of bumblebees. They swarmed inside my head, their droning boring through my brain.

"Katrina."

The bees are calling me?

"Katrina."

No, a man. Whispering.

The bees parted as light sliced through the slits of my eyelids.

"Katrina, wake up."

The voice. I recognized it. Brom.

I slowly rolled over, my head thundering with every move. Brom was crouched near the locked cell door.

Where is Fallon?

Brom grimaced as I slithered on forearms and knees. "Holy God," he gasped. As I reached the bars, he quickly pulled a flask from his coat.

"Thirsty," I managed.

He tilted it to my lips. Whiskey. It was hot cinders going down.

"I only have a moment," he said. He tugged a cotton scarf from his neck and doused it with whiskey. "Listen closely." Reaching in, he wiped at the blood on my face.

"How…how?" How did you get in?

"I don't have time to explain." He raised my chin so that my drooping eyes met his. "I'm coming back for you tonight. About midnight. Do you understand?"

My eyelids fell.

"Katrina." He shook me, causing a pain, like a bullet had shot through my skull. "Do you understand?"

"Yes," I croaked, the taste of blood and whiskey mingling with the word.

"Keep this." He slid the flask through. "But just take mild sips. I'll need you alert."

"Brom." I rested my head onto my arm. "They're going to hang me."

He reached in and brushed back my hair. "Not as long as I'm breathing."

I closed my eyes and he slipped away.

* * *

Shouting roused me from sleep. I briefly blinked my eyes open. Dark smoke swelled through the cracks in the wall, the room held an amber glow. *Fire.* I tried to stir, even a little, but my head screamed like I'd been kicked by an ox. *Fire.* Through blurry eyes I looked at the waxy wooden chair. Then the cornhusk mattress. Kindling. All kindling. *The witch won't hang, she'll burn.*

My stomach heaved twice, then vomit shot out, slapping the floor. I closed my eyes, steadied my breathing. The world slowed again. *Brom. He'll come.* I felt around for the flask, but it wasn't there. My mind drifted downward. Had he really been here, or had I only imagined him like before? I slipped into darkness again. *This time tomorrow, I'll be nothing but ashes.*

* * *

I awoke to a dead quiet—in my head as well as the room. I lay still, my eyes fixed to the back wall. The room smelled smoky and singed like the Horseman had slashed it. But what did I care? I was already marked. Night had fallen, but the glow of sconces lit the cell.

I listened to the sound of my steady breathing, then realized someone else was there. I lifted and turned, blinking my eyes. Beyond the bars, the notary sat, his hands folded in his lap, his mournful eyes watching me. He rose and walked forward, his face slack.

God help me, I haven't the strength for more bad news.

He voice was low and soft. "I thought you'd want to know that Peter Bottoms is dead."

"Dead?" I felt suddenly lighter. "How?"

"Knife to the throat."

At least it wasn't the Horseman. I was spared that accusation. "Who killed him?"

He shrugged his weary shoulders. "No witnesses."

Brom?

I waited for more, wondering why he was the one to inform me. After a moment, his stature slumped. His eyes glistened. "My son liked you."

Was that meant to compliment or shame me? "I liked him too. I loved him. You know he was a very dear friend."

He looked down, studying his clenched fists. "I remember

when you and Garritt were children—about eight years old, I think. He broke his arm tumbling out of a tree. You made a sling out of your petticoat and helped him inside. Then you waited with him till the doctor and I got there. When I walked in, you had his head in your lap, petting his hair, and singing softly to soothe him."

The memory pierced my heart. "He was very brave. He barely cried."

"Garritt was like that. Always strong." His face pinched. "He got into mischief a lot, though I'm sure Brom was behind most of that."

I didn't tell him that it was Brom who'd pushed Garritt out of the tree.

The notary raised his head and looked at me. "But he was a good boy. A strong boy. Do you know how powerful something would have to be to terrify him that much?"

I nodded agreement. "Yes, sir. His tortured look still haunts me."

He pursed his trembling lips. "Katrina, do you know why the Horseman killed my boy?"

I shook my head. "No. Nor do I know why he killed Marten. Or Nikolass. His brutal path makes no sense."

He blinked his weak and watery eyes. "I don't know what the Council will do with you, Katrina, but they'll no longer have this." He opened a fist. My talisman lay curled within his palm. "I'll toss it in the river."

I slumped, tears stinging my eyes. "Bless you, notary."

He closed it back in his hand, then straggled to the door. Just before exiting, he turned back. "Katrina, if I thought it would've saved my son's life, I would've dug those bones up myself."

* * *

Once he was gone I made an effort to rise. My bones ached, but the effort was easier than I'd feared. Upon standing, my foot kicked something under my skirt. The flask. *Brom had been here.*

I scooped it up and shook it. The sloshing liquid was like the peal of a bell. I removed the cap, filled my mouth, and swished it around to kill what remained of Fallon. A broad, dark smear leading out of the cell told me his body had been dragged away. *By who?* I vigorously spat the whiskey into the chamber pot, ridding him for good. Then I took a hearty swig for myself.

What time is it? I looked up, trying to judge by the degree of darkness, but the canopy of trees made it an impossible task. I sat down on the chair to wait. Eventually, someone would come for me—one way or the other.

* * *

At last there was a great disturbance within the courtroom. Scuffling, shouting. A single hard knock thwacked the door.

Someone's head has cracked against it.

The door flew open and Brom rushed in. He called behind him, "Get the key."

"Brom," I cried, hurrying toward the bars. "You came back."

He gripped my hand. "Yes, and I've brought someone to help."

It was then that Ichabod rushed in, fumbling with the key.

Oh God! Ichabod.

He unlocked the cell and rushed to embrace me. The feel of him was heaven to my touch.

"I'm so sorry," he said, squeezing me to him. "I tried to get back to you, but they were holding me."

"Come," Brom ordered. "You can explain once we're safe."

Ichabod placed his arm around me, guiding me out. We stepped over a guard, sprawled unconscious at our feet, and passed another lying face down on the floor.

At the back door, Brom peered out, and then hurried to a patch of overgrowth. Moments later, he led their horses out.

"Where are we going?" I asked Ichabod.

"First to the schoolhouse. We've hidden Dewdrop in the woods."

He helped me onto his horse then mounted, straddling behind me. As quietly as we dared, we trotted around to the road. Feeling it safe, they kicked the horses into a gallop, and we flew against the frigid wind.

Ichabod had both hands on the reins, his body warm against me. My mind urged the horse to move faster—to spirit us from danger.

But we'd barely made a quarter-mile when I heard a third set of hoofbeats behind us. *We've been discovered!*

"Don't look back," Ichabod said, but I already had.

Dear God!

My breath caught and my heart froze. The Horseman trailed us, his steed kicking up sparks as he quickly gained ground.

"Ichabod," I murmured. But he kept his eyes forward, spurring his horse on.

Brom was soon beside us, his face as pale as moonlight.

"Continue to the school," Ichabod said. "He never dismounts. We can find refuge there."

If we make it!

We cut off the road and across a field, our horses side by side. Within seconds the schoolhouse came into view. But the Horseman rode with ghostly power. As we entered the schoolyard, he bore down on Brom, reaching across and snatching Daredevil's bridle.

When Ichabod didn't slow, I grabbed the reins. "Brom!"

The Horseman held Brom by his hair, the scythe raised. But instead of sweeping it across his neck, he raised his foot and kicked him off his horse. Brom hurtled to the ground, landing on his back. His breath *whumped* from his body.

"Ichabod, we cannot leave him." I turned the horse and before it fully halted, leapt off.

"Katrina!" Ichabod yelled, bounding down and coming after me.

"Brom, get up," I urged. "Hurry!"

Brom struggled to his feet, but to our astonishment, the Horseman dropped from his horse and stalked toward him.

He dismounted.

I raced toward Brom, but the Horseman was there. Ichabod caught up and restrained me.

I turned, pleading. "We've got to help him."

"How?" Ichabod said, holding me tight. "Going closer would be suicide."

I struggled, but he held me firm. "We must try. Surely there is some weapon."

"Against a ghost? Katrina, we are powerless." Ichabod backed up, pulling me with him toward the school. Our horse had fled into the woods, leaving us helpless and exposed. But I would not desert Brom. I pushed forward against Ichabod's grip.

Brom's eyes met mine, fear masking his face. We were just yards apart when the Horseman strode up, kicking Brom back to the ground. Before he could make another move, the towering ghost raised his foot and stomped down on his chest. Steam rose as it seared though his shirt and into his flesh. Brom screamed, his face twisting in agony.

"Brom!"

I fought against Ichabod, but he would not loosen his hold. "Katrina, he will kill you if you interfere!"

The Horseman brought the tip of his scythe to Brom's neck, piercing his flesh. Brom's shrieks grew louder as blood seeped from the puncture.

I scoured the yard for something, anything to help him. When I raised my eyes again, the steam from Brom's chest had cleared, allowing me a glimpse of the Horseman's shoe. A shoe, not a boot. A gray leather shoe with a brass buckle. I went limp as realization struck.

No one wears shoe buckles anymore.

This was not our legendary Hessian. It was the ghost of our former schoolmaster.

"Nikolass?"

He relaxed his stance when I said his name, though he still held Brom at bay.

"Good God, Nikolass, what are you doing?"

Brom's face opened with recognition, then froze with new fear. "Devenpeck!"

"Nikolass, please," I begged. "Let him go."

But he gripped the scythe with both hands and pushed it deeper into Brom's neck. Brom winced as his blood sprayed forth. He gritted his teeth, the cords of his neck stretched tight. "Nikolass!" he yelled, "it was an accident! I swear!"

I flailed against Ichabod, but he was too strong. "It's Nikolass," I sobbed. "He was kind."

"And yet he holds a blazing weapon," Ichabod argued.

"Please," Brom pleaded. "It was an accident. We were drunk."

An accident? "Brom, what have you done?"

Nikolass grabbed Brom by his coat and lifted him to his knees, twisting him around to face us. He held on to Brom's hair as he placed the crescent blade to his throat. Then he pressed his own knee into Brom's back, just below his shoulders.

"Brom," I called again. "What did you do?"

Nikolass pushed harder against Brom's back, bringing the

scythe tighter. A necklace of red formed beneath it. Yet he only applied enough pressure to maim, not kill.

Ichabod placed his mouth to my ear. "He wants a confession."

"Brom!" I urged.

Brom clamped his eyes shut, tears squeezing through. "Katrina, it was an accident. I swear to you."

"What did you do?"

Nikolass pressed the scythe harder against Brom's neck.

"It was late. We'd been drinking." He paused, gasping for breath. "It was just that stupid prank we've always pulled. We'd stretched wire between the trees."

When he paused again, Nikolass brought the blade up to his jaw, leaving a crimson scrape.

Brom clenched his teeth against the pain. "We only meant to knock him off his horse." He lost strength, wilting against Nikolass's grip and looking up at me with sorrow in his eyes.

"Confess it," I said, hoping this was the ghost's only motive.

"We sent Marten to fetch him. He cooked up a lie that the schoolhouse was on fire.

Marten.

"But we'd misjudged. We'd strung the wire too high. When Nikolass rode through, it caught on his neck."

"Nikolass," I said. "You heard him. It was an accident. Can you not show mercy?"

But he tugged Brom's hair and dug his knee in harder. There was more for Brom to tell.

"The wire had cut so deep, he dangled from it. He thrashed and finally fell. Katrina, there was so much blood. Garritt pressed his coat to Nikolass's neck, but it was useless. He pitched and croaked. There was nothing we could do."

Brom lolled his head back, but Nikolass jerked it forward,

urging him on.

"After he died, we panicked. It wasn't the first time we'd pulled this prank. The village would know it was us. We had to do something to cover our tracks." Brom's eyes closed as he openly wept. "We found a scythe and cut off his head. Then we burned the grass . He made it look like he'd fallen victim to the Hessian."

I shivered within Ichabod's grasp, imagining their alarm and despair.

Nikolass released Brom, kicking him to the ground. Brom pulled himself up on hands and knees, weeping. It was done. He'd gotten his confession.

Ichabod dropped his arms, setting me free. I was never so weak and exhausted. "Nikolass," I moaned, stepping softly toward them.

But my sympathy meant nothing. With a savage thrust, Nikolass brought his blade down, severing Brom's head from his shoulders.

"No!"

Ichabod grabbed me, yanking me back.

I froze with shock, my eyes locked on Brom's body, a corona of blood spreading around his neck.

Nikolass stepped forward and kicked Brom's head, sending it rolling across the dried grass. Then he placed his scythe upon his shoulder, as though satisfied.

Ichabod slowly stepped backward, inching us away, though I wondered if there was a need. Nikolass had his revenge. His three slayers were dead. He could now rest in peace.

But instead of riding off, he strode toward us with a determination that spiked my blood.

"Nikolass…"

He continued marching our way.

"Nikolass, what are you doing?"

Ichabod grabbed my hand. "Run, now." We turned and fled.

I glanced over my shoulder. Nikolass still advanced at a hurried pace.

Ichabod tugged me along. "The cellar," he said. It was just ahead.

We can make it.

He opened one of the doors and shoved me inside. I lost my footing on the steps and stumbled to the bottom. Ichabod barred the doors and ran to me.

He encircled his arms around me, holding me tight. We stood, blind in the darkness.

"What is unfinished?" I whispered.

I felt him shake his head.

We waited, apprehensive, our breathing thick. Then the first blow struck the doors.

I yelped as we cowered back. Nikolass struck it again.

We inched into a corner as he axed the doors with his scythe, smashing and splintering the wood.

"We're trapped," I uttered.

With one final strike, the doors exploded and moonlight revealed us.

Nikolass kicked aside the remaining wood, and then tramped down the stairs, scythe raised.

My mouth tasted of ash as the blood drained from my face. *Heaven, help us.* We waited, pinned in the corner with no means of escape. Ichabod moved in front of me, attempting to shield me from Devenpeck's wrath.

"Ichabod," I said, clutching his arm as the Horseman raised his weapon high. But instead of thrusting it down upon Ichabod's neck, he dug it into the dirt just a few feet from where we stood.

He brought it down again and again, kicking up plumes of

dust all around us. I gripped Ichabod's waist, peering over his shoulder as Nikolass continued pounding the earth.

When he'd made a hole about a foot deep, he knelt to his knees and burrowed with his hands. And though his body cast a darkened shadow, I could still make out the strings of hair he'd uncovered. This drove him to dig faster, flinging the soil in handfuls. And when finally he reached it, he carefully placed both hands on the jaws, and lifted his head from its grave.

I barely blinked, my heart thumping. He cradled the filthy, withered thing in his arms. Then, leaving his scythe lying there, he turned, facing us. Facing *me*.

"Nikolass," I whispered.

He stood for a moment, his stature relaxed…weary. Then he shifted back and ascended the stairs.

"Ahh," I gasped, sinking against Ichabod. He spun, gathering me into his arms.

After a couple of minutes, Ichabod said, "He's gone by now. Let's hurry." He helped me up the steps and into the moonlight.

Once outside, my eyes fell upon Brom's body, soaking in its blood. His horse stood near him, braying and nickering in distress.

The ache inside me was heart-wrenching. "I am free because of him."

"Not yet," Ichabod said. "We must go."

I rushed to Daredevil, gathering his reins. "Here. This horse is faster than yours."

Leading him along, we brushed through the woods to where Dewdrop was hidden. Quickly mounting, we sprinted away.

Without interference, we raced off. Away from the school. Away from the village. Away from my home. When we reached the hilltop some distance away, I slowed, turning my horse. I gazed upon Sleepy Hollow one last time—now just misty shadows dwarfed by the rolling Hudson. Through all the years I'd dreamed of escaping, I never imagined it would be like this.

My breath quivered.

"Katrina," Ichabod urged. "We must hurry."

I nodded through tearful eyes.

We spurred our horses and fled into the night, not knowing where dawn would take us.

But as we rode away, a chill embraced me and a question came to my mind…

If it was Nikolass rising, who was that outside my window, beckoning to me?

Want More Dax Varley Books?

Try these:

RETURN TO SLEEPY HOLLOW
BLEED
SINFUL
SPELLBOUND AND DETERMINED
NIGHTMARE HOUSE
BREATHE
LOST GIRL
SECOND SIGHT
UP ON THE HOUSETOP

Dax Varley writes the kind of young adult novels she wishes were around when she was a teen. She's a lover of humor, horror and all things paranormal.

When Dax isn't writing, she's collecting odd photos online, reading recaps of her favorite shows or kicked back with a good book. She lives in Richmond, Texas with her husband, a shelf full of action figures and about a dozen imaginary friends.

Real or imaginary, you can find her at the following locations:

DaxVarley.com
Facebook.com/DaxVarley

Printed in Great Britain
by Amazon